CW01631851

Cake and Cocktails at Café Swan
Mary-Grace Burinski

Follow me on Instagram and Twitter
@mgburinski
www.mgburinski.com

To Craig for supporting me with my crazy notion of writing a book xx

And to Mum and Dad. Love you xx

PART ONE
CONFRONTATION

Chapter One

NOW

"So despite everything ...... EVERYTHING ...... we're right back here?"
"No Becca, we've been through a lot but we've never been *here*."
And with that, Tony slammed the front door behind him just as Becca's legs gave way and she crumpled to the floor, the realisation that she just might have witnessed the end of her marriage crushing her chest like a wrecking ball.

Chapter Two

SEVEN MONTHS EARLIER

The thing about the changing of the seasons as they move from one to another is it brings with it a sense of anticipation and hope. When asked what her favourite time of year was, Becca Swanson would always give the stock answer, "Easy. December. Because I love Christmas." But as time has moved on she has come to appreciate the beauty of each season and how each has their own unique qualities. Yes, the cold dark mornings and limited hours of daylight associated with winter are happily cheered by the twinkling of Christmas lights but by the time the spring months come along, the budding blossoms offer a welcome respite from the fear that the trees could never possibly look alive again. Then the temperature ramps up and summer begins, the air fills with the laughter and giggles of children making the most of their freedom from school.

This passage of time seemed to have amplified ever since Becca's two children (Emily eleven and Max seven) came along and Becca and Tony feel forced to think about Christmas earlier and earlier. This morning, it was the dawn of autumn which triggered this train of thought.

In recent years autumn was fast becoming Becca's favourite season (not to be confused by favourite time of the year, this was still Christmas and always would be) but autumn was set apart from the other seasons. At the start of the season, you could still feel the warmth of the late summer sun in the air and then as the temperature dropped the changing colours on the trees gave it a beauty unrivalled by any other time of the year. It was also a very settled time for Café Swan. Schools had just recently returned so parents and children alike were still reminiscing over their summer adventures while adjusting back to weekday routines. For most, Christmas is still a mere speck on the horizon. However running a business means you're often a step ahead of what the customer sees. It may only be the start of September but Becca had the autumn menu firmly established with Frankie White, her assistant. Frankie had even come up with a range of stunning Halloween themed cakes that were sure to be a money spinner. The thought reminded her to get Frankie to make a batch for counter taste-testing freebies and pin him down on a date to move to their autumn menu. They would also have to start thinking about Christmas soon, but that could be a discussion for another day. Becca opened the door to Café Swan, the warmth of the autumnal sun on her neck as she picked up the milk and bread delivery and moved it inside.

Her café. Her saviour.

Situated in the Hillhead area of Glasgow just a short walk from the Botanic Gardens, the café was never short of customers thanks to the nearby schools, university buildings and tourist attractions. Every morning as she walked over the threshold, her mind subconsciously wandered briefly back to that low point in her life when she didn't know what the future would hold for her personally, her marriage or family. Little did Becca know that on this innocent, bright and sunny September day in the west end of Glasgow, a chain of events would be set in motion which would lead Becca and Tony's relationship to breaking point once again.

Chapter Three

NOW

That clock in the lounge is ridiculously loud. Becca wondered why she chose this particular moment to notice this. She also realised she had absolutely no idea how long she had been lying on the floor in the hall despite the taunting ticks of the bloody clock. She wondered if she had fallen asleep - or more accurately passed out. When she got home she had been tired and was more than a little bit drunk. Everything was such a blur; Tony had hardly spoken two words to her in the car and then he walked ahead of her into the dark lounge without a backward glance. She knew something was wrong, she felt it in the air. Then came the discussion which somehow escalated to an argument; the accusations; the misunderstandings. Oh God. What a mess.

Like a baby deer, Becca tried to find her feet. She was still wobbly from a combination of alcohol, hunger, adrenaline and fear. She staggered through to the kitchen tucking her long caramel coloured hair behind her ears as she moved. Water. She needed water and paracetamol. Outside the birds were beginning to sing their morning song and it was starting to get light. Spring would soon be giving way to summer. Thankfully Frankie was due to open up the café this morning, but Becca was due in to help for a few hours with the lunchtime rush. Right now she could not see that happening.

"Tony. I need to speak to Tony." The image of her husband flashed to her mind. She could see his lopsided grin framed by his five o'clock shadow. His piercing blue eyes and his once jet black hair now generously flecked with grey.
She dialled his mobile number, fidgeting with her necklace as it rung. It went to voicemail. Not really surprised she hung up without leaving a message as she had no idea what to say. She tried to formulate her thoughts into a coherent process which would allow her to make sense of the situation and somehow figure out what she needed to do. Her mobile rang. She answered without looking at it.
"Tony?! Oh. It's you. What do you mean have I told him? Told him *what* exactly? There is *nothing* to tell! Hang on, have you seen him? Where is he? Is he with you……..HE DID WHAT?!"

Chapter Four

SEVEN MONTHS EARLIER

Becca was absentmindedly singing along with the radio as she collected the ingredients for scones from the pantry. Frankie might be a genius with the cakes, but scones would always be her forté. Along with daily plain or fruit scones, Becca always produced a special and today's was raspberry and white chocolate.

"Good morning Boss!" Frankie chirped as he walked into the kitchen.

"Morning Frankie." Becca answered with a smile as she tied her hair back into its trademark high ponytail. "There's a fresh pot of coffee just made and I'm just working on the first batch of scones if you want one?"

"Nah, I'm more in a savoury mood today." He patted his stomach. "I'm going to fry up some bacon if that's ok?"

"Of course. You know where it is. So how was your day off yesterday? Did you get up to anything exciting?"

"No. Why do you ask?"

"Frankie, I've known you for around five years now and you're a pastry for breakfast person. So I know when you rustle up a bacon sandwich *before* the café opens, it usually means there's some gossip on the go. Spill."

Frankie looked sheepish. "OK. But you can't get mad. I met Mark for lunch...."

"Frankie! No!"
"Becca just listen. No, please don't look at me like that. He was really sorry. He actually said the words. He actually said he was sorry and I believe him and not because I wanted to, but because he was. And we had lunch and we talked. And we had a couple of drinks and we talked more, then we had dinner and a few more drinks and it felt good. It felt really good."
"Frankie........"
"Look I know he treated me like shit....."
"That's putting it mildly," Becca muttered.
"But he was really messed up then. He was freaked out by being committed to someone. He wasn't ready."
Becca shook her head in disbelief "I don't like the sound of where this is going."
Wincing slightly, Frankie said, "So he's asked me to think about giving it another go."
At this Becca erupted. "Are you kidding me Frankie?! Mark? The guy who broke your heart by sleeping with your flatmate's boyfriend? So not only destroying your relationship and leaving you emotionally broken, he simultaneously ruined your flatmate's relationship too, who then unsurprisingly moved out of your flat with no warning, leaving you screwed for money? *That* Mark?"
"You make it sound a lot worse than it was."
"Oh Frankie! Do you hear yourself?"
"Hellloooooooo! Anybody around?" came a voice from the café.
"We're in here, Wendy!" Becca turned back to Frankie, "This discussion is not over Frankie. We are

going to talk later." Becca gestured to the kitchen. "Could you get this batch of scones in the oven for me and get the counter set up please?"
"Yeah sure boss." Frankie answered, deflated.
Becca stopped halfway towards the door, turned around and said gently, "He did a number on you Frankie. I wouldn't be your friend if I didn't feel anger towards him and protective of you. Just promise me one thing."
Frankie looked up and steadily held her gaze, "Name it."
"Just go at your pace on this and only if it feels right. Don't let him push you. You know I'm here for you."
"Thanks Becs," and relief flooded his face.
"Oi! Are you actually opening today?" The voice from the café sounded more impatient this time.
"I'm here, I'm here! We were just in the middle of something." Becca called over her shoulder to Frankie, "Scones, oven, now. And just when I remember - autumn menu and Halloween taster cakes for the counter. We need to get them sorted."
"How about a few taste samples today and we can launch the new menu on Monday?"
"Sounds good to me."
Walking into the café, Becca addressed Wendy. "Sorry about that. Something unexpected cropped up. How's you?"
"Oh, you know. Usual drama getting out of the house, won't bore you with the details but it involved a missing shoe and somebody using someone else's toothbrush. Anyway I'm just going to head through and get set up."

Wendy moved towards the back room of the café which she rents from Becca to run her 'TwinkleStarKydz' dance class and called to Becca, "Could I get a coffee and one of your scones when you have a minute? All the classes are fully booked today, so heaven knows when I'll get the chance for a break again."
"Yeah sure. Will a fruit one do you? I'll bring it through and help you set up."
And with that, Becca opened the door to welcome the first customers of the morning.

Chapter Five

NOW

The adrenaline following the phonecall from *him* had long worn off and Becca's hangover was back. She sat on a bench across the street from the Police Station cradling her takeaway coffee, waiting for Tony. When she contacted the Station to find out what had happened, a Police Officer told her that Tony would probably be released soon as it wasn't looking like any charges were going to be brought against him. "A bit of handbags," was how the Officer described it, but a smashed shop window sounded more than just a testosterone-fuelled pissing competition to her. She couldn't get her head around this. She knew he was angry but a response like this was completely out of character for Tony. However, she was relieved that *he,* Dan Lehmann, wasn't going to take it any further. The longer she waited the colder the coffee for Tony became and the more the memories from last night flashed through her mind like a strobe light, playing out the events in fits and starts to match her patchy recollection of an evening which went so badly, badly wrong. She angrily rubbed at her face, hoping the action would erase it all from her head. It didn't. Her hand instinctively went to her necklace and she toyed with it between her fingers.

She couldn't see him but he could see her.

Tony stood just inside the door to the Station and watched Becca for a while not really knowing what to do. He wanted so much to walk over there and just put his arms around her, hold her and tell her it would be alright. He could see even from this distance the anguish she was in and it pained him. But then in his mind's eye, he could also see the smirk on Dan's face as he relayed the details of his kiss with Becca, the anger flowed back through him and he struggled to contain it without lashing out again. Suddenly he let out a hollow laugh, aware of his surroundings and the reason why he was stood on *this side* of the Police Station door. Not being able to control his anger was exactly the reason he was here.

His outburst and actions had caught him completely off guard.

After slamming the door on Becca he had got into his car and drove to Lehmann's Wine Store without thinking. He had no idea what he was going to do until he got there, he certainly didn't expect to see Dan still in the shop at that time of night. When Dan looked at him, grinned and put his two fingers to the side of his head in some kind of mock army salute, something inside of him just snapped. Tony hadn't even noticed the skip full of debris outside the shop until he was holding the broken brick in his hand and before he knew what he was doing, it was flying through the air.

The crash from the breaking glass was followed swiftly by the siren of a passing police car. Fast forward a few hours and after a firm wrap on the knuckles, he was told he was "lucky that Mr

Lehmann wasn't going to press charges as long as he paid for a new shop window". It stuck in his throat, but he swallowed it along with his pride to get out of there without any further ramifications.

Back on the park bench, Becca routed in her pockets to find her phone which was vibrating furiously; it showed Wendy's number on the screen and she swiftly answered. "Hiya, everything ok?"

"Hey doll. Everything's fine, the kids are devouring their lunch right now. It's just Max has mentioned he needs to get to his football by 2pm and Tony was supposed to pick him up and take him….."

"Shit. I totally forgot."

"Look don't worry, if Tony heads over now he'll still make it."

"Erm, well there's going to be a slight problem with that."

"Becca, what is it?"

"I'm outside the Police Station. Tony's inside."

"WHAT?"

"It's a long story and I really can't get into it now. I know it's a huge ask but Frankie has a spare key to our place along with his café keys. Max's kit bag is sitting in the hall just as you go in the front door."

"I'm on it. Look, I wouldn't be a friend if I didn't ask, but are you OK?"

"Physically, yes. Apart from a monster hangover. Things just got out of hand after you and the girls left last night. Dan kissed me."

"Oh, Becca."

"I didn't invite it Wendy, you've got to believe me."

"I do sweetheart, I do. And I'm guessing this is all related to Tony somehow ending up with B&B courtesy of the boys in blue?"
"Yeah, it sounds worse than it is......" Just then a shadow fell over her and Becca looked up and met Tony's eyes. "Look hun, I've got to go. Are you OK to keep a hold of Emily for a bit longer too? Thanks Wendy, I owe you. Yes, yes I will. I just can't right now. Ok, yes ok. I'll phone you when I'm on my way."
Tony looked away. "Are the kids ok?"
"Yeah, it's just Max's football...."
"Shit."
"It's sorted. Wendy's going to take him. She's going to go past our place to get his kit bag on the way and she'll hold onto Emily for us until later."
Tony let out a sigh and slumped down on the bench next to her.
"I got you a coffee. It's probably stone cold by now."
"Thanks. Even a cold coffee will be better than the dishwater they serve with breakfast," he nodded in the direction of the Police Station.
They sat for a few moments staring straight ahead. Becca's hand went to her necklace once again. Neither one dared to look at the other nor knowing what to say. It was Tony who broke the stalemate first. "So are you going to tell me what's been going on, because trust me it can't be any worse than the versions that's been going through my head all night while I was banged up in there."
Becca's eyes filled with tears. "Yes. But not here. Can we go home first?"

Chapter Six

SEVEN MONTHS EARLIER

The phone in the café was on its fifth ring by the time Becca got to it. "Good morning, Café Swan."

"Hey gorgeous, take it you're having a busy morning? I didn't think you were going to answer."

"You could say that! Wendy's classes are all fully booked this morning and Frankie's finally gotten around to making some of his tester Halloween cakes which have gone down a storm."

"Halloween? Becs, it's only September!"

She giggled. "You know how this works Tony, we've got to be a step ahead and hook them in with a sneaky peak! Anyway, I'm guessing you're not phoning to discuss the café's current cake selection."

"No, I'll leave that to the experts. But I do have a business proposal for you. You know that networking group I go along to? Well a new guy joined a few months back - Dan, Dan Lehmann."

"Is he something to do with the wine store on Great Western Road? I thought that had closed down?"

"Not closed down completely, it was just shut down for a refurb. Anyway, the builders he was using let him down and left him with a job half done, so he asked me if I would be interested in taking on the job. I know it's not what I usually do, but one of the properties I had been working on was just about to go on the market - you know the three bed apartment on Belhaven Terrace? I had a few guys going spare and didn't want to turn down the work.

Plus I've been out for a few beers with him and he's pretty sound."
"Awww, how sweet! You've made a new friend! Do you want to ask him over for a play date? What did you have in mind, a soft play? Climbing trees in the park?"
"Oh you are hilarious."
"Sorry, couldn't resist. But I'm still not too sure what any of this has to do with the café."
"That's the best bit! But will take longer to explain. How about I bring Dan over to the café later this afternoon, around three? And we can go through the idea with you?"
"Hmmm. Sounds mysterious. Yeah that's fine, kids have after school club today anyway so no rush to get them. Look I need to go, Frankie's starting to look a bit frazzled. See you later, love you."
"Love you more."
Becca put down the phone and mulled over the conversation. What on earth did Tony have in mind that could involve her café and the wine store?

She didn't have too long to wait as the next few hours passed quickly with the lunchtime rush and before Becca knew it, Wendy's final class for the day ended bringing with it the last few orders for afternoon coffee and cake. It was just a little after three when the door to the café opened and in walked Tony.
"Hi!" Becca said brightly "You on your own?"
"No Dan's just parking his car. I'll grab a table for us....oh hey Frankie. Not seen you in a while.

How's things? I see you've gone green now!" Tony was referring to the ever changing colour of Frankie's hair, he never opted for 'ordinary'. He's been a vivid letterbox red, a striking cobalt blue and was currently sporting an emerald green.
"Cheers Tony! Oh did I show you my latest ink? And he pulled up his t-shirt to reveal a fresh tattoo on his upper arm. Tony nodded in approval. "Sleeves about done now. Really pleased with it. Although at the rate your good lady wife is working me I'm not sure when it'll get finished! Do you know she had me baking Halloween cakes today? It's only September! Honestly she'll have me churning out mince pies before bonfire night. Anyway, can I get you a coffee?"
"Yeah, a couple of cappuccinos, please mate. I'm waiting on someone and Becca's joining us too - here he comes now.......Frankie, this is Dan, I've been working on a project at the wine store with him."
Frankie turned around and locked eyes with the most gorgeous man he had ever met. Thick dark brown hair, lightly tanned skin that didn't come from a bottle or sun bed, chocolate brown eyes and clean shaven. His clothes were designer which covered a well-toned body, and he smelled divine.
"Hey, good to meet you, Frankie. You're the creator of the cakes that I've heard so much about!"
"Oh I just throw the ingredients together. Nothing too special," spluttered Frankie.
"That's not what I've heard, your cakes are legendary around these parts. I'm embarrassed it's taken me this long to come and try them for myself." Dan flashed a smile towards Frankie and he instantly

went crimson from the neck up.
"Coffees for everyone!!" squealed Frankie in a voice that made Tony choke down a laugh. He clumsily made his way back to the counter, bumping against Becca on the way.
"What on earth got into him?" Becca asked as she joined them, giving Tony a peck on the cheek.
"I think Frankie has a new crush," chuckled Tony.
"Oh no, not again!" groaned Becca. "Hi Dan, lovely to meet you, I'm so sorry about Frankie. He can be his own worst enemy sometimes. It took him months before he was able to hold a conversation with Tony without turning scarlet."
"No need to apologise. Good to meet you Rebecca." He shook her hand.
"Becca, please. We're all friends here."
"Then Becca it is." A smile spread across Dan's face.
"Ok enough of the small talk!" Tony couldn't hide his excitement any longer. "Dan has a unique business proposition for you."
"So I hear. Although I'm not sure how a run-of-the-mill café can help a high end wine store."
"Ok. So let me explain." Dan picked up the conversation as the three of them took their seats. "As you know I recently moved back from London to take over running my Dad's wine store. Well I had....have....big plans for it. But unfortunately the local authority haven't bought into my vision quite yet. The first phase of my plan was a complete renovation. I wanted a total overhaul of the property bringing it up to date to encourage a new clientele into the store. This alone took a lot of discussion with the planners as the store is a listed building, and

then to add the complexity of the renovation, I realised my builders just weren't up to the job so I had to get rid of them. Which is when Tony stepped in and saved my neck, otherwise I would have really been in trouble with the money I had already invested in a half finished project. I need to get the store up and running. And soon. Which is where I hope you come in, to help kick-start phase two of my plan even before phase one begins. Once the store is open, I want to run events using my experience from London - wine tasting nights, gin tasting nights, cocktail making classes.....but to do this, I need to do some further renovation work in the rooms upstairs and again the local authority are dragging their heels over the plans. All of which is costing me even more time and money. So one night when I was having a well needed drink with Tony, offloading the latest developments, he had a genius idea. We hold the events here." Dan made a sweeping gesture with his hand. "At the café."

"Oh! I did not expect that. Erm, Dan, I feel for you I really do, I know exactly how difficult it is to get a business up and running. And I wish I could help, but I'm sorry I don't have a licence for alcohol."

Tony cut in, "Babes, you don't need to. That's the beauty of it. Dan has a licence, so it's done under his licence and run as a private function, a closed event with no-one walking in off the street. All perfectly legitimate. And the best bit is we can advertise the events to the customers who come into the café so we have a ready-made audience. You can work out a theme, Dan can take care of the alcohol and I was thinking Frankie could do a bit of food......"

Dan picked up, "And in terms of the money, we split the profits from the ticket sales fifty-fifty once all the overheads - such as food - are deducted, plus I give you 10% commission for the total amount of wine orders people make on the night."
Becca waited a few moments before replying. "It's certainly an interesting and unique proposal. But I would really need to think it through. It's a lot of information for me to make a decision on the spot." She smiled at them both. "Excuse me a second, I'm just going to check on our coffees. Can you give me a hand?" She indicated to Tony to follow her which he did.
Once they were at the counter and out of Dan's earshot, Tony asked, "What do you think Becs? It could be real winner. Think about how busy this place is and the number of regular customers you have. You could easily sell out the events."
"You may be right Tony, but it's not just about the potential money. I don't know the guy and you're asking me to start up a business partnership with him. It's all just a bit out of the blue, don't you think? I hadn't even heard of Dan Lehmann until you phoned this afternoon and now you're suggesting I start running events with him."
Tony nodded his head. "Sorry. You know what I'm like. When I see an opportunity, I just go for it. I was also thinking it would give you a chance to get to know some of the regulars a bit better, you know? Get a bit more of a social life again. You've told me a few times you miss that. This could be the chance you're looking for plus make a bit of money at the same time. That's all." He stroked her face. "If you

don't fancy it, it's entirely your call.
She sighed and jerked her chin in Dan's direction.
"How long have you known him?"
"About six months give or take. The wine store renovation only came up in conversation a few weeks ago when we were out for a beer."
"And that's another thing! You never told me about the whole wine store thing either!" She playfully punched his arm. He shrugged in response. "Do you think we can trust him? I mean if I'm going to get my business involved," she asked.
"Yeah. He seems pretty switched on. He's got a really clear vision for what he wants to do. And it wouldn't be a permanent arrangement, just until he's up and running."
She considered this. "Ok. Let me go and talk to him again."
"Hey. Everything ok?" Dan asked as they approached.
"Yeah, I was just pressing Tony here for a reference for you," she joked. "OK. So here's the deal. You've talked me into it. But I have one condition. We run the first event as a trial night and if it works, then we look at a programme of events. Deal?"
"Deal!" And Dan flashed that winning smile again and called over to Frankie, "Cancel those coffees, I have something a bit stronger in the car that's more fitting for a celebration! I'll be back in a minute, guys."
As Dan left to get the champagne, Tony kissed Becca and looked into her deep green eyes. "This is going to be the start of something for us, a new phase, I just know it."

Chapter Seven

SEVEN MONTHS EARLIER

Decision made, Becca didn't lose anytime. The next day she spoke with Dan and agreed a date and theme for the trial night. They opted for Friday nights to host the events as the café was always a bit quieter on a Friday afternoon on account of Wendy finishing at lunchtime, so there was no footfall from TwinkleStarKydz classes. This would let Becca close slightly earlier to get the café ready. After discussing several options, they settled on a theme of 'Late Summer Sun' which would allow them to capture the essence of holidays: cocktails and delicious wines from around the world. She also worked with Frankie to put together a menu of food platters (tapas and antipasti) which would complement the drinks and again create the holiday vibe.

"So all we need to do now is get the posters and flyers for advertising in the café and we'll use the same poster design for social media promotion. Dan's working on that today and he's going to come over tomorrow to see if I like what he's done." Becca sighed.

"Don't worry about getting bums on seats!" snorted Frankie. "That's going to be the easy bit. I can think of at least half a dozen of our regulars who would be up for it not to mention the girls from your old workplace, my mates and social media promotion. The difficulty is going to be how we fit them all in!"

"I hope you're right, Frankie. But I'm not making any promises that it's going to be a regular thing. Although I admit I did have a very tentative conversation with Dan about potential future themes. It's a really good time of the year to start a venture like this, we've got Halloween, Bonfire night and Christmas all coming up. Lots of potential over the coming months. That's why I want to get this first one right. I just don't want to jinx it. Zoe's coming in today for a lunch, I'll chat to her and see if she can get a group from R&Ds interested in coming along."
Just then, Wendy plonked down at the table next to them, her mousey brown curly hair even more unruly than usual. "What have you two been up to? You've been thick as thieves all morning. Go on, spill."
"I suppose there's no harm in telling you now it's all pretty much sorted. I'm starting a new venture in the café, a kind of partnership with Lehmann's Wine Store." Becca answered.
"The wine store? I thought it closed down?" asked Wendy.
"No, turns out it it's just been shut for renovation." Becca moved over to the counter and made a round of cappuccinos for the three of them. "Tony's firms been working on it and he's struck up a friendship with the new owner, Dan. I got a bit more info from Tony about him last night. Dan's taken over the business from his Dad. Turns out he'd been working down in London as a qualified mixologist and sommelier for around ten years and moved back up here to take on the wine store when his Dad retired.

He's planning to expand the business so it'll be more than a wine store, using the old storage space upstairs as an area to run private events: cocktail nights, wine tastings, that kind of thing. But he's had a lot of problems with the renovation and he's desperate to start bringing in some money rather than it constantly going out. Tony came up with the idea of using the café to run the events until the wine store is fully open. It would help bring in some badly needed money in the first instance plus get Dan known and build up some buzz around his business. I don't mind helping out, I mean I run a café so we're hardly in competition with each other. And I know how tough it can be to get a new business up and running."
"Wine events? Here? Rebecca Swanson you are a little genius! So when do they start and how much are the tickets?"
"I think we've just sold our first ticket!" laughed Frankie
"You absolutely have!" replied Wendy.
Just then the café door opened and in walked Zoe Powell, same age as Becca but a world away. All designer clothes which changed with the seasons, daily gym visits, high-end make up, dermaplaning and facials meant Becca always felt like the dowdy frump next to her. When Zoe was around she always became more aware of her hips and boobs which had filled out post-baby and put her firmly in the 'curvy' category. Zoe was Becca's oldest friend from her pre-Café Swan life when Becca was an accountant.
"Frankie, can you fill Wendy in with all the details?

Zoe's here for lunch."
Becca skipped over to Zoe and gave her a big hug. She enjoyed catching up with her old friend. Yes, sometimes she would feel a pang of sadness for her former life hearing about the goings on at Red and Davies Accountancy Firm (or otherwise referred to as R&Ds) not to mention remembering a time when she had money to burn on clothes and regular beautician appointments but the thoughts were always fleeting. No sooner would she think 'what if' than she would breathe a huge sigh of relief at not being under the constant stress and pressure to bring in clients and meet fee targets. No exuberant salary was worth that. Plus being a fully qualified accountant meant Becca was able to keep the café books and Tony's accounts in order for free. She left that old life behind her five years ago and although she didn't realise it at the time, it was the best thing that could have happened to her. As much as she excelled in her career, it was an impossible balance to meet the expectations of her senior position at R&Ds with the needs of her very young family.
At the point Becca was made redundant, Emily was six and Max was just about to turn two. It was a complete shock. She had given her all to that firm. She joined fresh out from Glasgow University and even after four years of study she wasn't finished and pushed herself through all the necessary exams to become a chartered accountant. Her hard work paid off when she was promoted to Senior Associate - the youngest ever at R&D. When Tony and babies came along she thought (perhaps naively) that she had worked hard enough for long enough to prove

herself and protect her position.
The day she was told she was being let go was still a blur. She thought the HR meeting was to discuss her request to further reduce her hours; she had been hoping to reduce down to three days from four days. Becca had heard the murmurs that the credit crunch was about to get very real and jobs were going to go so she thought she was doing them a favour by offering to drop her hours further. To leave the meeting with no job and an extremely generous redundancy package was not what she expected. Tony was apoplectic. His business had used R&Ds for years, in fact it was how he and Becca had met. He couldn't believe that after the years of commitment Becca had given them plus the small fortune his business had paid them they were letting her go. But the credit crunch had bitten and Becca was one of the casualties. Tony was determined it wasn't going to destroy her and to cut a long story short, Becca ended up with Café Swan.
The redundancy had also initially caused tension in Becca's friendship with Zoe as she kept her job. Tony long held a suspicion that Zoe had more of a hand in Becca's redundancy but he had no actual proof, just an uneasy feeling whenever she was around. Becca never entertained Tony's bam-pot theory choosing instead to defend her, reminding Tony that having no family ties meant that Zoe was able to commit the hours needed to the Firm. However, despite Becca's best efforts to keep the friendship business as usual, it just simply became the elephant in the room. A lot of the common ground they shared which defined their friendship

was based around their jobs and careers. They both started R&Ds at the same time, both straight from University but from different institutions. In that first nerve-wracking week of having a 'proper job' they were delighted to have someone to cling on to. They celebrated surviving week one with well-deserved Friday night after-work drinks and the friendship was cemented. Over the years that followed, they shared a healthy competition for new clients and fee targets but supported and helped each other when their backs were against the wall. Now Becca had moved on from the corporate world they've been forced to recalibrate their friendship and find new, different reasons to stay in touch, despite now leading very different lives.

"Hey lovely, how's things?" Becca asked as she embraced Zoe. "You've changed your hair! It looks gorgeous."

"Oh, you know. We're of a certain age now when a good haircut can make the difference between looking 30 something or like we're kicking 50! How's things with you? How's Tony?"

"Yeah we're ok. Just plodding along. The cafés doing great and Tony's taken on a bit of a side project which is a move away from his usual property developments." Becca gestured to the comfy sofa which is situated in one of the bay windows of the café and they took a seat. The heat of the autumn sun flooded the area and felt warm and pleasant against their backs.

"Is this something to do with Lehmann's?" Zoe asked.

"How did you know about that?" Becca was taken

aback not to be the one breaking the news to her friend.
"Well someone's got to do his accounts," smirked Zoe, "and it makes it all the better that Dan's a total hottie!"
"Ah. Of course. I should have known he would be with R&Ds. So did you recommend Tony to Dan when he ran into trouble with his original builders?" Becca enquired as Frankie approached the table.
"Hey Zoe. Fab hair! It takes years off you!" Frankie chirped.
"Thanks Sweets. That's the idea!" She flicked her hair and picked up her Louis Vuitton handbag to retrieve her phone and check her emails. Frankie fought against the urge to roll his eyes but caught Becca's gaze in the process and they both suppressed a giggle.
"So do you guys know what you're having? We've got a Slow Roast Pork Roll with Apple Sauce or a Spicy Bean Burger with BBQ sauce on special today."
"Oh I've been desperate for the Roast Pork and Apple Sauce Roll all day!" said Becca. Zoe wrinkled her nose and picked up the menu to scan over it "Oh err, just the smoked salmon salad for me. Without the dressing? And just a water."
"Of course. I'll bring it over. Have you told her your gossip?"
"Lehmann's has already come up in conversation yes, but I haven't gotten around to our big news quite yet." Frankie went back to the kitchen as Becca turned to Zoe. "So, you were saying you already knew about Tony's involvement in the Lehmann's refurb but there's a bit more to the story. You'll

probably know about Dan's plan to run wine tastings once the store's up and running? Well, Tony and Dan hatched a plan to get the nights up and running a bit sooner, especially as the renovation has been held up. We're going to do them here, in the café."

Zoe couldn't hide her surprise. "Lehmann's events? Here? Wow. That is a bit of a curve ball. I knew Dan was getting really frustrated with all the problems with his builders which is the reason I recommended Tony. Turns out they were going to the same business network meeting so already knew of one another. Dan had already been thinking about approaching him so when I mentioned I knew him it was confirmation enough. But I didn't have a clue things had developed even further. That's exciting for you!"

"Yeah. I can't really take the credit for it though," smiled Becca. "Tony and Dan cooked up the idea between them, they only spoke to me about it yesterday."

Just then Frankie returned with their lunch.

"So Tony's up to his old tricks again making decisions for you, huh?" remarked Zoe. Becca shot her a look and replied sharply. "I think that's a bit out of line." Frankie, sensing the tension, sat the food down and retreated quickly to the kitchen. Becca continued, "They might have come up with idea but they hardly had my arm twisted up my back to agree to it. It makes a lot of business sense."

Zoe rolled her eyes. "I was only playing with you Becca. Jeez. So tell me, what's the big idea? Go on, I want to know, really. It sounds great and could be a lot of fun."

Becca took a deep breath to bring her heart rate back down to normal then shifted in her seat to explain the whole plan to Zoe. By the time they had finished eating, Becca had brought her up to speed. "So there you have it. What do you think?"
"Sounds brilliant! Count me in! And it's got the added bonus that I can put it through as 'business development' and claim it on my expenses. I mean, Dan is my client after all!" sniggered Zoe.
"Well, as long as someone pays for your ticket you can do what you like." Becca's reply had an edge to it but it was lost on Zoe who had already moved on and was chattering about buying a new outfit for the occasion.
"You know, sometimes it's really tough doing this job, Becca. I mean the nature of the work means I'm constantly meeting guys I fancy. You know my type, guys who have drive and ambition and look after themselves. But professionally it should be a no go. Dan's the perfect example of that."
"Well if there's someone you really like and it's mutual then you could always do what I did when I met Tony and hand your file onto someone else in the firm." Empathised Becca.
"And lose the fees? No way. No man is worth that! And talking of work, it's time I headed back. Loved our chat today." Zoe gathered her things together and stood up to leave. "I'll be in touch about the Lehmann's night, keep me ten tickets and I'll speak to the bosses about bringing some clients along. Right, need to dash or I'll be late for my afternoon appointment." And with that she kissed Becca on the cheek and swept out the door. Becca collected up

the dishes and returned to the kitchen.
"Honestly boss, I don't know why you put up with her," commented Frankie.
Becca sighed. "I've known her for a long time Frankie. And she's just booked ten tickets for the night for colleagues and clients from R&Ds which is calming my nerves about our venture with Dan."
"I get that, but she's wafted off without paying!" retorted Frankie, "She takes advantage of your fabulousness at times." His voice softened. "Just because you've known her for ages doesn't make her a friend."
Becca pinched Frankie on the cheek. "And that's why you're a real friend, Frankie. You tell me exactly what you're thinking. Don't ever change."

Chapter Eight

SEVEN MONTHS EARLIER

It was another autumnal sunny day and the soft sunlight which poured through the windows of the café gave the duck egg blue and cream interior a pleasant hue, it looked like someone had taken a photo and put a soft filter over the scene. The door opened and in walked Dan, bright and early, with the posters and flyers. Frankie was behind the counter and greeted him. "Well, what do you know, it's our new business partner! What can I get you?"
"A cappuccino, thanks Frankie. And what is that amazing smell coming from the kitchen?" asked Dan.
"Fresh batch of scones just out the oven not five minutes ago. Can I interest you in one to go along with the coffee? We've got our regular plain and fruit plus today's special: orange and dark chocolate." answered Frankie.
"Well, I've never had an orange and dark chocolate scone before. I've got to try one of those. How on earth do you keep in shape with all this temptation around you every day?" And there was that flirtatious winning smile once more which made Frankie drop the cappuccino mug he had just picked up from the shelf. Dan continued, "Is Becca around? I've got the flyers and posters for her to look at."
"School run," squeaked Frankie. "She should be here in about half an hour if you don't mind waiting."
"Yeah I'm happy to hang around. I've got a few emails to send and calls to make. Would it be cheeky

of me to ask for the wi-fi password?" asked Dan.
"Not at all, we have public wi-fi for customers. The password is Ca£e!Swan1. When you've logged in once you won't need to log in again." explained Frankie. "If you want to grab a seat I'll bring your scone and coffee over."
Dan moved over to one of the several booths which furnished the back wall of the café. He chose the booth furthest from the kids' play area to afford him some privacy to make his calls. Frankie delivered his order as Wendy walked through the door.
"Good morning, Luvvie!" chirped Wendy. "Could you give me a hand for a couple of minutes? I've got a car load of toy fish, octopuses and all things sea-life for today's 'Under the Sea' themed class and I'm double-parked."
"I'll help," came the voice from the booth behind Frankie. "Hi, I'm Dan and you must be Wendy?" He shook her hand.
"Yep, guilty as charged. I hope Becca's not been telling tales out of school?" she replied.
"Well, just enough to know you're the kinda lady who's a lotta fun to share a bottle of wine with." Dan gave her a warm smile and Wendy couldn't help herself and returned the smile back at him. "Ok Big Shot. Come on before I get a ticket. I swear the traffic wardens around here dress in camouflage and pounce when you're not looking, tickets just appear out of nowhere in a matter of seconds. Frankie, since you're off the hook, can I have a bacon roll and a coffee please?"
Fifteen minutes later, both Dan and Wendy were seated back in the booth tucking into their breakfasts,

chatting away. Wendy was giving him an abbreviated whistle-stop tour of her life story and how she ended up with the TwinkleStarKydz franchise, and Dan was returning the favour regaling Wendy with his exploits in London, including his decision to move home and take over the family business.
"So how does it work with you doing the classes from the café?" enquired Dan.
"Oh, simple really. I rent the backroom from Becca, although she could easily charge me double what she does but whenever I bring it up in conversation she always tells me that she looks at it as a steady flow of customers though the café. The majority of them either stay for something to eat, or grab a coffee on the way out. She's quite happy she gets the money into the café that way instead. She's a pretty shrewd business woman."
"I'm beginning to see that," replied Dan.
Neither of them noticed Becca enter the café. She went through to the kitchen to dump her bag and coat. "They look cosy," she commented to Frankie and nodded her head in the direction of Wendy and Dan.
"Yeah, he was in here early doors to see you. Something about the flyers and posters?" replied Frankie. "He's been hanging around for about an hour now."
Becca made herself a latte and approached the booth. "Hey. So sorry to have kept you waiting. I didn't realise you would be in as early or I would have asked Tony to do the school run this morning."
"It's honestly no problem. I've enjoyed having the

opportunity to get to know your colleagues." Dan gestured to Wendy who replied, "I'll leave you two to it. I need to go and set up anyway before the first class starts. I'll catch up with you later Becs, nice to meet you Dan."
"You too Wendy, no doubt you'll be seeing a lot more of me once we get started on these wine tasting nights!"
Dan turned his attention to Becca, "So I have the posters and flyers.....what do you think? If you're happy with them I'll email the PDF to you to use on social media." Becca took a poster from the pile and studied the image carefully. Although she had never been, it was what Becca imagined Santorini or Ibiza would look like at sunset with the sun burning bright orange as it sets, reflecting off the white buildings. A table and two chairs were prominent in the foreground, complete with a half drunk bottle of wine, two glasses, a discarded pair of sunglasses and stylish ladies straw Fedora sun hat. It certainly evoked feelings reminiscent of holidays, perfect for the theme. The all-important details of where, when and how much for a ticket were present too.
"Yeah, I like it." said Becca, "I'll put some up today and put a pile of flyers on the counter. Send the PDF to the café email address and I'll get Frankie to put it up on our Facebook and Twitter accounts. I've sold about a dozen tickets already."
"You're a fast worker! That's brilliant. How have you managed that so quickly?" asked Dan.
"I'm surprised you had to ask," replied Becca. "She's a mutual acquaintance of ours - Zoe Powell?"
"Ah. Of course. I should have guessed," said Dan.

Becca thought she saw a flicker of something pass over his face, something she couldn't quite put her finger on. Becca continued, "She's taken ten tickets for colleagues and clients of R&Ds. It's certainly given the ticket sales a boost from the outset. Wendy has also taken a ticket and Frankie's boyfriend Mark, too. There's also a few Mums who frequently come into the café who I'm going to speak to and ask if they're interested. How many tickets do you think we need to sell to break even?"

"Well, we're charging £25 per ticket and if we've sold twelve already I would say we're almost there. I reckon once we've sold twenty we'll easily cover our costs. How many do you think we can fit into the café?" queried Dan.

"Until all the tables are filled?" laughed Becca. "We have a capacity of forty in the café section, the back room where Wendy runs her classes has a capacity of twenty, if seated at tables. So we have options depending on how well the ticket sales go."

"Woah. I didn't expect those numbers." Dan couldn't hide his delight at the potential profit.

"So that's the ticket sales, how much would you expect to make off the wine sales?" enquired Becca.

"Tricky to estimate," came Dan's response. "It really varies as wine is so subjective. What one person finds delicious, another can't palate. So it just depends on the audience, their preferences and whether or not the wine is to their liking. That's where the cocktails come in." Becca gave him a confused look. "The idea behind giving them two holiday themed cocktails at the start of the night is to get them loosened up. So by the time we get onto the wine tasting section of the evening, they'll already be relaxed and enjoying themselves, therefore...."

"More likely to order." Becca finished his sentence nodding her head. The conversation progressed to food and the menu that Frankie had in mind which met with Dan's approval.

"I can't believe how quickly this has happened." Becca said as she sat back in her seat. "I'm excited!"

"Me too," said Dan as he caught Becca's eye and smiled. Something in the moment caught Becca off guard and she subconsciously adjusted her position away from him. "So, how well do you know Zoe?" he asked.

"Oh I've known her a very long time. I used to work with her at R&Ds. That all seems like a lifetime ago now." sighed Becca.

"I still can't get my head around you being a former R&Ds accountant." Dan shook his head, "You seem so far removed from that corporate world, in a good way of course." he smiled.

"Yeah, you and me both. You know when I look back on that period of time I struggle to recognise myself. At the time I loved the identity it gave me, I felt like I was achieving and #WinningAtLife. I was so sure of myself and what I wanted, or *thought* I wanted. When I left, well, it felt like my world had ended. But then Tony invested my redundancy money in this place, and yes, it took a bit of adjusting, and it was not all plain sailing, but now I couldn't go back to that culture of work. The stress and pressure all over making money. Whereas here," Becca gestured around the café, "I'm so proud of this place and what I've created. It's a real haven for parents who need a well-earned non-alcoholic pick me up and reassurance. Yes, Zoe is welcome to the world of accountancy and fees! I'm so much happier here. It feels more real, like I really am doing something positive."

"Hah, and we're about to offer your clientele an alcoholic pick me up too." laughed Dan, then continued, "As for Zoe, she is very sure of herself that's for certain. Brash is a word my Mum would use to describe her! She knows what she wants and isn't going to let anyone get in her way, which is probably the attitude needed in her work environment. But I can see why you thrive here and love it. You've got a good bunch around you, Frankie and Wendy." Dan mused.

"Wendy is like the older sister I never had," Becca reflected. "I rely on her for so much, she does the school run for me, has my kids for sleepovers and it's never a bother even though she has four of her own! I always worry that having my two is too much, but her reply is always the same, Becca when you already have four, you don't notice another two!"

"And what's Frankie's story?" asked Dan.

"Ah, he was the missing piece of the jigsaw that I didn't even know was missing." smiled Becca as she wistfully looked over in Frankie's direction. "I thought we were doing ok in terms of competing with other cafés in the area, then I hired Frankie as an extra pair of hands and discovered he had this unbelievable flair for baking. It took us to a whole new level. When he started with me he was still at the Art College so he worked here part-time to help pay the bills. His artistic skills and natural talent for cakes combined to create something very special. When he graduated I thought I would lose him and I had no clue what I was going to do. Then one day he asked me if he could use the back room for a photography exhibition - which was his focus at college - and we hit off this idea that he could continue to work here, he even increasing his hours, and in return he had a permanent venue for hosting his exhibitions. He gets to do the two things he loves most: photography and creating our amazing cakes. If Wendy is my older sister, then Frankie's my younger brother."

"And do you have any other staff or is it just the two of you?" queried Dan.

"I've got a couple of high school kids who do a Saturday shift and three Art College students who work part-time through the week to give me and Frankie a day off."

"You've really got this business malarkey sussed. And not afraid to try something different by the sounds of it. Between subletting to Wendy, hosting photography exhibitions, and now you're about to expand your empire to wine tasting events!" exclaimed Dan.

"Oh behave! I'm hardly a candidate for Dragon's Den." giggled Becca

"No I'm serious, you're a real entrepreneur Becca. Willing to take a risk and try something new even if you're not too sure about it. I got the impression when we first met you weren't entirely convinced by my proposal." probed Dan.

"Well I can't lie, I wasn't sure. No offence! It's just I don't know you very well and going into a business venture with anyone is a big step. With Frankie's exhibitions, I had known him for a while and I completely trust him." Becca shrugged her shoulders apologetically.

"Hey! No offence taken. Honest. I get it. But I promise you I'm not going to do anything to harm you or your business. I need to get this right just as much as you do because I have my own business to get up and running. I think we can create something pretty special together." Dan put his hand on Becca's and for the second time in their conversation it triggered something in her. She swallowed hard. Just then Dan's phone rang and broke the moment. "Looks like your hubby is checking up on me," he said, "Hey mate! Guess where I am right now? Sitting across from Becca. Yeah, the posters and flyers yeah. Yep. Go on. Oh great, you're kidding? Ok, I'll come straight over. Yeah I'll leave now and meet you at the store." Dan hung up the call. "I've got to go," he said to Becca, "More problems at the wine store. This renovation is going to be the death of me! I'll email you the PDF and will be in touch about some of the other details. I gotta go. Bye Becca." And he smiled at her once more, holding her gaze for just a fraction longer than was necessary before getting up and moving towards the door, calling goodbye to Frankie as he left.

Becca sat for a moment staring at the posters although she wasn't really looking at them, she was trying to process the conversation she had just had. For the large part it was fine, business focused. But just now and again there were some fleeting moments of something else which tugged at the edges of her comfort zone and she didn't know why. Surely he wasn't coming onto her? Was he? No. He knows she's married with two kids. And he's mates with Tony for crying out loud! No. "Give yourself a shake Becca and don't be so ridiculous." She scolded herself. Dan could have the pick of any woman he wants. He used to be a mixologist in London, charm and being flirtatious is probably par for the course in his line of work. Just then, Wendy sat down.

"Penny for them," she said and Becca looked at her blankly. "You look like you're miles away," Wendy continued.

"Just trying to get my head around this whole venture with Dan Lehmann," Becca replied.

"Hmmm. Just be careful there, luvvie," Wendy said, "He's a smooth operator that one, got the smile and charm to render even the most level headed of us giddy and land us in trouble."

"Oh, you don't have to worry about me," Becca waved her hand, "You know me and Tony are solid. Anyway I better get into that kitchen to help Frankie or he'll be taking the huff with me. I've been sitting here chatting for most of the morning!" As she moved towards the kitchen, she couldn't help but think about why she felt the need to say to Wendy that her relationship with Tony was secure. Was it for Wendy's benefit or did she need to remind herself?

Chapter Nine

NOW

The clock in the living room continued to tick as if mocking Becca and Tony, drawing attention to how long they had been sitting there without speaking. Becca had decided she was getting rid of the goddamn thing at the first opportunity.

"I don't know how to start," attempted Becca as her fingers played nervously with her necklace.

"How about at the beginning, how it started. No, in fact, forget that. I know exactly how it started, I introduced you." Tony laughed bitterly. "So just cut to the chase. Was it.....is it.....a relationship or just sex? A quick fumble over the sink in the kitchen at the café or is there more to it?"

"Tony, don't," pleaded Becca.

"I mean you've had plenty of opportunity. All those cosy 'planning' meetings for your boozy nights, staying late to clear up while I was at Wendy's watching *our children*." His anger had taken over now and he was standing over Becca.

"Stop it, Tony!" Becca jumped up so she was level with him so as to salvage some of the power dynamic in the room.

"Well. You've hardly put up much of an effort to explain yourself." His tone was calmer now, he had realised he needed to regain control of himself. His anger had been his downfall in the last twenty-four hours. He turned away from Becca, unable to look at her. "Do you know the real irony in all of this?

When he first started talking about the 'New Woman' he was seeing, he even had the fucking cheek to tell me he met her at your booze nights. Straight away I thought yep, he's definitely Zoe's type. Never for one minute did I think he had both of you on the go." And there was that hollow laugh again.

"Oh shit. Zoe." Becca felt sick again.

"Yes. Zoe. God knows I've never been her biggest fan but she certainly didn't deserve her 'friend' doing the dirty on her. Congratulations Becca, it's not just our marriage you and Dan have screwed up, but Zoe's taken a hit as collateral damage too."

"I didn't sleep with him." Becca's voice was small, barely above a whisper. "If I'm going to be totally honest with myself……and you…..I'll admit a small part of me, just a tiny fraction of me did want him."

Tony, still facing away from Becca, closed his eyes and his shoulders sagged. There it was. Not a physical betrayal, but a betrayal all the same. "Was it building to it, Becs?" he asked, eyes still closed. "Would it have happened if he hadn't told me about the kiss?"

"I don't know." Her voice, still small, was stronger now.

"Yes you do." His anger was returning, he could feel it beginning to bubble up to the surface again. "You've just told me you liked the idea of it, so you do know." He turned to face her, "If you had the chance, if you had the opportunity, *you know* if you would have gone through with it. Tell me," he demanded.

"Tony, it was a kiss. A kiss that he instigated, not

me," Becca countered. She could feel her anger rising too.
"Oh come on. At best, you were using it as a cheap thrill having a younger man run after you. I mean it's not like we're at it every night anymore. I should have known when you were more up for it after the wine tasting nights than you normally would be after a night out."
"Tony, that's enough." Becca snapped.
"At worst, it was all foreplay and you were planning it all along," he continued, not letting up. "So what was it, huh? A bit of stimulation to help you along during our routine once in a while sex-by-numbers, or was it inevitable, Becs. Were you always going to do the dirty on me from the first time he flashed that smile at you?"
Her slap came out of nowhere and landed squarely on Tony's cheek with a resounding snap. Even that godamn clock seemed to miss a beat with the surprise of it. They both froze with the shock of the movement, holding their breath. Becca eventually pushed passed Tony and went into the kitchen. Hands shaking, she picked up a glass, filled it with water and drank the contents in three ugly gulps. She didn't hear Tony enter the kitchen but she felt his presence and turned to face him.
"You went too far. And don't think you're completely innocent here or have you forgotten where we've just came from?" She found her voice but was still unable to look him in the eye. "Yes, he's a charmer and attractive and I was flattered. But we," she flicked her hand back and forward between herself and Tony, "we were never in any doubt. The

kiss came from him, he read the situation completely wrong. I'm not denying the time we spent together but that was all about the nights at the café. Nothing more. During those discussions, yes we talked about other things including relationships and yes we talked about us," again she indicated to Tony, "but I was only trying to help him see that the right person would come into his life and he would know when it's right. I didn't think he would take it as meaning me. To tell you the truth, there might - just might - have been a bit of flirting." Tony snorted. "But not any different from what you do when you need a rush on a quote or an order pushed through." She met his eye and he shifted uncomfortably. She knew she had hit a nerve. "You know me, Tony. You know where my line is and I would never cross it. From day one you watched me hand over your file to Zoe so my integrity could never be questioned. Why do you think I would ever, EVER, jeopardise us?"

"See, this is exactly where I have the problem, Becs. I do know you. You don't just respond to the physical, you need the emotion. That's what makes me think there was more to this than empty flirting. What did you talk about?"

"I can't remember," she replied

"Yes you do," he pressed, "you talked about us, you said as much yourself. What did you tell him about us?"

She turned away from him her hand went to her necklace once more. She knew he wasn't going to like the answer. In many ways her full confession on the detail of their discussions was going to be worse for Tony than if she had physically cheated on him.

Part Two
CONFESSIONS

Chapter Ten

SEVEN MONTHS EARLIER

As the week progressed, Becca had the opportunity to promote the upcoming 'Late Summer Sun' event to some of her regulars.
First on the hit list was Susan who had been a regular at the café for a few years now. She discovered the café by happy accident one day as she wandered the streets of Glasgow pushing a pram in the rain, desperate to try to get her baby, Evie, to stop screaming. The glow of the café lights had been a welcome beacon.
When Susan came through the café door, her chin length auburn hair dripping wet and her brown eyes filled with tears, Becca's maternal instinct kicked in and without hesitation she took Evie and walked around with her. Then, out of nowhere a large coffee and exquisite carrot cake appeared in front of Susan (although she didn't remember ordering it). By the time she had finished her coffee and cake, Becca had sat down with a happy Evie and started to chat to Susan about everything and nothing, reassuring her it's ok, without actually saying as much. When it was time to leave, Becca took no payment and Susan has never forgotten Becca's kindness on that first morning. Evie is now a sassy three year old with a little baby sister, Olivia, who is already edging towards the six month mark.
"Morning Becca, you on your own today?"

"Yeah, for the moment. It's Frankie's day off. But Amy, one of the Art College girls, is coming in to help at lunchtime. What can I get you? The usual?"
"Please. What would you like, sweetie?" Susan turned to Evie who was pointing at Frankie's newest creation which was freshly baked the night before: a layered rainbow cake with each of the five sponges a different vibrant colour, covered in lashings of buttercream, neatly sliced into wedges with each slice topped with a tiny decorative rainbow. Becca couldn't help but smile as she knew what would happen next. Sure enough, an epic negotiation followed which would have brought even Alan Sugar out in a cold sweat. The deal was done as long as little Evie ate her toast and yogurt she would be allowed to take a slice of cake home for an afternoon treat. Susan turned back to Becca and rolled her eyes, "And that's just for a slice of cake. I dread to think what she'll be like when she's negotiating for her first girls' holiday to Ibiza."
"Ah now, interesting you should mention Ibiza," Becca picked up one of the flyers and handed it to Susan. "What's this?" she asked as she scanned the information, "A wine tasting?"
"So do you fancy it then?" Becca pressed.
"I don't know," Susan bit her lip, "there's nothing more I would like than a night out, but it would feel weird coming to something like this on my own."
"You wouldn't be on your own, you could sit with me and Wendy," Becca responded.
Susan smiled, "Ok. I'll need to check with Paul, find out what shift he's on. And how he feels about flying solo with the two of them." She nodded her

head in the direction of the play area of the café where Olivia was sleeping soundly in her buggy while Evie was drawing with chalk on the section of the café wall which was painted with special black paint.

"And how's it going?" Becca followed her gaze.

"Getting there," Susan's smiled weakened "the stress levels are definitely down. And Paul's got the date through for his vasectomy."

"Wow, you didn't hang around." Becca couldn't hide her surprise.

"Didn't I tell you? Paul had an appointment with the GP within a week of me bringing Olivia home. We just had to wait for the referral to work its way through the system and well, here we are."

"And you feeling ok about it?" enquired Becca.

"God, are you kidding? Yes! After everything that happened when I had Evie, well, we weren't really expecting to go through it all again. I mean you know how Paul was a bag of nerves from the moment I showed him the positive pregnancy test for Olivia." Becca nodded in understanding. "In fact, we were driving home from her twelve week scan when he first floated past me that he was going to get it done. I told him it was fine with me but could we just get through this birth unscathed first!" and she laughed. "But we made it, in one piece and no emergencies. So he was straight down that surgery as soon as he could get an appointment." Susan looked down at the flyer in her hand and Becca could see her mind wander, she presumed back to that terrifying time when little Evie made her dramatic entrance into the world. "Oh what the hell.

I'm definitely in need of a night out," she said as her head snapped up to look at Becca. "I'm sure I'll make it, even if Paul's working I'll ask Mum to babysit the girls. I'll take a ticket."
"Excellent!" and the smile spread across Becca's face. "I'm going to speak to Carol too, she's always up for a laugh."
"Carol? I'm trying to think if I know her."
"You do. She's got a little boy, Dylan. I think he must be around eighteen months old now. She goes to Wendy's Tuesday morning class?" Becca responded. "She has jet black shoulder length glossy hair?"
"Oh yes, I know who you mean now. I never knew that was her name though."
"She usually pops in today on her way to work. I'll hopefully catch her this morning."
Just then Evie wandered over, "Mummy, I'm hungry and I can smell Olivia's bum."
"Oh! Alright sweetie, thanks for letting Mummy know. Here, take your juice and I'll bring your toast and yogurt over. Becca's put your cake in here for later." She gestured to the cardboard takeaway box she was holding. Susan turned back to Becca with a sigh, "I suppose I better go and get that sorted then. Thanks for this," and she waved the ticket at Becca. "I'm looking forward to it already!"

Shortly after Susan left the café, Carol came in as expected for her usual take away latte.
"Ah-hah! I was just talking about you earlier." Becca announced as Carol approached the counter.

"I don't know if I like the sound of this." came the response.
"Oh you will," and Becca pointed at the poster which was now prominently displayed on the 'Local Community News' notice board.
"I saw the post on the cafés Facebook page this morning and I was going to ask you about it. I have to say this is a very exciting development, Rebecca Swanson!"
"Tell me about it! It's legitimising a social life for me, under the cover of it being 'work'. Game changer as Max would say!" laughed Becca. "Do I take it you're interested then?"
"Oh absolutely. You can count me in."
"Great! It'll be a fun evening. Wendy's coming and I spoke to Susan earlier too."
"Perfect! Listen I've got to run. Dylan's going through a clingy phase when I'm dropping him at his childminder's, took me ages to detach him from my leg so I'm already running late for work."
"Oh poor Dylan." Becca empathised.
"Thing is when I text her to check he's ok, I always get a photo back showing him happy as Larry. Like it never happened. It's all for my benefit. Or guilt. Anyway, better shoot off. I'll be in tomorrow, bye now," and she picked up her coffee and rushed out the door.
Becca's phone beeped while she was still saying bye to Carol. Once she had left, Becca went to check her messages. It was a text from Tony: Been thinking about you a lot today. God, you're one amazing woman. Just wanted to tell you that xx
Becca smiled to herself. It wasn't so long ago that he

would never have sent her a message like that. There was no denying it, they had come a long way in their thirteen years together and this whole Lehmann's venture had definitely added a new spark between them. Tony was thrilled for her and now the tickets were starting to sell, any misgivings and hesitation she had was gone. She could feel the anticipation and excitement start to build. Something she hadn't felt in years. Yes, this was definitely going to be the start of something big for her.

Chapter Eleven

NOW

Tony watched her from his seat at the kitchen table. She was on her mobile talking in rushed, whispered sentences while playing with her necklace and pacing back and forward in the hallway. He felt exhausted. Although he tried to sleep in the cell last night, he couldn't. The closest he got was a stream of jumbled almost hallucinogenic thoughts that came and went whenever he closed his eyes.

First of all, it was him and Becca on a weekend away to Venice before the kids came along. He could see them sitting in Café Florian in St Mark's Square sipping champagne.

Then the scene jumped to the day he bought her engagement ring. He had looked in four different jewellers before going back to the first shop to buy the second ring he looked at.

Then on to the morning after their wedding when he woke up really early, dehydrated, and with a banging headache. He remembered taking some paracetamol and instead of falling back asleep just lay next to her, watching her as she slept soundly with her wedding make-up still intact.

He was still struggling to make any sense of what had happened this weekend and how they had found themselves in this situation. He was at a loss trying to figure out what he had (or hadn't) done that meant Becca had had her head turned.

He loved her. Still loves her.

That's when he felt the hot tears burn down his face.
"Wendy's going to keep the kids another night for us. She's told them we're having a date night," she said then halted abruptly at the kitchen door. Her husband slumped over the kitchen table openly weeping is a sight she had never seen before. She stood stock still, unsure what to do. Her heart was beating so hard she could feel it thump against her ribcage and hear her blood in her ears.
"Tony?" she said gently as she ventured forward and put her hand on his shoulder. He moved away. Her hand felt like it had been burned by the movement. Undeterred, she knelt on the floor next to him and pulled him round to look at her. "I'm so sorry," she whispered, holding his face in her hands so she could look him in the eye. "I'm sorry," she repeated, louder this time.
He put his hands on top of hers, "I just don't understand, Becs. Are you unhappy? I know we've not had a picture perfect relationship and more than our fair share of ups and downs but I didn't for a moment think you would be considering someone else. Is that my mistake? Did I get complacent, lazy? I've never been great at telling you how I feel or what you mean to me. I know that's always been one of my biggest faults, but ….."
"I'm not unhappy with you Tony," she shook her head and cut him off mid-sentence, they were so close now he could feel her breath on his face and she whispered, her voice full of emotion, "What we have is real. It's not supposed to be perfect - it's a marriage. It's supposed to be difficult, we're supposed to make mistakes and then sort it out. In

doing that we learn more about one another and that's how it's supposed to be. You know every little detail about me and I know every little detail about you. That's where we get our strength in being together. The fact that we still want to be with each other, knowing the imperfections and accepting all the faults. That's what I was trying to get Dan to see. The real, raw reality of a relationship, not the social media-ready vision which he thinks a relationship should be."

She looked away and dropped her hands which were still clasped over Tony's.

"Maybe he took it the wrong way, like I was telling him I wasn't happy with you. When I was just being honest. Trying to get him to realise that to have a true relationship with someone, to open yourself up to being with them in every sense, it means taking the bad with the good."

"If what we have is so real, then why did your risk it?"

"I didn't imagine for one second this would happen."

"But it has Becca."

She turned her head to look at him again squeezing his hands tight, "Tony, I love you. Yes that love has changed over time, it's been thirteen years and two children, for God's sake. I maybe don't love you the way I did when we first met and started dating, when it was all butterflies and expectation, but I still love you. In a different, deeper way. We've got all this history to our story now."

Her eyes searched his face looking for just a flicker of something, anything to let her know it was going to be ok.

What happened next was quick and unexpected.
Tony's mouth was suddenly on hers as he pulled her towards him. She responded, relieved he had reacted to her.
There was a real urgency in their kiss.
They moved together, standing now. The kissing becoming more intense. Becca perched herself on the edge of the kitchen table as Tony manoeuvred himself between her legs. She fumbled at his belt, it loosened and she undid his jeans. She stroked her hand along the outside of his underwear. He pulled back momentarily, his eyes scanning over her face catching on her necklace then back to her face again, she looked directly into his eyes silently pleading with him not to stop. He didn't. Instead he kissed her again, moving his hands to pull up her dress and then he slid his hands along the outside of her thighs until his fingers hooked around her underwear, he pulled them down and discarded them on the kitchen floor.
Becca returned the favour and tugged roughly at his underwear. Tony pulled her towards him and entered her, she let out a low groan as he did and wrapped her legs around his waist and her arms around his shoulders, holding on to him. His hands gripped her hips as they settled into a familiar rhythm. The intensity increased until moments later they both let out a final moan. Now it was over, they continued to hold on to one another, like they were scared to let the moment go.
Eventually, Tony staggered back confused at how he could be so angry with Becca but at the same time want her so badly. He was also embarrassed at what

they had just done on top of the kitchen table where they usually sit as a family to eat meals together. They were both panting with the exertion. Becca quickly arranged her clothes to cover herself again and Tony pulled up his underwear and jeans. He buckled his belt and then ran his hand through his hair.

Becca watched him, unsure what to say.

"It's all such a mess." Tony stared at the floor and shook his head.

"We'll get through this. It's been a misunderstanding that's gotten out of hand," she tried to reach for his hand but he moved away. Becca felt spurned by the action. It was now her turn to feel confused after what had just happened.

"I don't know if I can move on just like that, Becs." he snapped his fingers. "There's still so many things that bother me. First of all, how much detail about us did you go into with him? How many of our private secrets did you share?"

She held her breath.

"And more importantly. The kiss. You said he kissed you. That he instigated it."

"He did, he misread what was going on and….."

"Did you kiss him back?" he raised his head to look at her.

She didn't say anything.

"Did you pull away from his kiss Becs, or did you respond to him the way you just did to me," he gestured between them referring to what they had just done.

"I can't remember, Tony. It was the end of the night, I was tired and had drunk more wine than I had intended to. When it happened it was unexpected and caught me off guard."

"That's not an answer, Becs. It's a deflection. Yes or no is an answer."

"Tony...."

He turned fully towards her now, "Rebecca, did you kiss him back or did you stop it?"

"Yes." She blurted out and instantly her eyes filled with tears. Tony staggered backwards. "Yes to what?"

"Yes I kissed him back."

Chapter Twelve

SEVEN MONTHS EARLIER

Two weeks later and the inaugural 'Late Summer Sun' Lehmann's Wine Store Event had arrived. Ticket sales had gone well, not quite a sell-out and mostly friends and acquaintances but Becca and Dan had both agreed that was no bad thing as it was their first attempt at running an event together so they were expecting some teething problems. They looked at it as a soft opening which would let them iron out any problems in front of a friendly audience so they would know what they would need to work on and improve if they were to agree to a programme of future events.

Becca had closed the café an hour earlier to set up and also give herself some time to get ready. She wouldn't have time to go home and change so she had brought a change of clothes and make up with her. Tony and Dan were due any minute to help set up. The kids were with Wendy and then Tony was going to do a tag-team number, swapping over and he would sit with the kids so Wendy could come to the event. Mick (Wendy's partner) is a taxi driver, so he would bring Becca and Wendy back at the end of the night and Tony would take them home, leaving the kids at Wendy's to have a sleep over.

Becca felt slightly guilty at the thought of Wendy dealing with six kids (four of her own plus Becca's two) potentially with a hangover but Wendy told he not to be so ridiculous and reassured her that she had worked so hard on pulling the event together at such short notice that she absolutely deserved to enjoy it. Not to mention having a well-deserved child-free lie-in the morning after, which she knew Tony was looking forward to the most.

The thought made her smile as she moved around the café rearranging the tables so they were in a semi-circle formation to face the counter where Dan would mix the cocktails and give an overview of each of the wines they were to taste.

She had borrowed some white table covers from a neighbouring restaurant to cover the tables (and the toys in the corner) which helped change the atmosphere within the café. Becca made a mental note that she would need to order table covers if tonight went well as she couldn't rely on the kindness of neighbouring businesses indefinitely. Amy, the Art College student, had put together some very simple but effective floral table decorations using pink lilies and white roses which Becca had bought at cost price from the florist in the next street. The flowers gave off a beautiful scent which was helped along by several scented candles placed throughout the café (all of which were previously gifted to Becca which she had rescued from her cupboards at home for tonight). Numerous tea-lights were scattered on the tables, along the counter and on various other surfaces. She had even sent Tony up into the loft to dig out their plain white Christmas tree lights which she had hung around the walls of the café.

Becca was pleased with the overall result.

With the main overhead café lights turned off, the

candles and fairy lights would provide the perfect atmosphere to enjoy a relaxed wine tasting event.
She was just admiring her handy work when the café door opened and Tony and Dan walked in.
"Wow Becca! This is seriously impressive!" Dan was genuinely taken back by what he saw, "the café looks completely different. It's just perfect."
Tony beamed at her and gave her a wink.
"What can I say, I've got a lot of good contacts!" she smiled but was secretly very pleased with herself. "So, do you guys need a hand?"
"No, we got this," Tony replied. "You need to go and get yourself ready, it won't be long until everyone starts to arrive."
Becca looked at her watch. It had taken her longer to dress the café than she had anticipated and she was now regretting sending Frankie home to get changed when he had offered to stay and help. "Ok, if you don't mind, I didn't notice the time! Dan, all the drink you brought along this morning is in the kitchen. The red wine and spirits are on the counter, white and rosé wines are in the fridge. Vodka for the cocktails in the freezer. Help yourself to whatever soft drinks you need as mixers. Tony will show you where the glasses are stored. Frankie prepped the food platters before he left and he'll be back any time……"
"Becca, go!" Tony spun her around and gently pushed her towards the TwinkleStarKydz room where her clothes and make up were waiting. He followed her into the room and closed the door behind them.
"I just wanted to get a quick moment alone with

you," he said and he produced a small box from his trouser pocket, "and give you a little something to say congratulations."

Becca took it from his hands and smiled. Some habits die hard she thought. He had gotten better over the years, especially since the kids came along, but Tony was always much more comfortable in giving her presents as a way of showing how he felt rather than saying it. The café she was standing in was the ultimate example of that, but in addition, she had a wardrobe full of designer handbags, shoes, perfume and jewellery. Not that she really had the occasions to wear any of it anymore. Although she had rescued her favourite pair of Jimmy Choo's from the wardrobe for this evening.

"Go on, open it." he encouraged. The box snapped open and inside was a gold necklace, the pendant was a small bottle of wine lying on its side with a glass attached to the top of the bottle and some diamonds placed as if falling out of the open bottle into the glass, representing the wine being poured.

"Oh Tony! It's lovely."

"I thought it was just perfect for tonight. Here, let me." He took it from her and draped it around her neck, fastening the clasp. "You've done an amazing job and I thought you deserved a little surprise."

"You really didn't need to, but I love it. I'll never take it off. Thank you." She kissed him and he wrapped his arms around her to continue the moment. After a few minutes she broke away, "I was enjoying that," he groaned. "Yes I could tell!" she joked and her eyes glanced downwards to his groin and they both laughed. "But I really need to get

ready. You can hold that thought for later on tonight."
"Oh I will! I suppose I better go and help Dan, I'll need to head to Wendy's soon to take over babysitting duties." He moved towards the door.
"I won't be long, I'll be out before you go," she said as she started to busy herself with her make up. Twenty minutes later, she re-emerged wearing her go-to black dress which sucked in and skimmed over the right places, her silver Jimmy Choo's glistening as she walked. She had taken her long caramel brown hair down from its trademark high ponytail and quickly run her straightener plates through it using them to give her hair a slight curl. She had a particular way of doing her 'going out' make up which she had refined over the years. It brought out the sparkle in her green eyes and took her ten minutes max to apply. To complete the transformation she had used her Ralph Lauren Romance perfume which she had worn on every special occasion from her wedding day onwards.
When she walked back into the café Tony and Dan had been busy with the final touches. A drinks menu was placed on each table. Four glasses were placed at each seat: one for white wine; one for red wine; a champagne flute; and a glass for water. A small side plate, knife, fork and napkin was also laid out so guests could help themselves to the food sharing platters. Music was playing, Frankie had created a playlist of chilled house dance music which wouldn't be out of place playing at Café Mambo at sunset.
"Looks like we're ready, it looks great." Becca felt a mix of excitement and nerves in the pit of her

stomach.

"And so do you!" said Tony as he walked over to her. "We're pretty much sorted now and I really need to get to Wendy's so she doesn't miss the start." He leaned in for a final kiss and whispered in her ear, "I'll be thinking about you all night. That dress always does it for me."

He turned to Dan and wished him luck. She chuckled as they did some sort of macho high five handshake thing as Tony walked towards the door. Dan had been busy doing the prep work for the cocktails which would kick off the evening. She could feel his eyes on her, so she turned to face him.

"So, what are we having?" she asked.

"I thought we would start with a classic Mojito and then go a bit retro with a Sex on the Beach, but with a contemporary twist."

"Oh I used to love Sex on the Beach!" Dan caught her eye and her cheeks coloured. "It was the first cocktail I ever tried back in my early 20s. So what's the twist?" Becca gushed trying to cover her embarrassment.

"Well, it's traditionally made with vodka and peach schnapps. But I'm using a gin peach liqueur in place of the schnapps. Here." and he passed her one which he had just made.

"Oh wow! It's like the cocktail has grown up. It's delicious, not as sweet as the traditional version."

"Exactly. Hopefully by the time they've enjoyed the cocktails they'll be nicely loosened up and ready to buy some wines. I've got a great selection for tonight two whites, two rosés, and two red, finishing off with a fizzy. Oh, that reminds me, can you put these on the tables?" Dan handed her the all-important order forms, the target for the evening was for everyone who attends to order at least one bottle of something.

"Sure." Becca took the forms and walked around placing them on each table. Dan continued to work on the cocktail prep, watching her as she moved.

"So how long have you and Tony been together?" he asked.

"Oh, mmm. Emily is eleven and we had just had our one year anniversary when I found out I was pregnant, so around thirteen years now." She could see him trying to do the mental maths. "When I say one year anniversary, I mean since our first date, not our wedding anniversary. We actually got engaged after just three months together and were married six months after that."

"So you just knew?" he probed?

"Well, yeah. It's not all been plain sailing, believe me. After the whirlwind at the start we had a lot to find out about one another so we did a lot of learning along the way."

"I can barely get someone to go on a third date with me, let alone an engagement after three months! I'd love to know your secret." He smiled at her just as there was a knock at the café door. It was Frankie bringing with him the first of the guests.

"Oh believe me, I'm no expert! But I am a good listener if you need a friendly ear. I've had plenty of practice in here." She walked over to open the door.

He watched her go, his eyes wandering over her and murmured "I might just take you up on that offer."

Chapter Thirteen

SEVEN MONTHS EARLIER

They were well into the night and Becca was delighted with how it was going. The cocktails had gone down a storm and did the job of getting everyone in the mood for the wine tasting section. Dan's charisma and easy charm had instantly won over the crowd and he had them hanging on his every word as he explained the tasting process and described each wine.

The conversation at Becca's table was flowing as freely as the wine and she was really having fun being in the company of other like-minded Mums. It wasn't unknown for her to share a bottle of prosecco with Wendy but she didn't know Carol and Susan too well so she was enjoying the opportunity to get to know them better. The chat had turned to partners and Becca had just finished explaining how she and Tony had got together. "So what about you guys?" she asked.

"Well, you know all about me Becs!" Wendy laughed, "but for the benefit of the ladies here, I've been with my partner Mick for almost six years now. He's a taxi driver. He was a friend of my cousin and we met at my cousin's birthday party. I wasn't long divorced from my first husband and Mick had just separated from his partner. We ended up spending a chunk of the night comparing notes, and that was that! We got along, had stuff in common including a kid each, my Austin and his Lizzie," she shrugged, "it was nice to have someone to talk to who understood the single parent struggles. There's only a year between Austin and Lizzie, they're eight and seven now, but at the time they were both just toddlers so we had a lot to talk about. We've got another two boys now, too. Twins, Nicky and Sammy, who are four."

"Four kids? That's a handful! I've only got Dylan and I'm exhausted!" exclaimed Carol as she took another sip of her wine.

"Ah well, to be honest it was a bigger jump going from one to two kids. When you've just got one they can have all your attention and you can nap when they do or just watch mind-numbing day time telly. When there's two to deal with, well, someone always needs something so it wasn't a huge jump to add more in the mix. Although to be fair, we weren't expecting to be outnumbered two to one after just one more pregnancy! When we found out it was twins, it was a bit of a shock. That's also the reason I started with TwinkleStarKydz, more flexible than a nine to five job plus I only work school term times. And with Mick being a taxi driver, it meant he could mostly work evenings. It all made sense. But enough about me, what about you guys?"

Carol was first to offer her story, "Well, my fella is Jason and we've been together for like, well, forever! We were at school together you see. I stayed on to do my exams but Jase left and got an apprenticeship as a plumber with the council. He's worked there ever since. He's a proper home bird, content with his

lot. He's got me and now Dylan and he feels like he's won the lottery." There was a chorus of
'awwws' and 'that's sweet' from around the table.
"We haven't gotten around to a wedding yet, it all costs money doesn't it? And money is one thing we just don't really have right now, especially as I can only work part-time with Dylan being the age he is," she sighed but then smiled, "one day though. So I just live out my wedding fantasies by watching 'Say Yes to the Dress'!" They all laughed.
"I guess that just leaves me," Susan picked up her cue, "Husband is Paul and I absolutely get where you're coming from Wendy. He's a train driver, which means shift work and awkward hours which can be tricky when juggling childcare." Wendy nodded her head in understanding. "We've got the two girls - Evie and Olivia - you've probably see them around the café. And our story isn't quite as traditional as the rest of you. We met online." The disclosure was met with reassurances from the girls.
"I'm ok about telling people that's how we met. It's much more the 'done thing' now. I guess you can say we were trailblazers! But back then when we did it, there was still a bit of a connotation attached to it, you know? Suspicion that if you found the guy online then there must be something wrong with him. But to be fair, I was getting no where fast in the pubs and clubs. I was quite happy to give it a try and I'm glad I did......."
"Sorry to interrupt ladies," it was Dan. He addressed Becca directly now, "We're ready for the final wine, the fizzy?"
"Yep, no problem." She spoke to the girls, "I'll be

back shortly, I'm just going to help Dan serve the final wine." and she followed Dan to the kitchen to get the bottles of fizz out of the fridge. "It's going well." she said as they walked.
"It really is," he replied, "I know we haven't collected the order forms in yet but when I went around to serve the second red I could see that the forms on the two R&D tables were already looking healthy."
"That's great news! So what do you reckon? Would you be up for a programme of events until the store is open?" quizzed Becca as she popped open a bottle of fizz.
"Absolutely. I'm game for it if you are." Dan poured some of the wine into two spare glasses which were sitting on prep area, offering one to Becca which she took from him and smiled.
"Then I think a toast is in order," she said. "To the Lehmann-Swanson events!" and she held up her glass.
"To the Lehmann-Swanson events," Dan replied. They chinked glasses and took a sip of the fizzy. "Right, we're on the home straight now. Just get this final wine served and we're done."
They both left the kitchen carrying two bottles each. Becca made her way over to the table where Frankie was seated with his boyfriend Mark and some of their friends. She started to fill up their glasses. "So have you enjoyed the night?" she asked.
"Becca, it has been brilliant!" Frankie gushed.
"And how are you, Mark?" she asked as she filled up his glass.
"Yeah I'm doing fine thanks, good to see you again.

So Frankie's told you our news then?"
"Yes he has," she smiled coolly at him, "and he knows my thoughts on it."
Mark stood up to speak with her privately. "Look, I know you're not happy about this and I understand why. I was an idiot." Becca snorted. "But I told him I had been an idiot, and I'm telling you I was an idiot. And I also realised, well, that I love him. And I messed up big time." Becca's expression softened. "When I got back in touch with him, I didn't expect him to agree to meet up with me. I couldn't believe it. But I laid it all out for him, told him I knew I screwed up and that I had done a lot of growing up and well, I really wanted us to give it another go." He met her eyes. She scanned over his face taking in his dark hair and chiselled features. She sighed.
"You're both grown-ups. What I think doesn't really matter."
"But it does matter, to Frankie. And if it matters to him, then it matters to me. He didn't put me up to this. I want to put things right with you. You're like his big sister."
"Well in that case, I appreciate you speaking to me Mark. It takes guts. But just keep that in mind, I'm his de facto big sister. So you mess with him again….."
"Then I'm messing with you, too." he finished her sentence for her.
She nodded and asked, "So we're clear?"
"We're clear," he replied, "and are we good?"
She studied Mark's face one last time, "Yeah, we're good."

At that Frankie, who had been nervously listening into the exchange stood up and gave her a hug, "Thanks Boss."

She whispered in response, "I'm here for you," and gave him an extra squeeze, then let him go picking up the bottle once more. "I better go and get the rest of the room served or we'll never get finished tonight," she turned and headed for Zoe's table.

As she approached, she could see Zoe was well on her way. Becca wasn't surprised, she knew that Zoe ate a very carb-light diet and the mix of cocktails and wine meant she had probably consumed more alcohol than she could handle. "You doing ok?" she asked as she deliberately poured a smaller amount of fizz into Zoe's glass.

"Absolutely! Wonderful night Becs. You did amazing job," Zoe enthused. "Oh! I love your necklace!" Becca could definitely detect a slur in her speech.

"Thanks, Tony gave it to me tonight to mark the occasion. I'm glad you've enjoyed the night and it means a lot to me that you came along to support me," she replied. Zoe waved her hand.

"Oh not at all! It's what friends do. In fact, I was wondering if you could do me a favour. As a friend."

"Name it."

"Dan. Would you put in a word for me?"

"Zoe, we're not at high school! You're both grown-ups, why don't you just ask him out yourself?"

"Because if he turns me down I would be mortified! I don't know how I could ever face him again at work."

"Hang on, if you go down that road with him then you know you've got to hand his file on to someone else?"
"Well, technically I don't need to. I know it's frowned on but there's no official rule I would be breaking. And I wouldn't want to lose a client....and fees.....without knowing for sure it was worth it."
Becca shook her head. "No, Zoe. I'm not going to do it."
"Oh come on, Becs. I really like him. I honestly think I could make a proper go of it with him."
Becca paused for a moment and finally said, "I'll do it. But on one condition....."
"......Hand the file over." Zoe said flatly.
Becca nodded and said softly, "I'm just looking out for you. It's for your own protection, your job, your reputation....."
"Yeah, I know. And I know you're right too, as much as it pains me to admit. Ok. If he agrees to a date, then I'll pass on the file. There's plenty more fees in the sea!" she laughed at her own joke.
"Exactly." Becca couldn't hide her relief. "I'll go and have a word with him now. It looks like he's finished serving the fizzy," she gave Zoe a wink and walked off to speak with Dan.
"Well, I honestly don't think the night could have gone any better," he said as she approached him. He had collected the order forms and was skimming through them.
"How are they looking?" Becca asked, indicating the sheets of paper in front of him.
"Pretty healthy on first glance. On average we've sold one and a half bottles per head! That's smashed

my target of selling one bottle per head," he unleashed a dazzling grin on her. "That's a really impressive profit for the evening considering we didn't sell out the tickets."
"So lots of potential then. Once word gets out about tonight and we increase the ticket sales?"
"Absolutely. This is seriously going to help me, Becca. It's going to make a huge difference to the wine store to have some money coming in at this point in time. Now that Tony's taken on the renovation, I'm confident the store will be open by February and the upstairs function room ready by summer. If we can have some events running at the café between now and then, it's giving me a chance to generate an income ahead of schedule and build a clientele at the same time. I don't know how I can ever thank you. And Tony of course!"
"Interesting you should say that," she responded sensing the perfect opportunity to manoeuvre the conversation to Zoe, "I have an idea."
"Go on, I'm intrigued," he answered
"You mentioned earlier about your dating struggles. Well, I might also be able to help out there too." He looked at her confused. "Zoe," she said.
The expression on his face changed. "Look, I know she's your friend, but she's really not what I'm looking for. You know earlier when I mentioned to you that I struggled to get past the third date? I've worked out why. I always end up going out with the same type of person, self-centred and superficial....."
Becca sharply interjected, "Careful, that's my friend you're referring to."
"And you suggested the idea," he retorted. "I don't

mean any offence," he held up his hands as if defending himself, "but I'm ready for something real now. You know, like you and Tony. I'm ready to put in the effort to make a relationship work." He looked over towards Zoe. "She's just so obsessed with fees and meeting her monthly targets that she's never going to put time into building a relationship."

"What if I told you that she was going to hand your file onto a colleague so she could give it a go with you? She's forfeiting your fees."

"I don't know Becca…."

"Look, you said earlier you couldn't get past three dates. Give this three dates. If you don't feel it's working by then, well fair enough. And there will be no embarrassment from a work perspective as someone else will be dealing with your accounts, not Zoe." Dan considered this for a moment. Becca continued, "and you just never know, you might beat your own personal record and make it to four dates…." They both laughed, breaking the tension that had built during the conversation.

"Ok. Go on then. It might actually be fun. There's a few bars and restaurants I've been wanting to try out but haven't had the company."

"There you go!" she said, giving him a friendly punch on the arm. She looked over towards Zoe and gave her a thumbs up.

Zoe had watched the entire exchange from across the room. She was aware the alcohol had affected her faculties but despite that, she could see there was something in the way Dan was looking at Becca that she didn't like. Not that it would matter any longer. Becca's thumbs up gesture meant she would get her opportunity with Dan and that's all she needed. Once she was on her own with him she would make sure he would forget all about Rebecca bloody Swanson.

Chapter Fourteen

NOW

Becca was now seated at the formal dining room table which occupied a corner of their family lounge. This table was usually reserved for special occasions, such as Christmas dinners and birthday tea parties, or date nights between her and Tony. The irony of this was not lost on her. As far as her kids were concerned that's exactly what they were doing tonight. However, the reality couldn't be any further from the date night story which Wendy had given them.

Her mind wandered as she looked around the room taking in the high ceilings and period features which they managed to retain while still achieving a contemporary look. She still had to pinch herself that she lived in this gorgeous four bed, stone build semi-detached villa in Jordanhill, just a short fifteen minute drive from the café. They bought it just after their wedding when Tony heard through his contacts it was about to go on the market. He had warned her it was a 'do-er upper' which accounted for the knock-down price as they could never have afforded it otherwise but when he showed her around she could see the potential and fell in love instantly. Thankfully, with his team of guys they worked through the project in record time, which was just as well as she was pregnant with Emily by the time they moved in a few months later.

Her mind came back to the present and she

nervously checked her mobile, playing with the pendant on her necklace as she waited. She had texted Zoe and was waiting for a response. Thirty minutes had passed and nothing. She could see those two blue ticks in the corner of her WhatsApp message taunting her, she knew Zoe had read the message.

Her stomach rumbled, she had eaten nothing all day and it was now dinner time. They had ordered takeaway pizza, not from a fast food chain which the kids inexplicably prefer, but from a local Italian restaurant her and Tony both enjoy. She had set two places at the formal dining table for them. Not that she was trying to pretend this was a date night, she just couldn't face eating at the kitchen table after their earlier unexpected act. She coloured at the memory of it, how urgent and raw it was.

Tony had gone for a shower. He said he needed to freshen up as he hadn't washed since getting home from the Police Station. She wasn't sure how much he wanted the shower to wash off the grime from the cell or from the sex they had had. She felt grubby too, but right now her hunger was taking priority.

Tony walked into the lounge carrying the pizza takeaway box in one hand and a cold beer in the other. "The doorbell went just as I came downstairs," he said as sat down. She caught his scent in the air as he passed. His signature Giorgio Armani Acqua Di Gio freshly applied, the only aftershave he had ever worn, yet underneath the aftershave she could still detect his own scent. She often wondered if there was something primal about recognising the scent of your partner, if other people can smell it or if it's just you. A bit like the smell of your new born baby, nothing smells like the scent of your own child. In the few times she had been physically close enough to Dan, she could smell his aftershave and nothing more. Her train of thought was disturbed by the beep of her mobile. She snatched up the phone hoping to see a reply from Zoe, but it was from Frankie: Wendy told me what happened. WTF Becca! You OK?xx

She could sense Tony bristling as she read the message, "Don't worry, it's not from *him*." She spat the words out at Tony. He just looked at her, said nothing and opened the pizza box. "It's from Frankie. He's found out about what happened from Wendy. I was hoping it would be Zoe. I texted her when you were in the shower. I need to speak to her." She realised she was babbling now. Tony stayed quiet, taking a bite from his pizza and a sip of his beer. "I'm just going to text him back. I wish Zoe would reply." She fumbled with her phone and sent a quick message to Frankie: I don't know. Trying to fix it but it's a real mess. Can you keep the café running for me? I think I'll need a few days off xx

The response came back immediately to tell her not to worry, he would handle the café with some help from Mark. There was also some reassurance that he was available if she needed to talk. The offer brought a lump of emotion to her throat. She sat the phone down and took a slice of the pizza from the box. She was very aware of Tony's silence and it was killing her. She took a bite from her pizza but despite her hunger and knowing how good it should taste, it was like cardboard in her mouth. She picked up her can of Diet Coke and took a sip to wash it down.

"Not having a glass of wine then?" There was a definite edge to Tony's words. She paused with the can in mid-air, "No, funnily enough I'm not in the mood," she retorted. This exchange was met with silence and they finished eating their pizza without any further conversation. The atmosphere between them was turning hostile again which perplexed and unsettled Becca as she hoped they had turned a corner following their earlier act.

Eventually, when Becca couldn't bear it any longer, she broke the stalemate, "I feel like I'm on trial here for something I did wrong but we haven't talked about you last night. I'm not the one who ended up in prison! I'm not the only one who's made mistakes this weekend. What did you think you were doing going after Dan like that?"

"I broke a window, Rebecca. I didn't go behind your back and cheat on you with one of your friends. Don't try to compare the two." She noticed he had used her full name. He never used her full name. She felt chastised like a naughty child and got the distinct impression the broken window and subsequent trip to the Police Station was not to be mentioned again. He continued, "If we have any hope of moving forward from this, I need to know everything."

"Tony, I really don't know what else there is to tell you. He mistook our conversations.....our very general conversations.....about relationships as something else. I was just trying to help him figure stuff out with Zoe. I don't know what was going on inside his head, what he thought I was telling him, or what signs he thought I was giving out. All I know is he got it all wrong. I wasn't telling him I was miserable with you or that I was open to a having an affair with him. I really don't know what he was thinking. I'm not a mind reader."

Tony took another sip of his beer as he considered what she said. "So why kiss him back?"

She sighed, the pizza had started churning in her stomach in an unpleasant way, "I don't know why I did it. Yes, I was drunk but that's no excuse. And now, because of that very brief moment of utter madness, I think I've broken us." Verbalising her worst fear made it all feel frightening and real. She broke down, overwhelmed by the potential reality of what might lie ahead: her and Tony no longer together. Several minutes passed and she regained control of herself, she was conscious Tony had not moved from his position. He had made no effort to comfort her or reassure her. In all their years together, through her redundancy, having the kids, every time she had broken down with such emotion he was always straight to her side wrapping himself around her to make a protective bubble. But not today. Another bit of hope died within her as she registered this.

"Ok," he said, "so that's the kiss. You've also put your hands up to a bit of flirting and admitted to fleeting fantasy of being with him. But what about the other stuff?"

She looked blankly at him. He tried again.

"I can accept the fantasies, we all have them. I can even stomach the flirting because as you pointed out earlier, I've been guilty of that in the past too. And at a huge, huge push, I could maybe even get over the kiss. But you mentioned the 'benign' conversations you had with him. I want to know what you talked about. I want to know exactly what you told him about us. How much of our private life did you actually share?" He took the final gulp of his beer which drained the bottle.

This was torture for her. She knew she was going to have to come clean. She knew she was going to have to tell Tony everything if she was to stand even the smallest chance of fixing their marriage. She was going to have to admit that she didn't just share some general relationship advice with Dan. She had gone into real intricate details with him about her marriage with Tony and she knew that once Tony was aware of the full extent of what she had shared it was possibly going to push their marriage past the point of no return. She also knew she had no choice. She took a few deep breaths and another sip of her Diet Coke, stalling for some time and trying to figure out the best way to start the conversation which may well end her marriage.

"Ok. He had been out with Zoe a few times. He really hadn't been sure about going out with her in the beginning. She was keen, but I had to gently encourage him to give it a try with her. Anyway he had made a passing reference about being unable to get past a third date with a potential girlfriend, so I suggested he gave it three dates with Zoe and if it didn't work, then fair play to him he had given it a go. She was giving up his file so there would be no awkwardness with her still doing his accounts….."

"I know all of this. You told me this after that first wine tasting night back in September. I want to know what *you* talked about. How *you* exposed *our* marriage to *him*."

"I was getting to that. By the time the 'Autumn Festival' wine tasting night had come around, he had had his three dates with Zoe and he still wasn't sure whether or not the relationship was going to go anywhere. I suppose I became a bit of a shoulder to cry on for him. That's when it started."

Chapter Fifteen

SIX MONTHS EARLIER

The next event on their calendar was the "Autumn Festival" wine tasting night which took place the weekend between Halloween and Bonfire Night. It provided the perfect opportunity to encompass both celebrations into the one event and Dan had created two cocktails of his very own for the occasion. The first cocktail he called "Witches Brew" to represent Halloween. It was served in a high ball glass and comprised of vodka, Blue Curacao and pineapple juice; the combination of the blue liqueur with the yellow fruit juice turned it the most extraordinary green colour. The rim of the highball glass had some white candyfloss draped over it to look like spider webs and a black and white striped straw poked though the candyfloss to make it easy to drink through the decoration. The second cocktail was called "Toffee Apple" to represent Bonfire Night. It was served in a martini glass and used a salted caramel flavoured gin and apple flavoured vodka topped with grenadine to give it a bright red colour and finished with a splash of lemonade. The rim of the glass had been dipped into apple juice and embellished with crushed honeycomb. Both cocktails looked incredibly striking sitting on the counter of the café.

The rest of the evening would follow the same plan as the original night with tasting six seasonal wines and one celebratory fizzy to finish. Again, Frankie had put together a food platter themed for autumn providing small espresso mugs of butternut squash soup, hearty chunks of homemade bread, mini cheeseburger sliders, mini gourmet hotdogs and the infamous Halloween cupcakes.

Becca had dressed the café to tastefully reflect the time of the year, opting this time for coloured fairy lights which were peeking through pulled-cotton style spider web decorations which adorned the walls. Tealight candles were again on the tables with the addition of green, orange and black LED tealight candles adding an interesting change, and Amy had worked her magic with some colourful floral table decorations using autumnal colours of deep red roses, orange gerbera daisies and green foliage which popped against the newly purchased white table covers.

Word had spread about the first event and along with the longer lead in time to promote the night, the tickets had sold out with forty five people expected to attend. As a result they needed some extra hands for serving the wines. Wendy, Frankie and Mark had offered to step in and help with this. They had all been primed to pour only a third of a glass per wine (it was a tasting after all and there were six to get through) except for the final fizzy which would be a full glass. Becca felt that familiar feeling of excitement and nerves as the guests started to arrive. Although they had one successful event under their belt, the numbers attending tonight took it to a whole new level and would really make or break their plans for the months ahead.

"Ready?" Becca asked Dan as she toyed with her

necklace. Frankie opened the doors and the first guests started to filter into the café. Dan nodded decisively. Carol and Susan were some of the first to arrive, Becca welcomed them with a wave and indicated to them to come and sit at the table which was marked 'Reserved'.

"There was a queue outside!" Susan giggled as she approached the table, "hottest ticket in town tonight!"

"Oh don't!" Becca replied, "I'm nervous enough with it being sold out." She saw Zoe arrive bringing with her the clients from R&Ds, this time she had increased the ticket numbers to fifteen. Becca waved over and Zoe responded. "Excuse me ladies, I just need to go and say hello to another one of my friends." She made her way over to Zoe and they gave each other a hug.

"So, how are things going with Dan?" Becca didn't hold back, she was straight in with the all-important question grinning like it was a conspiracy between them.

"Well, we've seen one another a few times now and yep there's been some progress." She nodded in response.

"So would you say it's going somewhere then?"

"I'm taking it slowly but yes, I think I might just finally get what I want."

"That's great Zoe, I'm really pleased for you." At that point Dan joined them and gave Zoe a kiss on the cheek. "We were just talking about you," Zoe said as she playfully bumped her hips against Dan.

"I thought I could feel my ears burning," he replied.

"I've just been hearing that you've been out on a few

dates," Becca stated.
Zoe couldn't hide her excitement, "Yep, first time we went to the new Japanese place in the city centre, next time we just went to a few bars and last week we went to the Italian place you're always talking about Becs."
Becca addressed Dan, "So let me get this right, that's three dates?"
"You counted correctly," he answered.
"And can I presume there's going to be a fourth?" she pressed. This time it was Zoe who responded "Yeah. We're definitely going to be spending some more time together."
Becca nodded her head in approval. "Sounds like it's all working out. If you'll both excuse me, I'll leave you to it, I need to go and say hello to a few people before we get started."
Zoe watched her leave and asked Dan, "Why was she so interested in the fact we had been out together three times?"
"Oh, it was just something Becca had said when she first suggested I took you out." Zoe looked appalled and Dan laughed in response, understanding what Zoe was getting at with the reference to three dates. "No! Not *that*."
"So you've got some private jokes going on between you, huh?"
"Well yeah, but there's nothing in it. Just friendly banter."
Zoe watched Becca work the room, meeting and greeting her guests, laughing at their jokes and accepting their compliments. Her feelings towards Becca were gradually escalating and she was finding

it increasingly difficult to play nice with her but she knew she was almost there. With every night out and phonecall with Dan not the mention the constant text messages between them, she knew her plan was falling into place. It would just be a matter of time before she got what she wanted and she wouldn't need to have anything more to do with Rebecca Bloody Swanson.

Chapter Sixteen

SIX MONTHS EARLIER

A little while later and the evening had settled into its groove. The reaction to the cocktails was tremendous and Dan was rightly proud of himself. There were lots of positive reactions to the food too which gave Frankie an ego boost and he couldn't stop grinning. They had reached the wine tasting section of the evening and for the moment Becca had taken her seat with Wendy, Carol and Susan. Susan and Carol had met each other for coffee a few times since the first wine tasting night which meant everyone was at ease with each other. As a result, the topic of conversation for this evening had turned to comparing labour and birth stories.

Wendy had gone first. Her labour with Austin had been pretty unremarkable and straight forward with nothing exciting to tell. But when she had had the twins it was by a caesarean section and even that didn't go exactly to plan, "I wanted to go natural, but Sammy was lying breech you see, so we were advised it would be safest to have the c-sec. He was an awkward bugger at birth and nothing has changed ever since," she laughed. "I was booked in for a c-sec at 38 weeks, but started having contractions a few days before then so was taken into hospital and the docs decided it was too risky to wait any longer. Apparently a natural birth for twins when one is breech could be pretty disastrous. So it was all systems go."

"And did you feel ready for it?" Susan probed, "you know, if you had already got your head around having the c-sec instead of natural?"
"Well, that was the weirdest thing. You would have thought it wouldn't have really mattered. After all we were expecting to have the section in a few days' time, but I was proper freaked out about it. Mick had a real job on his hands keeping me calm. I just kept saying 'but what if they don't get me to theatre on time?' It was only once it was all over and the twins were safely tucked up in their cribs that Mick admitted he was shitting himself too."
Becca was really taken aback to hear this from her friend. She always considered Wendy and Mick to be completely unflappable. "Wendy I had no idea," and she put her hand over her friend's and gave it a squeeze.
Wendy smiled and squeezed Becca's hand in return, "I think it was just that final shred of control being taken away from me that did it. First off, twins weren't even on our radar so to be told at our ultrasound there were two babies, well, we needed to get our heads around that. Then I decided regardless of there being one or two babies, I wanted a natural birth but I was told nope, that couldn't happen. So we had 'Plan B' and a date for when we would have the section, but nope, that wasn't meant to be either. It was just the straw that broke the camels back for me. But hey! I survived."
"Yeah, I get where you're coming from," Susan reflected. Becca met her eye and gave her a smile of encouragement as she knew what was coming, "When I had Evie it had all gone so well. No

problems during the pregnancy or the labour and even the birth was pretty straight forward. It was once Evie had arrived that it all went wrong. I suffered a postpartum haemorrhage." There were some audible gasps around the table.

"What happened?" asked Carol.

Susan shrugged her shoulders, "It was just one of those things. Apparently there was a bit of trauma during the birth that caused the bleeding so I was rushed off to theatre to stop it, leaving poor Paul in bits in the room with Evie."

"Oh God! Poor guy!" Carol was stunned.

"The last thing I remember before passing out was alarms going off and the room filling up with doctors," she dropped her gaze to look at the table and continued, "Paul's face was just frozen in fear. When I came round after the emergency surgery he looked 5 years older. His eyes were red raw and bloodshot and he had black bags like I had never seen before despite his shift pattern as a train driver!" Her laugh sounded hollow. "When I opened my eyes he screamed and ran out of the room coming back with midwives and doctors, one of them started to explain what had happened. It was just a haze but I could pick out phrases like 'massive loss of blood'. It was a good while before they all left us alone and Paul was able to give me the hug I really needed. It was only then I remembered about Evie! In all the uproar, the very reason I was in hospital in the first place had totally slipped my mind!"

"I can't believe you were brave enough to have baby number two after all that," Wendy blurted out.

"Well, we didn't actually plan for baby number two."
"Ah."
"We went through the mill having Evie so we agreed that if there was even the tiniest risk then we wouldn't go through it again, especially now we had Evie to think about. So when I found out I was unexpectedly pregnant, we were honestly terrified. It was the longest nine months of my life. They kept a really close eye on me and thankfully this time it was a completely different story. No emergencies, no alarms, just Olivia. And within days, Paul was talking about a vasectomy." The girls all laughed.
"I'm not kidding you! He has his appointment at the hospital next week!"
The tension from Susan's story broken, Carol decided to take her turn. "Well, I don't really have anything dramatic to offer" she shrugged "It was all pretty straight forward with Dylan, other than a really long labour. My waters broke when I was getting ready for bed why does it always happen at night?!" the girls all laughed. "We phoned the hospital, they gave the usual advice 'take a paracetamol,' 'try to get some rest,' 'go for a warm bath' so I did that and not a lot was happening. We watched some TV, Jase tried to get some sleep and it was lunchtime the next day before things really started to kick off and we headed for the hospital. Once we were in the delivery suite it was all pretty straight-forward and by the time 'The Chase' was on the TV at tea time, I had baby Dylan in my arms."
"How long in total was your labour, Carol?" Becca asked

"Ooo, around nineteen/twenty hours, something like that?" There was an intake of breath around the table. "Yeah I know! I was certainly a bit tender and exhausted afterwards that's for sure. But it hasn't put me off doing it again. In fact, we've been trying. For a few months now but nothing seems to be happening."

"Aw honey I'm sorry, here was me babbling on about Paul's vasectomy ….." Susan apologised.

"Oh don't be silly." Carol waved her hand "You weren't to know. Jase keeps telling me my body's still recovering after Dylan and if I stress about it then that'll have an effect too. But I don't know ….." She trailed off.

"He's talking sense," Becca responded, "I know it sounds really clichéd but when you're ready …. and your body is ready, it'll happen." She squeezed Carol's hand.

"So what's your story? Go on, we've all shared!" Carol replied taking a gulp of her wine. Becca sensed she wanted to move the conversation on. "OK, well like you it was pretty uneventful both times. Only unlike you, both labours were pretty quick. With Emily, after I felt some contractions we stayed home and watched a few episodes of '24'……remember *that* programme? I'm showing my age now!" she shook her head and they all laughed. "I had a bath and once the contractions started to hit every five minutes we went to hospital and within a few hours I had a newborn baby girl. Then a few hours later, we were back home watching '24' again with Emily sleeping in her Moses basket next to us. It was all very surreal, the speed at which it happened.

I just kept peering into the basket and thinking 'what just happened and what do I do now?!" More laughter from around the table.
"Oh I think we can all relate to that!" Wendy said as she drained her glass.
"I still can't believe they actually let you *leave* the hospital." Carol added "I mean, you need a licence for your TV but you have a baby and they let you just walk right out without the first real clue of what you're supposed to do!"
"It's so reassuring to hear you all say that," Susan smiled, "I thought I was the only one who thought I didn't actually know what I was doing. When you're in the hospital, or later at a toddler group, you look all around and see these other Mums who just know what to do. You just think to yourself 'I definitely missed *that* memo!"
"I hope you've all never felt like that coming in here!" Becca asked in mock horror and she received reassurances from around the table. It was at that point she suddenly remembered she was in the middle of an event at her café. "Sorry ladies, I've forgotten what I'm supposed to be doing tonight! I better go and check in with Dan." She stood up and made her way over to speak with Dan.
"I'm so sorry. I completely lost track of time," she said. He waved her apology away.
"It's alright, between me, Frankie and Mark we've managed no bother. You looked like you were having fun and I didn't want to disturb you to drag you back to work. You've had a long enough day as it is working in the café and getting it ready without the extra time tonight. Go and sit down with your

friends and enjoy yourself, we've only got a couple of wines to go and we're done."
"Are you sure?" she pressed.
"Of course! You've worked hard behind the scenes getting it all set up, you're entitled to enjoy yourself. I've got this." He winked at her.
She played with her necklace and chewed her lip, torn between her professionalism and the free and easy chat she was enjoying with her friends.
Dan grinned, sensing her conflict, "Go," he said, "have fun."
"Ok, you've convinced me. But on one condition."
"Name it."
"I'm helping you to clear up tonight."
"Deal!"

Chapter Seventeen

SIX MONTHS EARLIER

The night was over. Mick had come to collect Wendy and unlike the previous night when he had taken them both back to Wendy's, Becca had stayed to help Dan with the clear up and Tony was going to come to the café to collect her. She had also felt the need to send Frankie and Mark home too as they had worked so hard earlier to let her enjoy the night with the girls. It was just Dan and Becca alone in the café.

"So I would say that was another resounding success!" Becca was wiping down the tables as they chatted.

"Oh absolutely! I can't believe the orders we took tonight. We've made a proper profit." Dan was stacking the dishwasher with the last of the glasses.

"And I was taking ticket bookings for the next night too," she added.

"You're kidding?"

"Nope, no joke. Quite a few actually. I think we're going to sell out quickly for the next event and with it being a Christmas theme, we really need to get our thinking caps on to figure out how on earth we're going to top tonight!"

"Oh, we're a Dream Team Becca, I'm sure we'll come up with something." He turned his attention back to the dishwasher, "I think we're just about done here. What time did you say Tony was coming to collect you?"

Becca checked her watch, "In about half an hour,

we've managed to get tidied up much quicker than I expected."

"Fancy a nightcap?" Dan picked up an unfinished bottle of prosecco.

"Oh go on, you've twisted my arm." Becca collected a couple of clean prosecco glasses from the shelf. Dan filled the two glasses and they took a seat at a table. Becca took a sip and nodded her head in approval. "That was a really tasty prosecco you had for us tonight."

"Yeah, it went down well with the crowd, it was really popular in the orders." He took a sip of his drink "It looked like you were having fun tonight?" he asked.

"I did. When I moved on from R&Ds I lost a lot of my social life. I'm not sure if it was the move away from there or the move into parenthood that did it, either way my social calendar emptied over time. It didn't really register at first, I was so absorbed in getting this place up and running," she gestured around the café, "between the café and kids, there wasn't much time for anything else. It's only been in recent months I've felt a bit, you know, lonely." She took a sip of her prosecco while Dan watched her closely. Becca was conscious of him looking at her. She continued, "I mean me and Tony are great, well we've had our ups and downs like every couple, but I've been missing some girly company. Other than Wendy…..and Zoe of course…..I don't have a huge circle of female friends. So Tony was spot on when he made the suggestion about these wine tasting nights giving me the opportunity to build up some friendships as well as a business opportunity."

Dan studied her for a moment, "And how would you describe your friendship with Zoe?"
Becca considered how best to answer this and played with necklace as she thought. "If I was being really honest, I don't think I could describe it as a friendship. Maybe once upon a time we were friends, but there's always been a bit of a love-hate thing between us. Our relationship was borne out of necessity really, we were both newbies with R&Ds. We started on the same day, did Zoe tell you that? Anyway, we would go out on Friday night after work for drinks together because we were the only single girls working at the firm. Plus we both had a bit of drive and ambition which meant we pushed each other, you know, friendly competition? Although not always friendly!"
"Yeah I could imagine. Having spent a bit more time with Zoe she certainly has a bit of a killer instinct about her. She tells me she's behind you and Tony getting together?"
Becca laughed, "Yeah, she likes casting herself with a bigger role in that story. But credit where credits due, she did have a hand in it but she was hardly playing Cupid. Tony was originally her client and she was due to take him to a business awards thing but she had a clash of dates with another client so she asked if I would mind going with Tony instead. I didn't want to, it was on a Friday night and I had put in a lot of extra hours that week already and was pretty exhausted but you know Zoe, when she has a plan in mind it's impossible to say no to her. So I went along having already decided I would stay for the dinner and awards then make my excuses and

leave. But we had a really good night." She played with her necklace as she thought back to the first night she met Tony, "And the rest is history. Zoe was quite surprised when I handed his file back to her the next week. She expected I would just keep him on as my client but I couldn't do that. It didn't feel appropriate if I was going to get involved with him, which is the reason I insisted she did the same before going out with you." She sipped at her prosecco. "So, is it going well between you?"

Now it was Dan's turn to consider his answer, "Well, since you're being honest with me, I'll be honest with you. There's definitely something there, but what I'm not sure yet. You knew pretty quickly with Tony, didn't you?"

"I did. But don't take us as the benchmark! We are by no means the perfect couple. And if we're putting cards on the table and full transparency, then me and Tony have been through some dreadful rocky patches."

"You're kidding!"

Becca shook her head and picked up her glass, Dan had refilled it without her realising. "No it's true! In hindsight we did everything way too quickly. We didn't give ourselves time to be a couple first, you know, to get to know one another properly. We were engaged within a few months so we went from 'dating' to planning a wedding almost overnight. I didn't think about it then but looking back I can see how crazy that was. But we were just so wrapped up in each other we didn't think anything of it at the time. I would freak out if Emily came home and told me she was engaged to some guy she had just met a couple of months ago. Ok, fair enough she's eleven so that's pretty unlikely but you know what I mean." They both laughed.

"We went from being single, to a couple, to engaged, to married *and* expecting a baby all in just over a year." She shook her head at the recollection of it all. "We were still getting to know one another by the time Emily came along. It all put a pressure on us. We were still essentially a new relationship but now we were responsible for another human being. The daily chaos, exhaustion and panic that comes along with babies was not what I expected. When I was working for R&Ds, I always felt in control. There was no situation they could throw at me that I couldn't handle. But with Emily, I felt way out of my depth. In a lot of ways I was pretty relieved to get back to work after my maternity leave was over."

"You and Tony obviously figured things out though, I mean you're still together? And you had another baby too."

"Well yeah but back then Tony wasn't one for talking about hearts and minds. He's much better now the kids have come along. When Emily was just a baby and then especially once Max came along, I was struggling. And he struggled to see me struggle if that makes sense? He really wanted to fix it for me but he just didn't know how to so most weeks he would come home with a bunch of flowers or a gift. That was his way of showing me that he cared and wanted to make it alright for me." She suddenly stopped, aware of how much detail about their marriage she was sharing with a friend of Tony's. She picked up her glass but noticed it was empty again. She set it down on the table, cleared her throat and in an effort to shift the conversation said, "So you mentioned earlier there is something between you and Zoe. If you want my relationship advice, not that I'm an expert by any stretch of the imagination, don't rush things. Take your time to figure each other out. And talk to one another. Yes, actions speak louder than words, but in my experience an honest conversation will actually go a lot further."

She stood up and stumbled. She had drunk much more than she had realised and the effects were clearly showing. "I'm just going to give Tony a ring and check if he's on his way." She made her way through to the kitchen to retrieve her mobile phone from her handbag. She was suddenly very conscious that she was drunk. She fumbled in her bag and took out her phone. There was a missed call and a text from Tony telling her he was en route. She returned to the café, switching off the lights as she went. "Tony should be here any time," she said.

"Then that's my cue to leave too," Dan answered "I'll help you lock up and wait with you until Tony arrives. It's getting late and I don't want you waiting on your own."

Dan washed out the two prosecco glasses while Becca went to retrieve their coats and turned off the last of the café lights. They left the café and locked up, the cold early November air providing some welcome respite to the earlier stuffiness when there had been so many bodies crammed inside the café. Becca also hoped it would help to sober her up slightly. Dan helped her with the gate which pulls across the door of the café to secure it. In doing so he stood close enough to her that she could smell his aftershave which she noticed was fruiter than Tony's. They waited by the door watching for Tony. There was an awkwardness between them now. Becca was conscious she had said too much. But over and above her loose tongue, there was an energy between them that was making the wait feel almost like the end of a date when you were waiting with anticipation to see if the other person wanted to kiss you. Becca played with her necklace and checked her watch, praying Tony wouldn't be much longer.

A few moments later Tony's car came around the corner and pulled to a stop in front of them. Becca let out a sigh of relief as Dan stepped forward and opened the door for her. He greeted Tony as he did so.

"I hear from Wendy that it went really well," Tony said as Becca climbed in. He noticed out the corner of his eye that she was moving a little clumsily.

"Honestly it couldn't have gone any better," Dan offered in response and he watched Becca as she leaned over and gave Tony a kiss on the cheek.

"Do you need a lift?" he asked.

"No I'm fine, thanks mate. I'll just walk along to the junction and catch a taxi." He spoke directly to Becca now, "I'll be in touch in a couple of days' time with the final numbers but as I said earlier, the orders were really healthy."

"Thanks, Dan," she smiled, "take care getting home. Night."

"Night guys." He closed the car door and watched as Tony's Audi A7 pulled away into the night. He waved before turning in the opposite direction. He decided to walk home instead of catching a taxi as he needed some time to think. He reflected back on his conversation with Becca as he walked. He was surprised at how candid she had been about her marriage and hadn't expected her to open up so quickly. He was sure the alcohol had a lot to do with it but nevertheless he had welcomed the opportunity to pry into their private life. He had plenty to report back to Zoe now. Now that he had her trust, he was sure he and Zoe could use what he had learnt tonight. And if he was to play things right over the next couple of events, he was certain he would be able to push things further with Becca next time.

Chapter Eighteen

NOW

Becca had finished telling Tony about the Autumn Festival night. There was more she needed to say but for the moment she wanted to pause and see what the initial reaction was to her confession so far. It had been a few moments now and Tony had said nothing. He had rubbed his chin as she talked but otherwise stayed silent. Now she had stopped, he pushed back his chair and started to pace the floor. The clock kept ticking and with every second it counted, Becca grew increasingly nervous.

"I honestly don't know what to say to that Rebecca."

There it was, her Sunday name again that he had never used until tonight. Now it was her turn to keep quiet. She needed to hear what he had to say so she would know how to approach the next part of her confession.

"That's some really private stuff you talked about."

"I know."

"What were you thinking? Sharing details like that with him?"

"I wasn't thinking. It just all came out. Maybe it was because earlier in the night me and the girls had been comparing notes from when we all had our babies – you know labour and birth stories? Maybe my guard was already down after sharing those experiences. Or I could blame the alcohol but I know that would just be an excuse to hide behind rather than taking responsibility for what I did." She looked up at him,

"I really am sorry. I've broken the trust between us now and I'm not sure how I can fix it."
"Well that makes two of us." He replied coldly. "You told him you were 'lonely' for Christ's sake! No wonder you sent him down the track of thinking you weren't happy. Albeit unintentionally."
"But I explained I meant lonely for female company. I specifically said we were good."
"Yeah, but then you followed it up by admitting you rushed things between us at the start and looking back now it was a mistake that we did things so quickly. In your head you were playing Agony Aunt telling him that in all relationships, even the ones that work, mistakes are made but you were using words like 'lonely' and 'rocky patches'. No wonder he thought you were starting to send him signals." He shook his head as he spoke to her. "I'm going to get another beer."
He went off to retrieve a bottle from the fridge. She could hear him moving around the kitchen, first the fridge for the beer then the drawer for the bottle opener. She fidgeted with her necklace and picked up her phone checking for a reply from Zoe. Still nothing. Tony returned to the lounge.
"So, were we a mistake? Is that what you really believe but you've just been too scared to say it out loud all this time?"
Becca recoiled at the question.
"God no!" she shouted.
"I'm just repeating what you said to him. Those were your words."
"I said that first year, eighteen months we were together was overwhelming. I never once said we

were a mistake. You're putting words into my mouth now."
Tony took a gulp of his beer and shifted his weight from side to side holding her gaze as he moved. She could detect he was agitated and she grew apprehensive, she could sense something was coming. The atmosphere had changed in the room again and she knew it was building towards something. Tony took another gulp of his beer, never breaking eye contact with her the entire time. Eventually he said, "Was this you finally getting your revenge on me? Five years later?"
They were finally going to have *that* conversation. The one they had managed to avoid for years. Becca exhaled slowly. "So, are we finally going to go there?"
"I think we need to," replied Tony. "If we are going to have any chance of working through this, then we need to get it all out there. You've just taken responsibility for breaking the trust between us but it's not been the first time one of us has broken that trust. Only the last time it was me."
"That was five years ago, Tony. A lot has changed since then. Is it really going to help dragging it all back up again?"
"We never resolved it."
"But we're still together."
"And you've just kissed some other man."
"It's not related to *that*."
"Are you really certain, one hundred percent sure? Then tell me the truth. If it wasn't for the kids being so small when it happened and you being so constantly exhausted, would you have left me?"

Becca considered this for a moment. "But I didn't leave you. So how can I even answer that? That's beyond hypothetical, it's a completely ridiculous question to ask me. I'm going to get a drink."
"I thought you weren't in the mood."
"Well that was before I realised we were going to do *this* but since you brought it up, then fine. We'll do this but I'm going to need a drink." She went to the kitchen. She didn't really want a glass of wine but she did need a reason to step away for a second, to pull herself together and regroup. The evening had taken a turn she did not expect.

Chapter Nineteen

NOW

The broken trust to which Tony referred happened just after she was made redundant. Tony, in his usual clumsy way, wanted to fix things for Becca in the only way he knew how - to throw money at the problem.

When Becca lost her job, Tony was furious. His property business was worth a small fortune to R&Ds, not to mention Becca had worked for the firm since graduating and was bloody good at what she did. Tony did what he did best and went into survival mode. Always the businessman, when he heard about a premises with planning permission for a café which was about to come on the market after a previous deal fell through, he didn't hesitate and within three months Café Swan opened its doors. It was a complete whirlwind (they were good at those) which put incredible pressure on them personally. However he knew it would be worth it in the long run, as long as their relationship survived the strain of those initial months.

Like every business at that time, Tony's had also struggled as a result of the credit crunch. The bottom had just fallen out of the property market, people just weren't buying, and a number of properties within his rental portfolio were also in negative equity so Tony could understand Becca's nuclear reaction to him taking on yet another property, especially as he used 'her' redundancy money for the deposit. That

was the biggest mistake he made. He didn't tell Becca his plan until it was all signed and sealed.
Due to the state of the market, the building was for *sale* at a rock bottom price, whereas just a few months before, it was only on the market for *rent* at an astronomical rate. The owner needed a quick sale but the only cash available was Becca's redundancy money, and as it was in their joint savings account, Tony was able to access it. The building was then bought under Tony's property development business to keep it separate and protect their own personal money and home.
It was all done legitimately and legally, albeit without Becca's knowledge.
It also gave his own building team a project to keep them busy as work was drying up. So for Tony it was a win-win scenario all round. However Becca had a completely different view. She felt betrayed that he had used her money like that and then he had thrown himself into the project, like it was his way of running away from the problem he had created.
It didn't matter how often he explained to Becca that he had to act quickly to secure the property at the knock-down price, or that having her own business and being her own boss would fit around the kids plus give her the focus in her professional life that she needed. To Becca it was a matter of broken trust. He had taken a major decision about her redundancy nest egg and her future career without any discussion. It took them almost a year to truly heal that rift. But their marriage survived and Becca stayed with him. Although, if Tony was being honest with himself, there were times he was sure

that the reason she stayed was actually down to her being so exhausted between the kids and getting a new fledgling business off the ground that she was simply unable to summon the energy to actually pack a bag and walk out the door.

She returned to the lounge to face Tony.

"Ok, so here it is. I hated you back then." She began. "I was exhausted with the kids. Constantly. And instead of being here, at home, where I needed you, you were at work. Every day. From seven o'clock in the morning until eight o'clock at night. You would then sweep in the door playing the part of the Doting Dad, kiss the kids goodnight and put them to bed. And that was it. Day done. We would eat, sleep and get up the next day to repeat. Day after day after day."

Tony's face drained of colour. He hadn't expected Becca to be this brutal. She continued.

"I wanted you to listen to me, to talk to me. I wanted, no *needed* reassurance that it was going to be ok. That we were going to be ok. I *needed* support with the kids, I *craved* intimacy - which didn't just mean sex - but what I had was a husband who was never here. Your life pretty much continued as normal, whereas I went from having a career and an identity which was my own, to being known as 'Mum' or 'Tony's wife' and becoming, well, just a cook and a cleaner. Nothing more." She threw her hands in the air in exasperation. "There were times when I would question if that was all I was to you, a live-in maid, not your wife or equal partner so when you took on the café, it pushed me to breaking point. I thought brilliant. Not only does he want me to cook and clean for him and the kids, but now he expects me to do it for other people too!"

"But Becca….."

She put her hand up to stop him from saying anymore. "No Tony! For once listen to me! I didn't want the café! I wanted you!" She screamed the words at him, snapping the chain from her neck and throwing the wine bottle necklace at him as she did. The necklace bounced off his arm and landed the coffee table. Her words hung in the air like a bad smell.

"I wanted you." She said the words again calmer this time.

"After I got over the initial hurt and shock from what you did with my redundancy money, I understood your reasons and then once my rational brain kicked in again when I wasn't feeling so vulnerable and sensitive and low, the penny dropped and I *really* understood what you were trying to do when you bought the café. But in those very early days when you did it, it wasn't what I needed from you. You messed up back then because it was easier for you to open up your bank account than it was to open up to me. But I forgave you. Whether or not I thought about leaving you doesn't actually matter because I stayed and now you're trying to make what happened last night at the wine tasting about *that* and it's not. Last night was not about me getting cold revenge on you. You know that's not my style or who I am and quite frankly the fact that you even think I would be so manipulative and calculating to do that to you makes me really question how well we truly know one another."

The room fell silent as Tony tried to process what Becca had just said. "You *hated* me. Is that true?"
"Yes. No. I don't know," she sighed and rubbed her face. "I was a mess. I had just lost my job. I had two young kids and a husband who seemed more interested in property than me. Maybe 'hate' is a strong word. I certainly resented you. You would get up in the morning, go and be an adult and a professional, swaggering around Glasgow - The Big Hot Shot Property Tycoon while I got to sit at home all day watching Mr Tumble and Loose Women. My career, my identity, gone," she snapped her fingers, "I didn't know who I was anymore."
"But that's why I bought the café. To give you that sense of purpose back, but only better. Because this time you would be in control of your own business."
"But you didn't *ask* me if that's what I wanted, or more importantly, needed. You decided for me. Now, five years down the line I am so grateful you did what you did. I wasn't in a good place back then to make a major life decision like that. The café has given me so much more than I could ever have imagined. It's given me a focus, a career and new friends. It saved me from an abyss but it was the *way* you did it that caused the problem. If you had just spoken to me. If we had just had a conversation about how I was feeling, what I was going through, and what you thought we could do about it, then it could have saved us both a lot of pain."
Tony sat down on the light grey L-shaped couch and put his beer down on the oval glass coffee table. Becca crossed the room to sit next to him, placing her untouched glass of wine down next to his beer. He

had never felt this ashamed in his life. To hear his wife, the woman he loves and adores, the person he would give his own life for, tell him in such a stark, brutal way just how miserable she had been and it was all down to how he behaved, made him feel like someone had hollowed out his soul.

He felt a raw pain like never before.

To make it even worse, he had let this situation fester between them for years for his own selfish reasons. He knew he had done wrong and didn't have the guts to talk to her about it. He realised then that somewhere along the line, Becca had taken the decision either deliberately or subconsciously, to bury all of her pain for the sake of their marriage and the kids. He hung his head too embarrassed to look her in the eye.

"I didn't realise you felt like that."

She sighed, "You never asked. We never talked about it. In fact for weeks we just didn't talk at all which made me feel even more isolated and alone."

He nodded, "I know and it's something I've never been able to forgive myself for. I could see you were in bits. I knew you weren't eating properly or sleeping well. You had lost so much weight and became a shadow of yourself. Your spark, your vibrancy, it was gone and I just didn't know what to do about it. I had never been in a situation that I couldn't fix with a well-timed business transaction so that's what I did." His head dropped further. "It's *all* I know how to do but when that didn't work and the one person that meant the world to me was so badly broken and I had somehow managed to make it worse and push you even further away, well, I was

out of ideas. I was out of my depth." He finally brought himself to look directly at her with his piercing blue eyes, which for only the second time in their thirteen years together, were filled with tears. "Becca," he said her name so quietly she could barely hear him, "did you have depression?" he stumbled over the word, terrified to finally say it out loud.
She met his eye and softly nodded, "Yes. Looking back at how I was then, I'm sure I was depressed but when you're so low, when you're so down and broken you don't see it. You don't understand what's going on or what you're feeling - or not feeling is probably more accurate. Nothing makes sense anymore and everything, *everything,* is an effort. There's just a numbness that goes so deep. From the outside, what did I have to be depressed about? A Mum to two gorgeous children, a husband who had just bought a business for me because I was out of work.....what did I have the right to complain about? I was being a fraud for being so melodramatic." She looked away.
"That's what I would keep telling myself, 'stop it Becca, pull yourself together,' 'you're being a drama queen,' 'snap out of it,' 'you're better than this, you're stronger than this'......the internal monologue inside my head would just go on and on and on. I should have asked for help. I should have spoken to you or gone to the GP but I didn't. There was just so much going on between losing my job, the kids and then taking over the café, I didn't have the time to deal with the emotional fall out from it all and on reflection, I didn't realise how unwell I actually was until I was through the worst of it."

They sat for a few moments in silence. The clock on the wall seemed to be muted as if respecting the mood in the room.
"I'm so sorry, Becca." Tony ventured, "You shouldn't have needed to ask for help. I should have just been there for you. I should have recognized that I couldn't just buy my way out of the situation. You needed more than that. You went through hell back then and I just stood by and watched you suffer from the side-lines. I behaved terribly and let you down so, so badly. I really messed up."
She took his hand in hers, "You didn't just stand by. The café brought me back to life and now I get to do that for the other Mums I see coming into the café who are lost or overwhelmed and just trying to make sense of the new role they have as a parent or the old life they've left behind. You gave that to me," she squeezed his hand gently. "That's why I love you and why the café means so much to me. You knew I could do something special with it when I had zero self-esteem and zero confidence. Yes, it was a very rocky road and neither of us knew it at the time, but when you bought the café you showed that you believed in me when I didn't believe in myself."
Tony had looked away just after she had started talking. They had finally opened the Pandora's Box of their marriage and he had found it painful and difficult. He realised he had to take responsibility for his actions of five years ago, in particular how they had affected her. He had got it all wrong back then. The decisions he made, his arrogance thinking he knew best. His ego and pride had gotten in the way of their marriage. He knew he should have done

better by Becca and that was something he was going to have to reconcile with. Right now he didn't know how to even begin to atone for his actions. What he did know was his wife was clearly the strongest out of the two of them. When he should have been protecting her, she had to pull herself out of darkness. He shuddered realising he had been so superficial and selfish. He played the part of the big man but that's all it had been, a role he had cast himself into. The reality was he was actually too weak and self-centred to really step up when Becca needed him most.

"I can't change what happened, Becca, or how I did you wrong back then. I know how I can come across. I'm not oblivious to it. All big gestures and showy. I know it's no excuse but I've always found this stuff, the raw emotional stuff, just too difficult. So when I buy you something, even if it's just a bunch of daffodils......"

She laughed, "You've *never* bought me *just* a bunch of daffodils! It's always pink lilies, pink peonies and white roses!"

He smiled weakly, "I just find it an easier way to show you how I feel." He shrugged his shoulders and looked down at his hands, the embarrassment again flooding through him. He looked back up at her, "But you have to believe me that you and the kids are everything to me. If I could turn back time, if I could just find a way...."

"Are you quoting Cher at me by way of an apology?" she tried again at a joke to break the mood. He laughed this time and turned to face her.

"You and your God-awful taste in music!" He

paused then continued, "I am really sorry. This conversation has been a long time coming. I shouldn't have let it go unsaid for this long. I really messed up and hurt you. You deserved better from me. I'm just dumbfounded you stuck with me after that."
"Like I said earlier tonight, its part of our shared history which makes us stronger. We found our way through it and I really, really want us to be able to find our way through what happened with Dan too."
He nodded, "Becca, there's one more thing I need to know."
She held his gaze, knowing what the question was going to be before he asked.
"How much of this did you tell Dan?"
Becca swallowed hard. It was time for part two of her confession.

Chapter Twenty

FIVE MONTHS EARLIER

The weeks which followed the Autumn Festival wine tasting went by in a blur. The run up to Christmas was always a busy time for Becca and the café as they would launch their Christmas menu in November to compete with the big coffee shop chains. Frankie worked extra hours preparing a Christmas menu which included all the traditional favourites but also with a few more contemporary choices. The Christmas themed cakes were always a big seller and as well as selling cakes by slice as usual through the café, they would take orders for customers who wanted to order whole cakes either as Christmas gifts or centrepieces for parties and this year, they had the added pressure of a wine night to organise for mid-December.

They closed the café early one Friday afternoon for a staff meeting, which consisted of Becca, Frankie, Wendy and Dan to discuss how they could up their game for the Christmas event. The first two wine tasting events had gone extremely well and had turned a healthy profit. However as it was Christmas (and Becca's favourite time of year) she wanted to really go for it and make this event something a bit extra special. After a lot of discussion and several bottles of wine provided by Dan under the auspices of 'approving the wine choices for the event,' they finally came up with a plan.

"So we're agreed then?" Becca asked as she toyed with her necklace and checked her notebook. There were nods from all around the table. "We'll start with the standard two welcome cocktails beginning with a small glass of mulled wine served with Frankie's mini mince pies. What's your idea for the second cocktail, Dan?"

"I'm thinking of something along the lines of a Clementine and Campari Bucks Fizz. Fresh clementine juice, pomegranate juice, Campari and prosecco. How does that sound?"

"Shame you didn't bring those ingredients for us to taste test that one," teased Frankie.

Becca continued, "Then we'll have the usual wine tasting section, but we're only going to do five instead of our usual six, but finish with a fizzy as normal?"

"Yep, and again I have a particular fizzy in mind. This one is pretty special as it's a red sparkling Shiraz which you serve chilled, just like you would a champagne. It's really popular in Australia at Christmas."

"A chilled red wine? And it's fizzy? That's a new one on me. At least I can justify these nights to Mick as being educational," joked Wendy.

"And what about food, Frankie?" Becca asked.

"Well, I was thinking we would go for proper Christmas buffet party food platters but up-market. So the humble sausage roll - I mean who doesn't love a sausage at a party, am I right?" he mischievously winked at Dan.

"Frankie, behave or your free wine is stopped," scolded Becca.

He tutted and rolled his eyes, "Spoil-sport. Sausage rolls, two flavours: pork and cranberry; squash and chestnut. We'll also have pigs in blankets, smoked salmon blinis, baked camembert with homemade bread for dipping and retro vol-au-vonts and for a sweet treat to finish off, I'll make a selection of white, milk and dark chocolate truffles."

"Sounds perfect," Dan approved.

"And this is when things get a little different," Becca picked up, "we're going to turn the TwinkleStarKydz room into a dance area so we can finish off the night with a bit of a party feel. When we start serving the red fizzy, we'll turn on the Christmas party tunes - we'll come back to the music in a minute and instead of just one glass of fizzy, they'll also get a top up. Then to finish off, they'll get a final cocktail which will make up for only doing the five wines. What's your thoughts on the final cocktail, Dan?"

"Going for a martini which I'm going to call 'Santa's Little Helper'. It's a take on a Cosmopolitan made with blueberry vodka, Chambord, Triple Sec and cranberry juice. When combined the ingredients turn the cocktail a deep purple colour."

"Cool! Now back to the music……" Frankie clapped his hands like an excited child.

"In a minute Frankie, there's one last thing I need to agree with Dan," Becca snapped.

"You're such a Grinch today," tutted Frankie.

"No, you're tipsy with the wine Dan kindly provided and I know why you're desperate to talk about the music because we've argued about it all week."

Frankie rolled his eyes and huffed while Wendy and Dan struggled not to giggle watching them argue.

"The price of the tickets. Will the usual twenty-five pounds cover our expenses? We've upped our game with the food and although we're only doing five wines plus a fizzy during the tasting, we're also giving a top up of the fizzy and providing three cocktails instead of two….."

"Yeah you're right," agreed Dan. "Spot the accountant! Nothing gets past you! Do you think we could get away with increasing the ticket price?"

"I think so especially as we're doing a bit of a party at the end of the evening. Do you think thirty pounds would be ok or should we push to thirty-five?"

"I think thirty-five might feel a bit steep," Wendy offered. "I know some places who do three course party nights for that price, fair enough they're a bit rubbish with crap food, but you know, just to give a comparison."

"Yeah, I think we would cover costs at thirty quid," Dan nodded.

"Ok, thirty it is. We've been taking mobile numbers and a £5 deposit to confirm places and advising there might be a slight increase in the ticket price for the Christmas night so it shouldn't be a big surprise. I'll do a group text tonight to confirm the cost."

"Music!" shouted Frankie and he drummed the table.

"Frankie, you are seriously pushing my buttons this week," Becca exhaled slowly, "we will get to the music in a minute. I just want to say that Amy can't help with the table decorations this time around so I was just going to pick up some poinsettias for each table. The café is decorated anyway with the Christmas garlands and we've got the tree in the bay window so I think the table cloths and poinsettias will be enough. Ok? Right Frankie, you're up. Music."

"Wendy has managed to source us some disco lights and a sound system from one of Mick's mates for the party room," Wendy gave a little firm wave of the hand to indicate her input, "so I was thinking we go full on Christmas cheese fest for the end of night party. We'll have Mr Christmas - otherwise known as the dreamy Michael Buble - playing at the start of the night and throughout the wine tasting, you know, tasteful to reflect the tone and atmosphere of the event but once that fizzy hits the glass, the heels come off and Christmas hits go on! I'm talking Elton, Slade, Wizzard, Shaking Stevens….." It was now Becca's turn to roll her eyes.

"Frankie, I know you love Christmas. *I* love Christmas but the point I was making is that Christmas music has been playing in shops and cafés and on the radio since the middle of November. Yes, let's have *some* Christmas music at the start and then the end of the night, it is a Christmas party after all, but can we not break it up with some other stuff, too? We can still do cheesy tunes, you know I have a terrible taste in awful music, but let's not do a Christmas overkill."

Dan looked from Becca to Frankie, "You guys have been *arguing* over this?"

"All the live long week and I'm sick of hearing it!" Wendy threw her head back in frustration. "I really don't care what the music is. I'll dance to anything. Dan, you've got the casting vote on this one." All eyes turned expectedly to Dan.

"Oh, I am not going to be responsible for this," he held up his hands in defense, "tell you what, we'll let fate decide. Toss of the coin?"

"Fine with me," said Becca.

"And me," agreed Frankie.

"Ok, here we go." He went into his jeans pocked and pulled out a 10p coin. "Heads: Christmas music, tails: party mix." The coin flipped in the air, landed on the table and spun dizzily for a minute before settling to reveal the Queens head. Frankie leapt from his chair and punched the air.

"That has made my day!" Frankie sang as he danced around the table where they were sitting.

"Sorry," Dan silently mouthed to Becca as she rolled her eyes and put her head in her hand in mock exasperation, then laughed.

"Right kids, if we're done here then I need to make a move and get home to make the cherubs their tea. Frankie, are you going home or to Mark's?"

"Going home, Mark's coming over later," he replied as he slipped on his coat.

"Do you want a lift? I didn't have any of the wine."

"That would be great as long as The Boss is happy with me heading off?"

"Yeah, on you go, I'll lock up. I'll see you tomorrow. Night guys." Wendy and Frankie left, leaving Dan and Becca alone in the café.

"Oh shoot!" Becca said suddenly. "I can't drive home. I've been drinking the wine with you and Frankie. I'll need to phone Tony and see if he can come and pick me up," she looked at her watch, "he'll be right in the middle of making the kids their tea."

"Or we could share a taxi and finish this bottle while we wait?"

"Now that sounds like a better idea." Becca pushed her glass across the table for Dan to fill up.

Chapter Twenty-one

FIVE MONTHS EARLIER

"Mick's going to come and get us at the start of his shift," Becca was referring to the text message she had just received from Mick, "so we're all sorted." She smiled at Dan.

"So you've got a terrible taste in music then?" he asked as he took another sip of his wine.

"Oh, it's awful."

"How awful?"

"You don't want to know."

"Try me."

"Well if we're talking 80s, we're not talking the good stuff. I was a huge Wham fan, obviously, but I also liked Bros and do you remember Milli Vanilli? Had their album, too."

Dan screwed up his face, "No Bowie? Or Queen?" Becca shook her head. "Anything more recent?" he asked.

"Well when we got into the 90s, it was Take That, of course, but I also loved a bit of Boyzone and Westlife."

"Where were you on the Oasis versus Blur debate?"

"Nowhere. I was Team Boyband all the way. Britpop was too cool for my liking."

He laughed, "You're right, that's pretty awful."

"Yep, warned you. Tony's always managed to keep his music tastes more current and relevant. He's always swapping songs with the kids. Not me, my music knowledge died circa 1999 when I graduated from university. Until Take That reformed of course.

He's also happy to sit with the kids and watch their favourite You Tubers for hours on end whereas I just don't get it."

"Now I understand why things got so heated between you and Frankie over the music. Do you always bicker like that?"

"Nah. It's just the time of the year. We're both working longer hours so we're in each other's pockets much more than normal. The café's busy and we're tired. That's also part of the reason I close between Christmas and New Year, we need the break."

"Tony mentioned you did that. I gotta say I was pretty surprised. You're pretty business-savvy. It's a bit of a risk closing like that over Christmas, is it not?"

"Not really. We're not a wine store like you where alcohol is a high priority for folk between Christmas and New Year. We did open with reduced hours for the first couple of Christmases but it really wasn't worth it. We're too far out of the city centre to get footfall from people shopping in the sales. The bulk of my customers are locals who live near the café and pop in on their way to work or parents who come in after the school drop off or before the school pick up and of course the footfall from Wendy's classes. At Christmas when the schools are closed and Wendy's classes aren't running, we're not busy. It's different during summer holidays. We're kept busy enough with our regulars and day trippers to the Botanic Gardens and Kelvingrove Museum at this end of town. We just benefit more from having the time off to recharge. Tony closes over Christmas too so it's really good for us to have that protected family time together when we're not working and the kids are also off."

"What are your plans for Christmas?"

"Well, we have Tony's parents and my parents over for Christmas day. It's much easier having them come to us to see us and the kids. Then at some point, the kids stay over at my parents to give me and Tony a night out. I think this year it's actually going to be New Year's Eve. Frankie and Mark are having a party and have invited us so I think we'll go out for a meal, then head to theirs. What about you?"

"Dad and I go to my sister's. She's married with a little boy, Caleb. He was six on his birthday so I'm very much Cool Uncle Dan in his eyes. We usually spend the day playing his Xbox or like Tony, watching You Tube." Becca noticed how his eyes lit up as he spoke of his nephew.

"Have you got plans with Zoe?" she pressed.

"Not at Christmas, she's going to stay with her parents for a few days but we're heading down to London for New Year. I'm going to catch up with some friends and I asked if she fancied coming along. Frankie had invited me to their party too but my plans were already made."

"Things must be going really well with you and Zoe then if you're heading off to London together?"

"Yeah but she blows hot and cold with me. I'm not entirely convinced she'll actually go, to be honest."

"Really?" Becca was surprised.

Dan nodded, "To tell you the truth, I don't actually know where I stand with her. I just wish she would

tell me what she's thinking. I'm not a mind reader."
Becca nodded in empathy, "I know how that feels."
Dan looked at her curiously, his chocolate brown eyes searched her face. "Do you want to talk about it?" he asked.
She chewed her lip as her hand subconsciously went her necklace. "I don't know if I should. You're friends with Tony. I felt a bit odd after the last wine tasting night. I think I told you things I shouldn't have."
"It's your choice, Becca. It strikes me that you listen to everyone else's worries and you help them figure out their problems. I just want you to know that if you ever need someone to help do that for you, then I'm a good listener. Just like you've had years of practice in here, I've got years of practice working in various bars and hotels across London." He smiled warmly at her and covered her hand with his.
"Oh, it's nothing really. Just what you said about not really knowing what Zoe's thinking. I had a similar experience with Tony a few years back just after I left R&Ds. I've already told you that Tony invested my redundancy money in the café? What I didn't tell you was I didn't know anything about it. We had no discussion, he didn't ask, he just went right ahead."
Dan was stunned, "He didn't speak to you about it first?"
"Nope. The first I knew anything was the day he brought me here to show me the café. It didn't look anything like this," she gestured with her hand, "it was just a shell, no counter or booths and had been taken back to brick. The kitchen had the basics. I thought he was just showing me another one of the

properties he was doing up. I did think it was a bit odd. As you know, he doesn't usually do commercial work, domestic properties are his thing - you've really been the exception to that - and that's when he told me what he had done."

"How did you take it?"

"Hah. Not well."

"I'm not surprised."

"It caused a huge rift between us. For quite a while actually. I really struggled to get over the fact he thought it was OK to make such a significant decision like that on his own. There were business reasons for it of course, namely a deal to be done and little time to act but for me it was about trust and us supposedly being a partnership together, both of which just didn't seem to be on his radar. I ended up in quite a bad place actually." She looked at the stem of her wine glass as she played with it. Dan didn't say anything, he wanted her to continue. "We came very close to splitting up. I was hurt, angry and emotionally I was all over the place. I was still reeling from losing my job and juggling the kids who were so small at the time then to be suddenly thrown into a business that I hadn't chosen. It all got a bit much." She smiled weakly.

"Why a café? Was it something you had mentioned you fancied doing?"

"No, not particularly. I've always enjoyed baking and really got into it after watching Great British Bake Off one year. I think possibly in one of my more stressful moments at R&Ds, I might have moaned to Tony about jacking it all in and doing something completely different, like baking cakes.

I'm also sure I also said I fancied looking after animals but it was only ever a throwaway comment. I'm just glad he opted for a café and didn't buy a zoo!" she laughed.

"So how did you guys work it out?"

"That really depends on your definition of 'working things out'. I decided it was better just to draw a line under it and we moved on." She shrugged her shoulders. "Now after all the initial heartache and soul searching, I'm extremely proud of what I've created here," she smiled, "anyway, we better get ourselves organised, Mick will be here for us any time." Dan got the impression the topic was closed to any further discussion.

"Yeah, I guess we should." They both stood up and put their coats on. Becca took the dirty wine glasses through to the kitchen and turned off the café lights.

"Listen Becca, I know I'm mates with Tony but if there's anything you want to talk about...." He let his sentence trail off.

"Then I know a barman who will listen," she smiled.

"Mixologist, actually."

She laughed, "Thanks, Dan," and gave him a hug which he held on to longer than she had anticipated. A car horn outside indicated Mick's arrival and allowed her to break away.

"After you," he said as he moved towards the door and opened it for Becca.

They locked up and climbed into the back of Mick's taxi, Becca greeting him warmly as she did. Dan gave Mick a few brief directions to his apartment which was slightly off the route they would take if going directly to Becca's. They travelled the distance with Dan making small talk with Mick. Dan noticed Becca had grown quiet and was gazing out the car window playing with her necklace. Five minutes later they arrived at Dan's building. "Let me get this," he offered, but Mick waved him away commenting about mate's rates. Dan turned his attention to Becca, "Have a good weekend. I'll pop in next week to catch up with you."

"I'll have the kettle on," she smiled.

He got out the car and waved them off as Mick did a u-turn to take Becca home. He took his phone from his pocket and sent Zoe a text: Just home from the Café. There's definitely been some trouble in paradise. You around tonight?x

The response was instant: Ooo interesting! Need to know more! Dinner? My treat.x

They made arrangements to meet later and Dan went into his apartment to freshen up. The conversation with Becca still very much on his mind.

Chapter Twenty-two

FOUR MONTHS EARLIER

The much anticipated 'Winter Wonderland Wines' event finally arrived. Becca felt pretty exhausted as it had been a full on week but her adrenaline kicked in as she dressed the café and now that she was changed into her party clothes, she was very much looking forward to the evening. After wearing her go-to black dress for the previous two nights, she had decided to treat herself to a new outfit for tonight and had purchased a tailored, sleeveless jumpsuit with a sweetheart neckline which showcased her necklace. It was a deep green colour which really brought out her eyes and with her caramel hair tumbling around her shoulders and favourite Jimmy Choo's, she looked quite stunning. When she walked back into the café, Dan couldn't help himself from doing a double-take.

"You look fabulous."

"Thank you. It's my new Christmas outfit." She did a little twirl and received a wolf-whistle from Frankie who had been in the kitchen gently heating the mulled wine. "Look at you, hot stuff!" he jibed gently as he began decanting the warm wine into the small latte glasses which were lined up on the counter. Becca gave him a nudge by means of a playful rebuke. Dan was prepping the Clementine and Campari Bucks Fizz watching the exchange. He was struggling to take his eyes off Becca. He cleared his throat, "Do you want me to unlock the door? I

think I can see the first guests starting to arrive."
"Oh! Ok, I'll get it." and she crossed the floor to open the door and greeted the crowd as they slowly filed into the café bringing the cold air with them. Dan and Frankie began serving the mulled wine which was very much welcomed by everyone as the weather had taken a cold turn earlier in the week. Wendy, Carol and Susan were amongst the last to arrive.
"So sorry we're late!" Wendy apologised looking a bit frazzled, "Mick's run off his feet already. Bookings are backing up and it's still early. He's going to squeeze us in later but we'll probably need to head off a bit sharpish which was going to be a problem for you but don't worry, I've spoken to Tony and he's going to come to the café to pick you up once I get home."
"Thanks Wendy, that's saved me from finding the time to make a phonecall to Tony. I have a feeling I'm going to be busy tonight."

The tickets had sold out quickly and the majority of the crowd were now 'regulars' at the events. Many had brought friends with them for the first time tonight and this combination of new recruits with seasoned attendees, plus the addition of the end of night party and general Christmas spirit resulted in an atmosphere of excitement and anticipation. Michael Buble's Christmas album crooned smoothly from the speakers. Becca caught Frankie's eye and she couldn't help but laugh at how ridiculous their arguments over the music had been. The Christmas party food platters were served as the crowd enjoyed the Clementine and Campari Bucks Fizz. Dan was asked for the recipe by several people and he happily obliged. As with the Autumn Festival night, Mark and Wendy had offered to help serve the wines. They all worked together efficiently to move through the tasting section of the evening as Becca was conscious of the party section at the end and she wanted to ensure they had sufficient time for people to have a dance.

Soon enough, it was time for Dan to wow the crowd with his exceptional chilled red fizzy Shiraz. Once he had explained the background and origin to the unique drink and everyone had a full glass, Frankie turned on the disco lights in the TwinkleStarKydz room transforming it into a dance area. The majority of guests immediately responded and filled the dance floor. It was at that point Becca was finally able to take her seat with the girls.

"The best night yet, Becca!" Susan enthused. "This red fizzy wine is amazing! I've never tasted anything like it before."

"You've not had the chance to stop all night," Carol observed.

"I know. I had the feeling as we opened the doors it was going to be full on. I've not even had the chance to say hello to Zoe either." She indicated to the table where Zoe was seated and waved over to her. "Thankfully that's the busiest part of the night over now and I can relax a bit. So what have I missed?" she asked as she took a long awaited sip of the infamous red fizzy.

"We were just saying what we've bought our other

halves for Christmas," Carol answered, "Wendy's got Mick a Laphroaig Single Malt Whisky gift set……"
"Courtesy of the lovely Mr Lehmann," interjected Wendy.
"And Susan's got Paul one of those gift voucher deals for a round of golf and overnight stay at a posh hotel."
"I figured he deserved something extra special this year after being brave and surviving his vasectomy!" giggled Susan. She continued, "What about you Becca? What have you got Tony?"
"Well, since you've asked I've actually got him something a bit special this year too. Cars are a big thing for Tony, he loves his Audis and used to drive an R8 model before the kids came along but a two seater coupe is not the most practical when you need to fit a baby seat so he swapped it for a more family friendly model. However, his dream car is an Aston Martin…."
"No, you didn't!" squealed Susan.
"No I absolutely did not!" laughed Becca in response, "but I have found a company where you can pick from their catalogue and hire an Aston Martin for a weekend."
"I think you may have just won the wife of the year award with that one," Wendy winked at her friend. "What about you Carol? What's on your shopping list for Jason?"
"Well, I was thinking along the same lines as Susan but I'm going to have to come up with something a bit more budget friendly," and she held up her left hand to show a glistening diamond engagement ring.

There was an explosion of noise from the table. Dan, Frankie and Mark who had been making their way around the room to give everyone their top up of fizzy headed straight over to find out what had happened.
"Carol's engaged!" Becca excitedly shared the news with the boys who responded with a round of congratulatory kisses for Carol. The bottle of sparkling red wine which Dan was holding was almost full. "Why don't I just leave this here for you?" he smiled as he sat it on the table. Zoe had also heard the commotion and came over to investigate, Dan told her what had happened. She smiled coldly at Carol wishing her well and quickly made her excuses to leave again.
"What's wrong with her?" Becca asked Dan. He shrugged his shoulders and replied, "I told you, hot and cold. I better go and speak to her, check she's ok. Congratulations again, Carol."
The girls all took their seats again eager to press Carol for the details. "Why didn't you mention anything sooner?" Wendy asked as she topped up everyone's glasses.
"I wanted to wait until Becca was sitting down to tell you all together," she replied.
"Well come on then! Details!" Susan pressed.
"OK, so he bought me the ring with the intention of asking me on Christmas day. I didn't know it but he had been saving up to buy me a ring ever since I found out I was pregnant with Dylan. He picked it up on Saturday and just couldn't wait any longer so he asked me that night. I had just put Dylan to bed and came downstairs and got all comfy on the sofa.

Next thing I know Jase was kneeling on the floor next to me. At first I thought he was looking for the controls for the telly or he had dropped money or something, then he just asked me. It took a minute for it to register what was going on. Then I cried. Then he cried.....then we heard Dylan starting to cry," the girls all laughed.
"That's lovely Carol, I'm so pleased for you," Becca smiled warmly at her friend.
"Have you thought about a date?" asked Wendy.
"And somebody better phone Randy Fenoli, we've got a bride that needs to Say Yes to a Dress!" giggled Susan.
"No, no date yet. I can see us being engaged indefinitely. The ring cleared out Jase's savings so we need to start again from scratch. It won't be a big wedding, Jase hates being centre of attention so we're thinking a registry office and somewhere informal after but even that isn't cheap. The second you mention 'wedding' to a venue, even for a small private room, they start adding zeros to their quote. Then there's a cake and a photographer. Not to mention a dress." She sighed and looked down at her glass.
"Why don't you have it here?" asked Susan.
Carol's head snapped up, "Could we, Becca? It's only going to be a small wedding, around thirty guests."
"Oh. Em, I've never done a wedding reception before Carol. It's a huge responsibility."
"Luvvie what are you talking about? Look around at what you've organised for tonight. Alcohol, food, party.....all that's missing is a posh dress for Carol,"

encouraged Wendy.
"I would need to speak to Frankie, see what he thinks. It wouldn't be right me deciding to take on something like this without discussing it with him first. Leave it with me and I'll chat to him." She gave Carol's hand a squeeze.
"Thanks Becca. It would actually be perfect!"
"No promises, but I'll see what I can do. I better go and catch up with Dan. I can hear him making up the final cocktails for tonight. Why don't you ladies go and enjoy a dance and by the time you get back to the table you'll have a 'Santa's Little Helper' waiting for you."

Chapter Twenty-three

FOUR MONTHS EARLIER

The girls headed off in the direction of the TwinkleStarKydz room while Becca went off to find Dan.

"Well, this evening took a turn I did not expect, celebrating an engagement. I'm so pleased for Carol," she commented as she entered the kitchen where Dan was putting the finishing touches to the cocktails. "Did you get a chance to speak with Zoe?"

"Yep," came the sharp response.

"Is she ok?"

"Nope."

"What's wrong?"

"How the fuck do I know!" he snapped. Becca took a step away. He sighed and looked up at her. "Sorry Becca, I shouldn't take it out on you. I don't know what's gotten into her recently. Ever since I asked her to come down to London she's been a bit off with me."

"Do you want me to have a word with her?"

"No, don't worry about it. It's a fortnight before Christmas. You've got enough on with Tony and the kids and this place. I'll speak to her again and see if I can get to the bottom of it."

"If you're sure?"

"Yes, I'm sure," and his winning smile returned again, "anyway let's get these bad boys served so we can enjoy the rest of the night." And as if on cue Frankie and Mark joined them in the kitchen.

"Wow! Those look amazing!" enthused Mark, "how did you get them that purple colour? I'm guessing there's some Chambord in there?"
"Good guess," replied Dan "Blueberry vodka, Chambord, Triple Sec and cranberry juice to be exact."
"Nice," Mark nodded his head, "I used to do some bar work while I was studying. I loved experimenting with various combinations although they didn't always work."
"You can say that again. You came up with some pretty vile concoctions," murmured Frankie.
"Yeah but it never stopped you from drinking them!" retorted Mark.
"Guilty! Never one to be accused of wasting good alcohol!" he turned to speak to Becca, "tell you what, things are getting a bit feisty out there." He nodded his head in the direction of the café, "I think that red fizzy stuff you served was some kind of rocket fuel. Are you sure you want to give them more booze?"
"I'm sure once they have a dance and burn some of it off they'll settle down but maybe we should re-fill the water jugs too."
"Good plan Boss. I'll see to the water jugs if you serve the cocktails." Frankie motioned to Dan and Mark who each picked up a tray of cocktails and headed out the kitchen. Becca took the opportunity to float the idea of Carol's wedding reception to Frankie. "So that was exciting news Carol had to share with us."
"Yeah, she seems really happy."
"She's asked if they could have the wedding reception here."

Frankie couldn't hide his surprise "Here. As in, the café?" Becca nodded. "Sheesh. I know we're a top tier café, but a wedding reception?"
"They don't want a big flashy, fussy do. They've been together since school. They're only having around thirty guests and want something informal so they can enjoy it and not feel uncomfortable and on show all day. What do you think?" Becca chewed the inside of her lip and started to play with her necklace.
"You're the boss, Boss. It's your call. I just bake the cakes and do what I'm told."
"No you don't! You're my wing-man. This place would fall apart without you. *I* would fall apart without you, and Wendy, of course. Unless you think we can do this, then the answer will be no so what do you think?"
"Thirty guests you say."
"Uh-huh."
"Informal? So a bit like what we've done tonight?"
"Yep."
"Then hell yeah, we can totally do that!" he smiled and put his hand in the air for a high-five which Becca responded to.
"Tell her I'll do her photographs too, and the cake, naturally."
"I think you've just made all her Christmas wishes come true. I'll go and let her know." Becca gave Frankie a hug then made her way back through to the café to find Carol and tell her the good news.
Their table was still empty. Becca figured they were still in the TwinkleStarKydz room dancing so she moved through the tables towards the dance area.

She noticed Dan was sitting in one of the booths talking with Zoe. It looked like a pretty intense conversation they were having and from the looks of it, Becca feared the worst for their relationship. As she approached the dance area The Darkness 'Christmas Time' was playing. "Oh Frankie," she said to herself, shaking her head. When she popped her head around the door she couldn't help but smile. The makeshift dancefloor was filled with bodies all hugging and singing along to the music. She saw the girls and waved over to Carol, indicating that she wanted to speak with her. Carol obliged and made her way over.

"Well, I spoke with Frankie," Becca began, arranging her face into a serious, straight expression.

"And?!" Carol pressed.

Becca shook her head, "I'm sorry Carol." Carol's expression dropped.

She continued, "But we'd love to do your wedding reception!" Carol's face lit up.

"You……you…..!" she gave Becca a crushing hug, "that was like something straight out of XFactor! You honesty had me thinking it was going to be a no!"

"Who are we to stand in the way of a 'happy ever after'? Frankie's also offered his services as a photographer and of course the cake. But we don't have to agree anything tonight, go home, talk to Jason, and if you're both happy with Café Swan as the venue then we would be delighted to have you as our inaugural wedding."

"Oh Becca! You don't know how happy this has made me! I'm sure Jase will be relieved to find somewhere that's so friendly and relaxed. He was totally dreading the thought of some posh stuffy hotel. Thank you! Thank you! Thank you!" she said as she hugged Becca again. Just then, they were joined by their friends.

"More good news?" probed Wendy.

"Becca's agreed to host my wedding reception!"

"Well I would say that's a cause for another drink to celebrate!" added Susan.

"Glad you said that as we've just served the final cocktail," laughed Becca and they all turned and headed back to the table to enjoy their final drink of the night.

A little while later the evening drew to a close. Mick came to collect Wendy and the girls as the crowd slowly dispersed. Becca began the task of clearing up, keeping one eye on the booth where Dan and Zoe sat. She noticed they didn't look as intense which she hoped was a good sign. Eventually they made a move away from the table and Zoe approached Becca.

"Another fabulous night Becca, you must be pleased."

"Yeah, they just keep getting better and better. We've only got one more to go now. I'll be sorry when they're over. They've been a lot of fun."

"Well you know what they say, all good things must come to an end."

"That sounds ominous. I hope you're not talking about you and Dan?"

"No, I think we're going to be ok," Zoe smiled,

"anyway, I just wanted to say well done again for another great night. Hope you have a lovely Christmas."
"You too, Zoe," and she gave her a hug.
"Better go, I'm sharing a taxi with some clients." Dan joined them and helped Zoe put on her coat. "I'll phone you tomorrow about the arrangements for London," she said to Dan then gave him a kiss on the cheek.
"Night babes," he said in response, "text me when you get home." She waved back to them as she left.
"So you guys sorted it out then?" Becca asked as she worked away clearing glasses and loading the dishwasher.
"It was all a misunderstanding over the London trip and she had gone into a sulk with me. We got it sorted though."
Becca was about to press further when suddenly a crash came from the toilets. Dan and Becca froze for a second before moving towards the source of the noise. When they opened the door to the men's toilets they saw Frankie lying on the floor, Mark kneeling next to him.
"What the hell's happened here?" exclaimed Becca.
"He's drunk," answered Mark, "he said he felt unwell and came in here. I gave it five minutes and came to check on him. He was really unsteady on his feet and put his hand out to hold onto the sink and missed."
"How on earth did he get *this* drunk?" she asked. Dan looked sheepish.
"There were quite a few spare cocktails going. When we went around with the 'Santa's Little Helper' a few

people said they were ok for drinks. I took them back to the kitchen and Frankie asked if he could have another one. I didn't think it would do any harm. Sorry."

"It's not your fault. He can be a bit of a guzzler when he's in the mood." Becca was clearly irritated. "Let's get him up and through to the café. Mark, try phoning a taxi so you can get him home."

"I've already tried. Everything's booked solid. We were going to walk home, maybe get some food on the way. I don't know what we're going to do now. He's in no fit state to walk."

As they manoeuvred Frankie into a seat in the café there was a knock on the café door. It was Tony who had come to pick up Becca. Dan let him in.

"What's going on here?" he asked.

"Frankie's had a bit too much Christmas spirit," Dan replied.

"Tony, could you maybe take him home?" Becca asked, "Mark's tried to get a taxi and nothing's available. There's no way he's capable of walking."

"Argh. Really?" Tony looked from Becca to Mark and finally Frankie. "Oh bloody hell. Ok. Mark, you get one side of him, I'll get the other but I swear if he throws up in my Audi ...."

"Thanks Ton," Mark was clearly relieved.

Tony couldn't help himself and laughed. "God, he's in a proper state! That must have been some cocktail you put together, Dan." He turned to Becca, "I'll be back as quickly as I can. Will you be ok to wait here? It's getting late."

"Yeah I've still got some tidying up to do," she replied.

"Don't worry mate, I'll wait with her," Dan smiled.

Chapter Twenty-four

FOUR MONTHS EARLIER

They all helped manoeuvre Frankie outside and into Tony's car. Becca and Dan returned to the café.

"What a night!" Becca shook her head, "Do you know what I could kill for right now? A cup of tea. Fancy one?"

"Only if there's a biscuit to go with it."

"I think I can manage better than that. There's still some of Frankie's truffles in the kitchen."

Becca busied herself making a pot of tea and collected the truffles from the kitchen. They took a seat.

"What about the rest of the clearing up?" asked Dan.

"I really can't face it tonight," Becca shook her head, "the dishwashers full and all the rest of the dirty glasses are stacked in the kitchen. I was going to handwash them but they can just wait until tomorrow and I'll re-fill the dishwasher. It's just really the tablecloths that need to be lifted, tables wiped and a quick sweep of the floor. Wendy and Mick are going to come in tomorrow first thing to sort the sound system and lights. Wendy's going to give me a hand to finish clearing up." She kicked her shoes off and put her feet up on a spare seat, sighed and took a sip of her tea.

"I think that has been the most eventful night we've had! I just mentioned to Zoe I'll miss doing them once you're open and running them at the wine store."

"You'll just need to come along then, won't you? You can be my guest of honour." There was a definite flirtatious, teasing tone to the question. "But first we need to get the place open." Becca felt relieved to be able to steer the conversation to safer ground and she toyed with her necklace as she spoke.
"Yes, Tony mentioned he has a definite date to finish the renovation on the store section of the project although he said the function room will take a bit longer. Have you thought about having an opening night?"
"Absolutely! I'm looking at early February, try to capitalise on the Valentine's Day market, you know, do some champagne promotions? You and Tony will be invited, of course."
"Thanks, Dan. We'll be delighted to come along. So, Zoe seemed much happier by the end of the night. You two looked like you were having quite an intense conversation earlier."
"Hmmm. Yes. She had completely got the wrong end of the stick about the New Year trip to London and had taken the hump with me. After she had agreed to go, I mentioned we would be staying with one of my friends. She had assumed we would be staying at a hotel so when I mentioned staying with a friend she thought we'd be kipping on their floor."
Becca laughed, "Yes well, I could imagine that would not be her style, a sleeping bag on the floor!"
"Exactly. The friend we're staying with part owns a bar in Soho. He's not exactly short of money and has a pretty impressive apartment in Pimlico. It has three bedrooms and it's just him so plenty of room

for a couple of visitors. Once I explained we weren't sleeping in a doss house she was much happier."

Becca let out a low whistle, "A three bedroom apartment in Pimlico? He must be doing alright for himself! That's much more in keeping with Zoe's standards."

"Absolutely. And you were absolutely right."

"About what?"

"Communication in a relationship. Being honest and transparent. Look how easy we got in a muddle over a short break to London." He shook his head. "I still can't get my head around Tony going behind your back like that with your redundancy money."

"His heart was in the right place and his intentions were all good. It was the execution that was all wrong."

"Even so. You must really love him to be able to put that behind you."

Becca let Dan's words hang in the air for a moment, "I do. But you can love someone and dislike them at the same time and I disliked Tony for a long time after he did that."

"Did you think about leaving him?"

"Of course I did. It wasn't just about the money. For a long time I just couldn't trust him and what's a relationship without trust? He pulled a pin in a grenade and threw it right at the heart of our marriage then to top it off he just walked away, or more accurately threw himself into renovating the café. I barely saw him for weeks and when I did, we never talked about it so when the grenade finally went off, I took the brunt of the force of it, emotionally speaking."

"So how did you get back on track?"
Becca shrugged, "To be honest, I don't actually know. We never had any big showdown over it. No ultimatums or marriage crunch-talks. Just gradually the days and weeks passed and we started to have proper conversations again. Immediately afterwards the only thing we talked about was the kids and it was purely an information sharing basis, for example, if they kids had been bathed already by the time he got home or if one of them wasn't feeling well, then I moved on to checking if he'd eaten or needed dinner, then slowly I started to ask about the café. It was a gradual thing."
"I gotta say, I'm in awe you pulled it back. Many couples would have just thrown in the towel."
"No relationship is picture perfect, Dan. All this social media #MakingMemories nonsense, it's all superficial. If you want a real relationship, with Zoe or anyone else, you need to be prepared to throw yourself over the odd emotional-grenade or two for the sake of making it work and not giving up."
"And what about now? How's things between you?"
"We're good. Solid. We seem to have found our groove."
Dan leaned forward and looked intently at Becca, "Would you say groove? Or is it actually more like a rut and you would be open to a change?" The atmosphere shifted. In previous exchanges Becca had wondered if Dan had an ulterior motive. This time there was no denying the line of questioning.
"What exactly are you getting at, Dan?"
"Well you've admitted things haven't always been

great between you and Tony and you did at one point consider leaving him. I just wondered if in some way by telling me all of this, you're actually telling me that you're still keeping your options open." He held her gaze so there was no misunderstanding.

Becca's heart started to race. She fidgeted with her necklace and despite her head automatically reacting with disgust at the very thought of an affair, she felt a flutter in her stomach and a stir of arousal which caught her off guard. She opened her mouth to speak. Just then the café door opened and in walked Tony.

"He was absolutely smashed. I don't think I've ever seen Frankie so drunk."

"Oh hey! You're back," Becca breathed a sigh of relief, "is he ok?"

"Yeah. I had to help Mark strip him and get him into bed though. I have seen enough of Frankie White tonight to last me a lifetime. I think he was hallucinating too. He kept garbling something about a wedding at the café?"

"Nope, no hallucination. Carol, one of the Mums, got engaged last week and has asked to have the reception here. She still needs to talk to her fiancé but she reckons he'll go for it. He's a really down to earth guy and they're desperate for a low key, informal setting."

"Nice one! That could be another business spin off for this place, bespoke bijou informal private functions." He turned to Dan, "Talking about business, how were the sales tonight then?"

"Yep, good." He looked at Becca, "With all the

potential excitement right at the end of the night I completely forgot about that." Becca detected the double meaning in his words which went straight over Tony's head. His tone change and he continued, "Sales were well up on the last event. We sold several cases of the red Shiraz."

"So that's three events down and just one to go. Don't know how you guys are going to top tonight though."

"Oh, I've got a few ideas. Don't worry about that," replied Dan and he smiled at Becca. She shifted in her seat as that tug of excitement in her stomach unexpectedly returned. "I'll head off, leave you two to it."

"Do you want us to drop you on the way?"

"No no, it's fine. Happy to walk home and get some fresh air, you know, wind down. Night guys," and he put on his coat and left the café.

Tony turned to Becca, pulling her up from her seat into an embrace and nuzzling her neck, "Sounds like it's been quite a night." He took a step back to look at her, his eyes twinkling, "And you, Mrs Swanson, look absolutely ravishing." He kissed her, Becca relaxed and sank into the moment.

"Let's go home," she murmured into his ear. He grinned at her, familiar with that tone in her voice and what it would mean once they got home. Tony knew he was on a promise but for Becca, she needed to do something to get Dan Lehmann out of her head.

Chapter Twenty-five

NOW

Tony sat slumped, defeated on the sofa.
"So pretty much everything then. He knows it all but what really hurts is that you spoke to him about it before you spoke to me. You even told him you thought about leaving me. When I asked you that same question earlier, you avoided it." He sighed, "Looks like we've finally had our showdown."
Becca felt the pizza she had eaten earlier churn in her stomach. She sat for a moment hoping it would settle but the combination of a hangover, lack of sleep, junk food and the confession to Tony was too much. She made a dash for the downstairs loo where she threw up. It was the ugly violent sort of sick - loud, painful wretches which felt like your insides were trying to escape. When she felt confident it was over and there was nothing left in her stomach, she pulled the handle to rid the toilet of the mess, put the lid down and sat there, clammy and sweating. Her hands shaking, she scraped her hair back from her face and tied it up into a messy ponytail. Next she stood up, splashed cold water on her face and rinsed her mouth to rid it from bitter taste left by the vomit. There was a knock at the door.
"You ok?"
The sound of his voice cut her in two. Earlier tonight when she broke down at the dining table he hadn't flinched. He had just sat there and looked at her like he was watching some random stranger have a

meltdown. Now, after everything she had admitted to him, he was back. Her protective bubble right at her side when she needed him. It destroyed her knowing what she had just done to him. "I'll be out in a minute," she croaked, her throat burnt from the bile. She took a few deep breaths and opened the door. Tony was stood in the hallway, leaning against the wall his arms folded, staring at his feet. When she stepped out, he looked up at her.

"Jesus, you look rough. Can I get you something?"

She shook her head, "I just need to sit down." She headed back through to the lounge and retook her seat on the sofa. She lay back and closed her eyes.

A few minutes later Tony appeared with a glass of water and a couple of paracetamol, "Here, take these," and he handed her the glass and tablets. She duly obliged. He took his seat next to her and began.

"I don't get why you went ahead with the final wine tasting. He pretty much propositioned you in December, yet you put yourself in a position where he could have another go and try again." He shook his head. "I just don't get why you would do that."

"It wasn't as simple as that though, was it?" She began, "It wasn't just the café and the wine store, your business was in the mix too. You were well into the renovation work and had finances and resources tied up in his place. He owed the property business money. In fact he *still* owes you money, you've not finished the function room yet. I just couldn't see a way to get out of it that wouldn't raise questions from you."

"Yeah, whereas this way has worked out so much better," his voice dripped with sarcasm.

She continued, "I thought I could handle it. I figured I just needed to get through the opening of the wine store - and we were going to that together - I didn't expect him to chance his luck that night. Then it would just be the final wine tasting. Knowing what *he* was thinking I thought I could mitigate for it, make sure we weren't alone and once it was over, I had no intention of doing *any* business with him. I was going to leave the wine and cocktails for Carol's hen night and wedding to Mark."
"Again Becs, that was a fool-proof plan well executed."
She sighed, "So what now?"
"Well, we've had the showdown. Now it's the crunch-talks I guess. Tell me, where do you think we go from here, Becca?"
"I....I....we can't give up. I made a stupid mistake and I am so very sorry," she stammered. He nodded his head slowly. "What about you? What do you want to happen?" she ventured.
"Honestly? I really don't know."
She felt the nausea returning.
"It's been a *very* long twenty-four hours. I've had no sleep. I'm exhausted and there's been a lot said tonight. I need time to think. I need time to process it all. I can't make a decision right now."
"But we're not giving up?" she pressed, desperate for a shred to hope to hang onto.
"I honestly don't know Becs," he shrugged, "it just feels like we've made a right mess of things. We're both responsible in our different ways for what's happened and where our marriage has got to. You said it yourself, we've got a lot of history and not all

of it's good."
The beep from Becca's mobile interrupted them.
"Aren't you going to check that?" Tony asked.
"It can wait. This is more important."
"It might be Wendy, something to do with the kids."
Reluctantly Becca stood up from the sofa and collected her mobile from the dining table. It was finally a response from Zoe: So uv decided to crawl out from under your rock & face me. Ur rite. We need 2 talk. Come 2 my place in the morning @10 Another wave of nausea hit her. She sent a response confirming she would be there. "It's Zoe. She wants me to go and see her in the morning."
"Well maybe you should go and get some sleep. You've got round two to face tomorrow."
"I don't know if I'll get any sleep not without knowing that we're going to be ok."
Another sigh. "I'm not going to promise you that, Becs. We've obviously had a real problem with communication in our relationship for a long time so if there's any chance of salvaging our marriage we need to be completely honest with each other starting now even when it means having really difficult conversations and facing things that we would normally run away from."
"So you think we're worth saving?"
He shook his head, "Becs that's not what I said. I said I can't promise anything and I need you to hear that even though it's not something you want to hear or something I want to admit. We might not make it back from this. We might need to accept that too much has happened."
They looked at each other, the enormity of Tony's

words weighing heavily in the air between them. She nodded her head and bit her lip fresh hot tears stinging her eyes. Tony stood up and went over to her, folding her into an embrace. She breathed in his aftershave and his scent as the clock on the wall counted the minutes while they quietly held on to each other.

They didn't speak. There was nothing more to say.

Eventually and somewhat reluctantly, Becca broke away. "I'm going to go and try to get some sleep. Zoe wants me to go round at ten tomorrow morning."

He nodded and tucked a strand of loose hair behind her ear then cupped his hands around her face, his piercing blue eyes meeting her deep green gaze. He kissed her on the lips and said, "The only reason it's *this* difficult is because I love you. But it's not just about me anymore, it's become more complicated than that. You understand that, don't you?" she nodded again unable to trust her voice. He continued, "Regardless of what happens next Becca, I'll always be in your corner. For you and for the kids. I won't let you slip back into that difficult place again. You won't be on your own. Go and get some rest. I'm going to wait down here for a while. I don't think I'll be able to sleep yet and I need to think."

Becca left the lounge and Tony listened as she made her way to their bedroom. He collapsed back onto the sofa and closed his eyes, straining to hear his wife move around upstairs. In his minds eye he could picture her carrying out her night time routine, getting changed out of her clothes into the comfortable pyjamas she preferred, then going into

the ensuite to remove her make-up and clean her teeth.
He found the familiarity of it both reassuring and unsettling following the events of the last twenty-four hours.
When he couldn't hear any further sound and was quite sure she was asleep he went upstairs to get ready for bed. He silently opened the door to their bedroom and waited. He could hear her deep even breathing indicating she was sleeping soundly. He quietly moved across the bedroom to the ensuite where he washed his face and brushed his teeth.
When he emerged a few minutes later he stopped for a second and looked at Becca. The dim light from the bathroom cascaded across her face and he was momentarily transported back to the day after their wedding when he had woken early thanks to a hangover. He had taken the opportunity then just to watch her, uninterrupted. He took the same opportunity now. He could see the fine lines on her face which betrayed her age and their years together but she was still the same Becca.
He had no idea what to do. He still loved her and struggled to see a life without her but he was beginning to realise that their marriage was very badly damaged and as much as he struggled to see a life without her, he also struggled to see how they could repair what had happened and by trying to find a way through it, would they really just be delaying the inevitable? He shook his head, unable to think anymore. The exhaustion he felt earlier had returned with vengeance.
He silently left the bedroom closing the door behind

him then opened the airing cupboard and removed the spare duvet which was used by the kids' friends when they had sleep overs. He returned to the lounge and made a bed for himself on the sofa. He stripped off his jeans and crawled under the cover.

Just as he was about to give into sleep, something under the coffee table caught his eye as it glistened in the street light which came in through the lounge window. He sat up and reached over to recover it. It was Becca's necklace which she had thrown at him earlier during their argument. He lay back down on the sofa, turning the wine bottle pendant between his fingers, the chain broken where she had pulled it with force from her neck. He suddenly realised that since he had given it to her at that first wine tasting event all those months ago, she had never taken it off. Other than her engagement, wedding and eternity rings, it was the one piece of jewellery he had given to her that she had constantly worn. He closed his fist around it and held onto it as he drifted off to sleep.

Chapter Twenty-six

TWO MONTHS EARLIER

After the Winter Wonderland wine tasting Becca hadn't seen much of Dan or Zoe. The café had closed for its annual festive break and everyone had disappeared into their own Christmas bubbles. She had only seen Wendy one night between Christmas and New Year when Wendy had invited her, Tony and the kids round for Christmas drinks on one of Mick's precious nights off. It had been a fun night as they ended up playing some ridiculous board game which one of the kids received as a present. The adults all made right fools of themselves much to the kids delight and dismay. Then Max and Emily went to Becca's parents on New Year's Eve so she and Tony could have a night to themselves. They enjoyed a meal out together and showed face at Frankie and Mark's party. They didn't stay long, they were present for the big countdown to midnight and wished everyone a Happy New Year but had cleverly booked Mick to come and get them shortly after twelve. They made their excuses and returned home to enjoy the peace and quiet and a bottle of Bollinger. She remembered Tony making a toast saying this year would be one to remember. If only he had known what the next year would have in store for them.

Becca was quite relieved to have avoided Dan given

how their last encounter had ended. She didn't want to voluntarily put herself in a vulnerable position with him and neither did she want to risk any awkward conversations with Zoe about how her relationship with Dan was progressing.

Becca felt increasingly uncomfortable knowing that Dan didn't seem to be as committed or honest about the relationship but she didn't know what to do about it. How could she warn Zoe without facing some very uncomfortable questions? She had received a couple of WhatsApp messages from Zoe with photos of their trip to London which seemed to have gone well. Becca just hoped the time in London would be enough to put his notion of starting something with her behind him and he would focus on Zoe.

Thankfully Dan had been pre-occupied with the final stages of the renovation work on the wine store. They had moved to the decoration and final touches and he was being pretty hands on, much to Tony's irritation.

Becca had learned through Tony that he had opted for quite an industrial look in the store, bare brick walls and bottle green paint, copper coloured shelves and bare lightbulbs with copper wire surrounds hanging low from exposed wires. The store was due to officially open for business on Monday which was Valentine's Day but at the launch night tonight the till would be open for the invited guests if they wanted to make any purchases.

The thought of the launch night made her stomach turn but she was reassured knowing she was attending with Tony so was pretty confident it would

be uneventful. She was putting the final touches to her make up when Tony announced his arrival by a rather loud wolf whistle. "Cut it out you!" she joked throwing the cotton pad she was holding in his direction. "Kids ok?" she asked. He had just dropped Max and Emily at Wendy's. Dan had invited Wendy too but Mick was working and she was adamant that Tony and Becca should both go to the grand opening. Frankie and Mark had also been invited but had a clash of dates with a friend's birthday so they would be on their own.
"Yeah Wendy had just taken a pizza out of the oven and Austin and Lizzie were watching You Tube so I didn't see Max and Emily for dust." He held out his hand to her, "Stand up until I have a look at you." she grinned and did as she was asked. She was wearing the green tailored jump suit which she wore at the Winter Wonderland wine tasting event. "'I'm so glad you decided to wear the jumpsuit again. You look stunning in it." He gave her a long lingering kiss. "You ready? We better make a move we're already a bit late." She nodded and tried to ignore the butterflies that were doing dive-bombs in her stomach.

The opening night was well under way by the time they arrived. When they walked in they were met by a wall of noise, a combination of some non-descript jazz music playing in the background and a bustling crowd who were clearly enjoying the free samples offered by Dan. Tony was holding Becca's hand as they manoeuvred their way through the throng to the counter where Dan was chatting with some guests and pouring samples to taste. He smiled warmly at them and offered Tony a firm handshake and Becca a kiss on the cheek. She deliberately took a step back following his greeting and positioned herself just behind Tony's shoulder.

"For a moment I thought you were going to blow me out and be a no-show," he looked pointedly at Becca.

Tony responded, "What? And miss all the glory for my hard work? Not a chance!"

"It looks amazing, you've done a really good job. Congratulations, Dan," Becca offered as she played with the pendant on her necklace.

"Thanks. I'm relieved to have got it over the finishing line." His smile softened "What can I get you guys to drink? I've got a whole selection here. Actually, let me choose. It's got to be a proper celebratory drink." He poured them all a glass of champagne. "I just want to say thank you. You've both really supported me over recent months. Tony, you really got me out of a hole. This place was turning into a proper money pit thanks to those cowboys I originally gave the contract to. And Becca, we created something special with the events at the café."

"And you've still got one night to go yet." Tony interrupted as he tipped his glass towards Dan.

"Yes. Yes we do." Dan continued his eyes on Becca, "They've allowed me to build up a ready-made clientele which is just amazing. But more importantly, I hope that that we can continue what we started." Becca felt a coldness creep across her shoulders and it wasn't from the chilly February

evening. "A toast. New beginnings. And Happy Valentine's Day." Dan indicated he was finished by holding up his glass.
"New beginnings!" Tony repeated and chinked his glass against Dan's then turned to Becca, "and
Happy Valentine's Day," he said as he kissed her. When he moved away Becca could see Dan was looking at her, his jaw set.
"Would you mind if I showed Becca what we're doing in the function room upstairs?" Tony asked as he took a sip of his drink.
"Not at all, be my guest. I've got a few sales to put through down here but you know where to go."
Tony took Becca by the hand and led her through to the rear of the store. "You've done an amazing job, Tony. I know residential properties are usually your thing but it looks fabulous. Are you pleased with how it's turned out?"
"Yeah, I think there were one or two things we could have done differently but it was Dan's choice, his vision, so you've got to go with that. He's pleased with the final result which is all you can ask for, a happy client."
"Would you take on a job like this again?"
"Well I've done a couple now, the café and here. This one was a lot more stressful because I was working to a client's specification rather than my own vision but I've learned a lot with both projects so yeah, I think I would be up for more commercial jobs if they came along. We're just up here," Tony indicated to the staircase.
When they reached the top, there was a small

hallway which followed similar décor as downstairs – the staircase, skirting boards and banister were a dark oak wood. There was a door immediately to the left, a door in front of them and a door down the corridor on the right. Tony explained to Becca that the door on the left was the toilets, the door along the corridor was Dan's office and the door ahead was the function room which was where he wanted to show Becca. He opened the door to reveal an unexpectedly large room.

"Woah! It's a bit of a Tardis up here, isn't it?" Becca stood for a second taking in her surroundings. She could see exposed oak beams holding up the vaulted ceiling, a few beams seemed to be covered by false walls. The floor was also solid oak which she could see was in the process of being restored. She turned around in a circle to take it in. "So are you covering or exposing the beams?" she asked.

"Exposing."

"Have you done anything like this before?"

Tony shook his head, "And if I'm being honest I was beginning to think my guys weren't up to it. It's pretty skilled work and we've just never taken on anything like this in any of our other projects. This is next level stuff. It doesn't help having the local authority breathing down our necks at every point but we seemed to have cracked the process so we're making headway now."

"Now I get why there were all the delays. What's the plan? The vision?"

"Well we need to expose the last few beams. Dan's Dad had covered them over and basically turned this entire area into a series of smaller rooms for storage.

The planning guys were *not* happy about that. He had done it without any consultation with them which came as news to Dan so when Dan first brought them in to discuss his plans and how he wanted to change the layout, there were a lot of questions to answer but as he was planning to restore it to what it was, it wasn't too big a problem."

"Sheesh. Must have been a bit of an awkward conversation."

"You bet it was and it held us up. We couldn't touch a thing up here until planning had re-checked their records and sorted all that out. We've removed most of the internal walls now," Tony made a sweeping gesture with his hand, "and we just have the final few beams to expose and treat. We've been lucky, they're all in good shape. We need to finish treating the floor too," he stamped his foot on the ground, "then we've got some bespoke shelves and storage to build over here," he gestured towards one of the long walls which had several alcoves between the beams, "which will have wrought-iron gated fronts on them and be internally lit. They'll double up as storage for the store downstairs but also provide a design feature for the function room. Then on the other wall, where we have the sash windows, which we need to replace, we'll build some bench seating areas. They'll be boxed in so again they'll have some hidden storage for stock. Then it'll just be decorating and job done. He's going for the same green throughout, that's what which pulls it all together, but with slightly different accents in each area..." Tony stopped mid-sentence, "what, why are you looking at me like that?"

Becca shook her head, "I've never seen you come alive like this before when talking about one of your projects."

He shrugged, embarrassed. "I've been doing the residential stuff for so long I don't really need to think about it. There's no problem we come across that we haven't dealt with before but here, here I really had to think. It really pushed me so yeah, I think I've got a taste for this stuff now. I would definitely do another one."

She walked over to him, put her arms around him and kissed him, "I'm so pleased for you. You've done an amazing job."

At that, the door opened and Dan appeared with a group of around ten guests behind him. "Not disturbing you, am I?" he directed the question at Becca and she took a step away from Tony in response.

"No, no! Just explaining the plans to Becca," Tony smiled.

Dan nodded slowly, "Well I hoped you were still up here actually, I was going to talk through the progress to date with the guys," he indicated to the group who had entered into the room, "would you mind doing the honours for me? You've got the technical know-how after all."

"Sure, I'd be happy to." Tony turned to the group and began recounting what he had just explained to Becca. Dan took his opportunity to join Becca.

"No Zoe tonight?" Becca took first shot.

"She's been and gone. Some dinner commitment with a client. She popped in on the way to show face."

"How was London?"
"Yeah, it was good. Seems like a lifetime ago already. The last few weeks have gone by so quickly with the final preparations for this place." Dan turned to face her so his back was to Tony and the other guests. "I haven't stopped thinking about our conversation at the last wine tasting before Christmas."
The tingling coldness crept across Becca's shoulders again.
"I haven't stopped thinking about you," his chocolate brown eyes searched her face. She hated herself but she felt the tingling coldness turn to arousal. "Everything you told me about you and Tony. About how he treated you. You're remarkable and deserve to be with someone who appreciates how incredible you are."
Becca shot a look over Dan's shoulder as Tony approached them. "What are you two whispering about?" he asked as he joined them.
"Oh, you know, just chatting to Becca about potential ways we can keep the relationship going once the function room is fully open. We've made such a good team I wouldn't want to lose that." He smiled then continued, "I was thinking, for example, with Carol's wedding and hen night coming up we could work something out where I provide the alcohol? Maybe even help out with some of the cocktails."
"Makes sense," Tony nodded, taking a sip of his drink and turned to Becca, "and if you're going to try and attract other private functions it would be a good move to continue the partnership with Dan so he could provide the booze."

"Oh, well I don't know if we're going to make it part of what we do at the café," Becca spluttered, "it's really just a one off, a favour for Carol."
"Well it was just an idea. Just think about it Becca."
Dan turned to Tony. "I better make my way back downstairs, hoping to make a few more sales before the nights out."
"I'll help you out there. We'll take a bottle of this," and Tony held up his champagne flute then
turned to Becca, "for Valentine's Day on Monday."
"No problem, I'll give you a discount on it too," Dan replied.
Tony turned to Becca "I gotta say I was kinda dreading tonight. I was actually nervous about you seeing the place. I'm really quite proud of this one. I'm glad you like it but I'll be equally glad when it's finished."
Becca smiled at Tony and thought to herself, 'you and me both'.

Chapter Twenty-seven

NOW

The next morning, Tony was awake before Becca. He lay on the sofa where he had slept and stared up at the ceiling. His body may have been refreshed after a night's sleep but his mind immediately began turning over the events of the weekend as soon as he opened his eyes. He had no idea how long he had been awake for before he heard Becca move around upstairs. He looked at the noisy clock on the wall and it showed it was just after nine. He stood up and pulled on his jeans then folded the duvet in preparation to return it to the airing cupboard before the kids came home. As he did so, Becca's broken necklace which had been tucked between the folds of the duvet fell to the floor. He picked it up and put it in his pocket.

He went into the kitchen and began making a light breakfast for them both. If he knew Becca, she would be feeling extremely anxious about facing Zoe and probably wouldn't want anything but after she had been sick last night she would have nothing in her stomach so she really needed to eat. He put four slices of bread in the toaster and boiled the kettle to make some coffee. He was busy getting the plates and mugs from the cupboards when she came into the kitchen.

"Nothing for me, my stomach still isn't quite right"

"I expected you would say as much but you are not going to see Zoe without eating. You only had a few bits of pizza all day yesterday and you didn't keep it down. You can manage a slice of toast." His tone was firm so she did as she was told and sat down at the table as Tony placed a plate in front of her with a single slice of toast on it. He sat the butter, jam and peanut butter on the table so she could choose her topping and returned to the counter to retrieve the cafetiere.

Once he was seated at the table with his breakfast, she ventured, "You didn't come to bed last night. Did you sleep down here?"

He nodded but didn't offer any explanation. She sensed she shouldn't push this particular line of questioning any further. They continued eating in silence. When they were finished Becca made to stand up when Tony began, "I've been turning a few things over in my head and there's one thing that's been niggling me. Well a few things actually but one thing in particular that my thoughts keep catching on." Becca re-took her seat and he continued, "Last night when you mentioned the opening of the wine store, you said you didn't think he would 'chance his luck' that night. It strikes me as an odd thing to say."

"What do you mean?"

"Well, if he *didn't* chance his luck, you would have surely said something like 'we went to the opening together and he kept his distance' or 'he stayed clear'. But you didn't say that and what I'm trying to figure out is....I was with you the whole night. It was just the two of us, no Frankie or Wendy."

"Not the whole night."

Tony's mind started to race as he replayed the events of the opening night in his mind on fast forward.

"What? When we were in the function room?"
Becca nodded.
"But I was right there, just a few feet from you." Becca saw the flicker in his eye as the realisation dawned on him, "Hang on, those comments about keeping the relationship going, he wasn't referring to the business relationship between the café and the wine store, was he?"
Becca shook her head.
"He was meaning you. He was meaning a relationship with you. Son of a bitch. I can't believe he would have the audacity and be so blasé to go there with you when I was *right there.* In the same room! Why on earth didn't you just out him to me there and then? We could have put a stop to it once and for all."
"How could I? I had just watched you light up talking about the work on the wine store and function room. You were so proud of yourself and rightly so. It had ignited a passion in you again. You've been doing the residential re-developments for so long you could do it in your sleep, take on a property and turn it around to make a profit no bother. It was becoming like a repetitive conveyer belt but the wine store pushed you. It challenged you and you had to use all that experience and all that knowledge in a completely new way. How could I taint that achievement for you?"
Becca stood up and cleared the breakfast dishes. "I need to go. I told Zoe I would be there at ten and I'm going to be late if I don't go now."
"You can't be serious? You're going to go to Zoe's now after your latest revelation? Don't you think

we've got more to talk about? Zoe can wait."
"There's nothing more to say Tony. You know everything now." Becca slapped her hands against her legs in exasperation. "You're not the only one whose been doing some thinking overnight. Last night you admitted to being arrogant when you tried to buy my way out of depression. You're not the only one who's been guilty of arrogance. I realise now that I didn't make just one mistake on Friday night when I kissed Dan, I've made poor decisions for months now but my biggest mistake was arrogance too, thinking I could handle it myself and keep it from you. I thought that after the last wine tasting event I would be able to find excuses to avoid going to the wine store for his events but then he dropped the bombshell at the opening night about doing the booze for Carol's hen night and wedding. I realised then I was in over my head but it had gone too far."
She stopped for a moment to catch her breath then continued, "I admitted to you last night that part of me wanted something to happen but it was the excitement, the possibility that something *might* happen I was actually attracted to, not Dan. As soon as he kissed me on Friday I knew I had made a disastrous mistake. All I could do was hope you wouldn't find out."
"But then he told me."
She nodded her head, "But then he told you." She looked down at the floor, overwhelmed by shame and unable to look Tony in the eye anymore, "I asked him to leave. Straight away. I told him it was a mistake and he had got the wrong idea about me but

it was too late, the damage was done. He was angry with my reaction and I needed him gone before you arrived to get me. I couldn't risk what he might say to you. It didn't occur to me to check outside, I was just so relieved he had left the café."

"He was waiting for me, primed to tell me what happened."

She nodded again, "I'm sure it was the rejection that did it. *That's* why he told you. He was furious. Had I not told him it was a mistake...."

"Jesus Becs, you were still going to hide it from me? If he hadn't told me, would you have told me?"

"I honestly don't know Tony. I would like to say yes I would have told you everything but I just don't know." She checked her watch, "I really need to go and get this over with Zoe. Wendy said she would keep the kids until lunchtime and she's giving them something to eat. Could you maybe head over after one to get them? I really don't know how long I'm going to be."

"Yep. Whatever." His tone was brisk, clipped.

She tried again to smooth over her need to go and speak to Zoe, "Look, it's no bad thing me going out this morning. It gives you few hours on your own before going to get the kids. You know everything now. It's all out in the open." He was avoiding looking at her. "Please listen to me Tony," the break in her voice made him finally look up. "I don't want us to give up. I want us to work through this but as you said to me last night it's become complicated and I understand it's not just about me and what I want. You need to decide what you want. Then and only then can we decide if there's a way through this." She took two strides over to his side and kissed him on the cheek, then turned sharply and walked out of the kitchen, down the hallway and out the front door without looking back, tears blinding her.

Tony watched her leave, the image burned into his mind. He couldn't help but wonder if this is what it would actually feel like if he did call it a day and all he would be left with was the ghost of her image and the ticking of the clock for company.

Chapter Twenty-eight

NOW

As Becca parked her car in front of Zoe's apartment building she thought in passing that the knot of anxiety in her stomach seemed fast becoming a permanent feature. She turned off the ignition and sat for a few moments, stalling herself for the inevitable onslaught from Zoe. She really had no idea how she was going to start the conversation. She didn't think a quick "sorry I kissed your boyfriend" was going to cut it, but neither did she relish the idea of having to re-tread the entire sorry tale again so soon after explaining to Tony. She decided to wait and see how Zoe played it and follow her lead. It didn't really matter now, the damage had been done. The tenuous friendship they had maintained since Becca left R&Ds was undoubtedly destroyed and all that was left was for her to face up to her actions, take responsibility and accept whatever harsh reality Zoe had to serve her.

Reluctantly she opened the car door and made her way towards the apartment block. Her hand was shaking as she pressed the buzzer for Zoe's apartment. As she stood for those few moments waiting for a response she wrestled with her fight or flight response but before she could give in to the latter, Zoe's voice coolly answered.

"Hello?"

"Hi. It's me."

"Doors open."

The buzzer sounded to indicate the door was unlocked. Becca entered the building. It was a new build on the Clydeside, sleek and modern all white walls and floors, frosted glass and chrome fixtures and fittings. The term estate agents would use to describe it would unquestionably be minimalistic. Becca personally thought it was cold and clinical.
She pressed the button to summon the elevator and again her fight or flight response taunted her. She held fast. She had come this far now and had to see it through. The door opened and she pressed the number to take her to Zoe's floor. A few seconds later and she emerged in the hallway which took her to the apartment. She was aware she shared a floor with two other neighbours. It was almost ten thirty now, still early for a Sunday morning. Becca silently prayed her neighbours were either out for early morning exercise or brunch as she expected the conversation to escalate to an argument and she hated the thought that when she did the unavoidable walk of shame to leave the building the neighbours would be able to see her through their peepholes.
She arrived at Zoe's front door and knocked quietly. She heard Zoe move around on the other side of the door and a few moments later the door opened and she was finally face to face. Becca was momentarily taken aback by the icy cold stare she was met with.
"Hi," she offered feebly.
Zoe didn't respond. Instead she just turned around and walked back into her apartment. Becca wavered then finally followed letting the door close behind her once she was on the inside. She emerged into Zoe's living area. Becca realised it had been a

number of years since she had last been invited here and she quickly scanned around the interior to familiarise herself with the layout.

It was an open plan apartment with the lounge, dining area and kitchen all occupying the same space. Two of the four walls boasted floor to ceiling windows, one of which opened onto a balcony area with a fabulous view of Glasgow city and along the Clyde. Back along the corridor towards the front door were three internal doors - the bathroom, the bedroom and a small closet. She noted that Zoe had redecorated since she had last been here. The interior had previously reflected the minimalistic, clinical style of the building with cream walls, sofa and soft furnishings completed with matching chrome and glass dining room table, coffee table and console table. The interior was now a palette of greys with a variety of different textures which gave the apartment a much more luxurious feel. A grey thick shag pile rug occupied the centre of the room which was surrounded by a chenille fabric corner sofa complete with chaise longue in a similar colour. The chrome and metal furniture had been replaced with high shine grey gloss furniture.

Zoe stood over by the door to the balcony, arms folded. Becca felt very small and vulnerable in Zoe's personal space and began to feel it had been a mistake having this showdown on her turf, she should have demanded they meet at a neutral venue.

"You look like shit. Rough night with Tony?" Zoe began. "Good. I'm glad. It's nothing less than you deserve."

Becca swallowed. No escaping it, this was going to

be brutal.
"Zoe, look….."
"Let me guess," she cut her off, "you can explain? It wasn't your fault? Or it wasn't what it looked like? Come on Becca. Don't take me for a fool."
Becca shifted her weight nervously. Zoe hadn't invited her to sit down which meant one of two things - either this wasn't going to take long or Zoe was going to make her feel as uncomfortable as possible throughout the ordeal.
"I'm not going to insult your intelligence," Becca fired back, "yes it happened. We kissed and I'm not even going to play a blame game of who kissed who first because it really doesn't matter. We both need to take equal responsibility for what happened but you have to believe me, I am so very sorry, Zoe. I didn't for one second intend to come between you and Dan."
Zoe started laughing manically. "Dan? You think all this is about Dan? I don't *care* about Dan," she spat the words at Becca, "it's always been about Tony. I love Tony."
As Zoe's words sank in Becca had a sudden onset of vertigo. The walls seemed to spin around her and she felt as if the floor had given way below her. She tried to regain her composure, her mind racing trying to make sense of it all.
Zoe continued to cackle. She was clearly enjoying the moment, "Oh poor Becca, you really don't get it, do you? Now who's taking who for a fool? Think back Becca, think back to the very beginning."
"What? The awards night?"
"Surprise! I had no other commitment that night.

There was no clash with another client. I had my eye on Tony from the minute he walked into the office but I knew I couldn't do anything about it as long as I had his file. I needed someone else to take him on. Why else do you think I would willingly hand over a high fee earner? Out of the goodness of my heart? No. I thought if I could get you to take him on it would leave the path clear for me to make a personal approach to him. I had been to so many of those boring awards nights. They're always sooo *dull.* I never for a minute thought I needed to worry about you two going together to something so excruciating. I couldn't believe it when you walked into the office on the Monday and handed his file back to me with that stupid grin on your face. At first I thought all wasn't lost. He was still my client. If I could maybe just do a harmless bit of flirting when we were catching up over coffee then I could maybe tempt him away from you but he caught on to me quickly and firmly put me in my place."

"He's always been suspicious of you and I could never work out why. Now it's making sense. But you and Dan, you've been together for months now……and your London trip……"

"You're right, I did fancy Dan in the beginning but after we started dating I realised quickly he was absolutely smitten with you," she growled the word at Becca. "Even on our first date he kept asking me all these questions about you. I thought no. Not again. Rebecca Swanson is not going to take someone else from me. Dan was like a pathetic puppy following you around. I watched him at the wine tasting nights. He was unable to keep his eyes off you. He was supposed to be with me! Then I realised I could actually use this to my advantage, play the long game. Put Dan between you and Tony then as a kindred wounded spirit offer Tony a shoulder to cry on and gradually over time become more than just a friend to him."

"You bitch. You played us all."

"Oh no, not all of you. Dan was in on the plan." Zoe inspected her nails. She was clearly having fun now. "When we got to that magical fourth date which *you* were so obsessed with, I knew it wasn't going anywhere so I started to tell Dan that maybe all wasn't well in the perfect world of Tony and Becca. I started to hint that there had been some problems in the past and you hadn't really gotten over it. I alluded that you were really just sticking it out for the kids but I wasn't sure you were actually happy and of course being the *lovely, caring, friend* I was really quite worried about you." Her voice dripped with mock concern and she put her hand to her heart in an over-the-top dramatic fashion to emphasise the point.

"Dan lapped it up. What made it all the more convincing was the fact there was a germ of truth in it. You had been so angry with Tony over using the redundancy money for the café I knew if Dan asked you the right questions, in the right way, at the right time you would spill your guts. All the while you would innocently be thinking you were helping him navigate and work out his relationship with me."

Becca sat down uninvited and perched on the edge of the chaise longue. Zoe moved from her position next to the window and was now standing in front of

Becca. "What's wrong, Becca? Two day hangover?"
Becca looked up at her, "I don't believe you. I saw you together at the wine tasting nights. The Christmas night, you fell out and then made up again. Dan said you had some sort of misunderstanding. And London. You went to London together and stayed with Dan's friend!"
"You stupid, gullible cow. You saw what I wanted you to see. The chaste kisses on the cheek? They were all friendly, nothing more. We did have a misunderstanding at the Christmas wine tasting night, I was convinced Dan was getting cold feet about our plan and he was reneging on making a play for you. I had to work hard that night to convince him to keep going but from what he told me it played off."
"That was the first night he made a move."
Zoe's smile looked more like a snarl. It twisted her features and made her look quite grotesque.
"But London…." Becca was clutching for any shred of information to discredit what she was hearing.
"We. Were. FRIENDS!" Zoe screamed the words at Becca, bringing the back of her hand to meet her cheekbone. Becca was thrown back on the chaise longue by the force. She rolled over to protect the side of her face which Zoe had struck. Zoe continued, "Dan told you his friend had a three bedroom place. A room for his friend, a room for Dan and a room for me although I didn't use it. I ended up getting off with his friend and slept with him instead."
Still dazed, Becca pulled herself into a seated position, her face stinging from the backhanded slap.

"But if you had this *plan,* why give up on it now? Why tell me? You've got what you wanted. Tony is barely speaking to me. He told me last night that he might not be able to forgive me. We might be over. If *this* was your plan all along, you're on the cusp of getting what you want! Why stop?"

"Because Dan messed up!" she grabbed a fist full of Becca's t-shirt and pulled her to her feet. Zoe may be petite but Becca suddenly remembered her daily gym work outs and was fearful of her unexpected strength.

"He wasn't supposed to tell Tony that he kissed you! Not yet! He was supposed to stick to the plan, not give up. Keep chasing you, flattering you, wear you down. Then once his charm had *finally* worked and he got you into bed so there would be *no* way back for you and Tony, then.....*then* I would turn up at Tony's door, in tears, after 'finding' the text messages between you both." Zoe threw Becca down on to the grey rug.

"But after you firmly rejected him last night he couldn't hack it. He thought it was done. He was convinced he had blown his opportunity. The sad thing is he genuinely thought you two had a future together! He can be just as gullible as you so I suppose you would have been well suited. He texted me to tell me what had happened but by the time I got his message and replied to tell him to hold steady, it was too late. He had told Tony. It was over. All that work. All that planning. Gone. So this.....*this* is my payback. Getting to see your face as you realise your marriage is in tatters and it's all thanks to me. It's not pleasant having your future

stolen from you by a *friend*, is it?"
Becca scrambled to her feet. "You're a psychopath!"
"It's revenge, Becca, and the only reason I've hung around you and that greasy café since you left R&Ds. I thought it would be enough when I convinced them to let you go as part of the efficiency savings and it was, for a while especially when you fell apart *so dramatically* but then Tony swept in and picked up the pieces for you, handing you a business of your own. I needed a new plan that would mean you finally got what you deserved for stealing Tony from me. I just needed to wait. And now it's done, *we're* done. Good luck with picking up what's left of the pieces of your pitiful life, Becca. Now get the fuck out of my apartment and get the fuck out of my life!"
Becca didn't need to be asked twice. She turned and ran out the front door of Zoe's apartment, no longer self-conscious about the potential of the neighbours hearing her or seeing her.
She needed to get as much distance between her and Zoe as quickly as possible.
This time she didn't wait for the elevator. She took the stairs, bounding down them as fast as she could, stumbling several times as her body was moving faster than her brain could handle. She burst out the front door and ran to the safety of her car. As she reached the driver's side, she couldn't help herself and took one last look up towards Zoe's flat. There she was, standing out on her balcony watching her, holding what looked like a bottle of champagne. Zoe's eyes met Becca's and she lifted her glass in a toast, a twisted smile on her lips.

Chapter Twenty-nine

THE DAY BEFORE YESTERDAY

Becca woke up with mixed feeling on the morning of the final wine tasting event. Despite the unexpected turn of events with Dan, she had very much enjoyed the nights. They had given her an opportunity to develop new friendships and she would miss having the dates in her diary but she had already resolved to keep the girls nights going so was confident there would be more to come. She had also enjoyed the chance to flex her creative muscles in order to pull the events together. Thankfully she had Carol's wedding in six short months which would provide her with a creative focus. Carol had also asked if she could have a hen night at the café the month before the wedding so she also had that to plan.

The hen night and wedding might mean she would need to maintain some further contact with Dan. This was the thought which troubled her most. Much to Becca's relief, their planning for tonight's 'Spring into Summer' wine tasting event had largely taken place via text and phone call on account that the wine store was now open so Dan's time to drop into the café was more limited.

The downside of this was that in addition to planning the event, Dan had started to send Becca text messages clearly indicating he wasn't giving up on his pursuit of her which made Becca feel uneasy. She had really hoped that following tonight's event she would be able to back away completely from

Dan and put some much needed distance between them.
Unfortunately, Carol and Jason had come into the café to have an initial discussion about their wedding and they had asked if Dan would be available to do a couple of rounds of cocktails. So far, Becca had managed to deflect this using the excuse that Dan's store and function room would be fully open by the time their wedding came around so Dan may not be available due to events he may be running. She had suggested as a 'Plan B' that Mark might be able to do the cocktails as he had previous experience of bar work. This seemed to satisfy Carol for the moment and allowed Becca to breathe again.
Despite the jumble of feelings, Becca was in a good mood. She opted to think positively and focus on the fact that in just a few hours she would be able to think about an exit strategy to untangle the café from the wine store once and for all. The day passed quickly and soon it was time to put up the 'closed' sign and get the café ready for the final wine tasting event. She checked her watch, Dan should arrive in an hour's time. She had deliberately sent Frankie home as soon as the lunchtime rush had finished to let him have a break and freshen up. She had asked him to return to the store at the same time as Dan was due to arrive, therefore avoiding them being alone together. She had also had a firm word with Frankie following his shenanigans at the Winter Wonderland event. He was only allowed to drink the cocktails and wine the same as everyone else, no extras. He had coloured in embarrassment at the memory of being told that Tony had helped to strip

him and put him to bed. He promised Becca there would be no repeat performance tonight.
Becca began the familiar routine of rearranging the tables and covering them with the white tablecloths.
It was late April and a couple of weeks after Easter. They had chosen to go for a spring theme but incorporate elements of summer, hence the title 'Spring into Summer'. For table decorations Becca had decided to go for classic spring flowers tulips, daffodils and white gerbera daisies. Dan had opted to start the night with a Pimm's cocktail he called 'A British Sunset' which combined a shot of Pimms and a shot of vodka with orange juice, lemon juice and apple juice. The second cocktail he called 'Elderflower Fizz' and combined a gin liqueur with lime juice, sugar syrup and topped up with prosecco. For the food, Frankie had gone for a theme of a summer's picnic pork pies, scotch eggs, sausage rolls and quiche followed by mini strawberry tarts and mini meringue nests. Dan had decided to focus on white and rose wines for the night and as it was the final event at the café, he was pushing the boat out and going for a rose champagne to close.
Becca had dressed the café and set out the glasses for the drinks and plates for the food before retreating to the TwinkleStarKydz room to get changed and do her make up. She took her phone with her as she had told Frankie the front door would be locked while she got ready so he would need to phone her so she could let him in. She had opted to wear a floral print maxi dress for the evening. It wasn't new as she had bought it for a family holiday to Portugal a couple of years ago but it was one she rarely wore

so decided to give it an airing for tonight.
Unfortunately her Jimmy Choo's didn't match the dress so she had to wear a pair of white sandals instead. She let her caramel hair down from its high ponytail, covered it in dry shampoo then threw her head upside down, spraying it with curling spray and hair spray. She used her fingers to encourage some volume before flipping it back so she was standing upright again. A final few sprays of hairspray and she was done just as he phone beeped to announce Frankie's arrival. She made her way through to the café to open the door.
"Hey! I had *the* best afternoon nap! Thanks for letting me head home earlier, I didn't realise I was so tired."
"It was only fair, you've been on early shifts opening up all week. Are you ok to go and get started on heating the food? I'm not quite ready yet. Dan should be here any time to make a start on the cocktails. He's coming straight from the wine store."
"You got it Boss! Go and make yourself beautiful."
Becca returned to the back room to finish getting ready, relieved he had arrived before Dan. Her plan not to be in a position where she was alone with him seemed to be working so far. Fifteen minutes later she re-emerged and heard the cocktail shaker signalling Dan had arrived. Her stomach flipped and she wasn't sure if it was as a result of apprehension or anticipation. She walked into the café and greeted Dan, trying to keep the conversation chatty and light.
"So here we are then, the final event and it's another sell out," she smiled.

His eyes flicked over her, "You look very pretty tonight."
She felt an unwelcome tingling creep across her neck and shoulders. Her hand automatically went to her necklace as if protecting herself. "I'm just going to go and check if Frankie needs any help." She moved past him heading towards the kitchen when out of nowhere he caught hold of her wrist.
"Can we talk?"
"Dan, please let go," she hissed, "Frankie is just in the kitchen."
"Sorry," he dropped her wrist, "I just can't leave tonight without speaking to you. I don't know when I might get the chance to see you again and there's some things I need to say."
"And what are you two whispering about?" enquired Frankie as he emerged from the kitchen.
"Oh you know, the wine store and my plans for the first event."
"Oh cool! So has Tony given you a date for when the work will be finished?"
Hearing her husband's name made Becca feel faint. She needed to put a stop to this.
"Eh, yeah. He's hoping to be clear within a fortnight so I'm thinking of having an event at the start of the summer to coincide with either Wimbledon or Glastonbury. Do a bit of a theme. That seems to have worked well here." Dan gave Frankie a weak smile which didn't reach his eyes.
"I heard it's looking amazing! I'm so sorry we missed the opening night. Can't wait to come and see it in all its glory. Becca, can you give me a hand to set up the sharing platters? The guests will

probably start arriving soon."

"Yep of course, I'll be there in a minute." Frankie retreated into the kitchen and Becca turned her attention to Dan. "I don't know what you want me to say Dan, or what you think is going to happen. As far as I'm concerned tonight will be the last event we run together."

"That's what I want to speak to you about. I want to continue the business relationship with the café. With you. You've got Carol's hen night and wedding coming up. I'll be starting to run my events soon. We make a great team, Becca. Just think about it." As he finished speaking, he traced his finger along the outside of Becca's arm which sent an explosive shock from the base of her spine to the nape of her neck. Her rational brain was screaming at her to keep away from Dan but elsewhere her body was desperately begging for him to touch her again.

Chapter Thirty

NOW

Becca made a beeline for the café which was closed on Sundays. She couldn't go home, not yet. She couldn't face disclosing Zoe's revelation to Tony and the inevitable questions which would ensue. She parked the car and adjusted the rear view mirror to look at her face which was now swollen and still throbbing from Zoe's backhanded slap. A large purple bruise was forming under the skin on her right cheek and it looked like it was going to extend to her eye socket. Her hands were still shaking as she gently prodded the affected area to check just how tender it was and she recoiled at her own touch. She decided she would go into the café, put some ice in a tea towel and lie down on the sofa in the bay window.

She didn't notice until she was out of her car that the iron gate, which should be pulled over in front of the door to secure the café, was open. That meant either someone was in the café or whoever was last to leave didn't lock up properly. As much as she didn't want to risk coming face to face with *anyone* right now, she couldn't walk away without checking the café was secure. As she approached she saw there was a light on and she could make out two figures moving around inside. She squinted, her right eye wincing with the movement and she finally identified it was Frankie and Mark. They must be doing a final tidy up from the weekend. Becca's recollection from the end of Friday night was hazy at best, but she did recall dumping the table covers and flowers in the TwinkleStarKydz room just to clear them from the café area. She wondered what state the café must have been in yesterday morning when Frankie opened up if they had to come back today to finish tidying up. She was just about to back away when Frankie turned around and saw her. She froze. It was too late to make an escape. Frankie practically fell over a nearby chair, he was in such a rush to open the café door to her.

"Becca!" he ran out into the street and engulfed her in a painfully tight hug.

The gesture of genuine concern and unwavering love pushed Becca over the edge and she broke down. With one arm around her shoulder and the other holding her hand, Frankie tenderly directed her inside the café and seated her on the sofa in the bay window. She sat with head in her hands uncontrollably sobbing. Mark, hearing the commotion, appeared from the kitchen and looked from Becca to Frankie - who shrugged his shoulders to indicate he didn't know any more than Mark. Frankie momentarily left Becca's side to retrieve some tissues and a glass of water. By the time he returned along with Mark, she had managed to compose herself. She raised her head to look at them and for the first time they saw the bruise on her face. Both of them instantly shot a look of horror at one other, Frankie instinctively went back to her side. Becca read their minds, realising how it must look after Tony's overnight stay in a Police cell.

"It wasn't Tony."

"Becca…" began Frankie.
"It wasn't Tony," she repeated, louder this time.
"Then who?"
"Zoe. It was Zoe."
Frankie visibly relaxed. "Thank God. Not that I mean thank God she clobbered you one, I mean thank God it wasn't Tony. It looks like she properly caught you square on the cheekbone. You're going to have a matching black eye tomorrow."
"Yep." Becca smiled, then winced as the pain ricocheted across her face, "I'm going to go and get some ice for the swelling."
"You'll wait right there," Mark stood up, "I'll go and do that. I think I've got some ibuprofen in my bag if you want some?"
"Yes, please Mark. Nobody's ever hit me before. It bloody hurts."
While Mark was busy in the kitchen, Frankie took Becca's hand and brushed a loose strand of hair behind her ear. "Do you want to talk about what's happened?"
She nodded, her eyes welling up again, "Oh Frankie, so much has happened since Friday and it's all such a mess. I really need to try and wrap my head around it and figure out what to do next but I don't know where to start."
Mark re-joined them and handed Becca the painkillers which she swallowed in one gulp. Frankie took the tea towel with ice and gingerly held it against Becca's swollen face. She flinched as the cold met her cheek then relaxed as it slowly numbed her aching face.
"Why don't you just start from the beginning?"

Mark offered. "What actually happened between you and Dan, how Tony ended up getting arrested and what happened when he got home from the Police Station yesterday."
Becca nodded. "OK, but it's going to take a while."
Frankie squeezed her hand. "We're here for you and in no rush to go anywhere."

Chapter Thirty-one

THE DAY BEFORE YESTERDAY

The night had flown by as the chat was predictably about Carol's upcoming wedding. Becca, relieved to be nearing the end of the night, had been more liberal filling the wine glasses on their table and as a result they had consumed a bit more than normal. "I can't believe I have *less* than six months to go!" Carol exclaimed.

"Are you feeling pretty organised?" asked Susan.

"Yeah, having the reception here has taken so much pressure off everything. I totally trust Becca and Frankie." Carol smiled in the direction of Becca who, along with Wendy, was working her way around the café serving wine. "Becca's given us several different possibilities for a buffet meal. Frankie has drawn me his vision for the cake and he's also given me a couple of options for the photos, we've got the invite list finalised, the registry office is booked, we've put a deposit down on the rings, Jase knows the kind of suit he wants to wear.....so we're pretty sorted!"

"Sounds like you're missing one key feature......your dress?!" Susan offered.

"Ah, that seems to be the tricky bit," Carol played with the stem of her wine glass, "our parents are paying for the wedding. Apparently both Jase's folks and my Mum and Dad have been putting money aside ever since we moved in together but it's on the condition that we pay for our rings and what we're going to wear. Jase is just going to rent a suit. I told

him he should treat himself and buy it but he told me it would be a waste of money as he would never wear it again. He would rather put the money towards a mini-moon, a couple of nights somewhere just the two of us. So when me and Mum went to look….."
"You've been wedding dress shopping? Tell, tell, tell!" Susan drummed the table excitedly.
"Seriously don't get excited. I didn't get the distance of trying any on. I looked at the price tags and just told Mum I didn't see anything I liked. I really don't know what I'm going to do. I've got less than six months - and the woman in the shop told me with less than six months to go I might be looking at extra payments for a rush order. I can't even afford the price if I had plenty of time to order," she sighed.
"Wait a minute, I was watching Say Yes To The Dress the other night and they were talking about these pre-loved wedding dress websites where you can pick up a wedding dress for a fraction of the cost." Susan took her mobile out from her bag and a few minutes later she had brought up several different websites. "What would you say your budget is? And did you have a style in mind?"
"I don't know, around five hundred pounds? I was thinking a tea length dress. It's going to be such an informal day and I don't want to feel uncomfortable."
Susan clicked on a few options to filter the results. "Look! Here you go!" She slid her mobile across the table.
"Oh my God! Why didn't I know about this? Susan thank you so much!"

Susan drained her glass, "Ah, just call me your Fairy Godmother."

Wendy and Becca took their seats and filled everyone's wine glasses. "All right, so what did we miss?" asked Wendy.

"Carol was filling me in on the wedding plans. She's hit a little glitch."

"Oh? Hope it's nothing to do with our suggestions?" Becca looked worried.

"No! Not at all! It's my dress. Or more precisely lack of one but Susan here showed me some pre-loved websites which are more within my budget so hopefully Cinderella shall go to the ball!"

"Well if you need a few adjustments I'm pretty handy with a sewing machine," offered Wendy.

"Really? I was looking at tea length dresses, so nothing too fancy or intricate."

"Yeah! I've got four kids so someone always needs something mending plus I'm always making props and costumes for my classes. As long as it's just a nip and a tuck I should manage it. Don't worry, I won't touch it if I'm not confident that I'll be able to do it."

"I can't believe how kind you've all been," Carol smiled, her eyes filling up with happy tears.

"Oh don't! You'll start me off!" said Becca, "it's already been an emotional day."

"I bet! It's the last wine tasting event at the café. How are you feeling about that?" asked Susan.

"A bit sad," Becca answered truthfully. "They've been a lot of fun to organise but the wine store is open and the function room will be ready in a few weeks, so it's over to Dan to keep things going."

"And will you keep working with Dan in some way?" pressed Carol.
"I know you're hoping he'll be able to do some drinks for your hen night and wedding but I really don't know. I expect he'll be pretty busy getting the business up and running," she shrugged her shoulders, "but don't worry, we have our 'Plan B' in place. Anyway, these are discussions for another day. Let's just enjoy tonight! Cheers!"
"Cheers!" came the response from around the table.

The girls had a lot of fun comparing stories about hen nights, wedding day memories and disasters. Before they knew it, the majority of the guests had left and Mick had arrived to collect everyone. It was only as Becca was waving the girls away that she realised Zoe hadn't come. She went to speak to Dan.
"Hey."
"Hey."
"I just realised, no Zoe?"
"No," his smile was tight, "she had another business commitment."
Frankie had just shown the last of the guests out and joined them. "What. A. Night. I'm knackered."
"Nightcap? A final toast to close the events?" Dan asked as he produced a rather special looking bottle of champagne.
"Do you know what, I really need to pass. I'm beat." Frankie turned to Becca, "I know I was supposed to stay behind to help with the clear up but I'm really done in. Marks just gone to the loo. If I promise to come in early tomorrow, can I just head off? Please?"

Becca felt her heart begin to beat against her rib cage. She had allowed herself to relax tonight chatting with the girls. She had drunk more than she intended to thinking she would have a Frankie-shaped safety net at the end of the night but she knew she couldn't refuse him, he had worked so hard in the run up to tonight. She reluctantly nodded her head.

Dan sensing his opportunity added, "I'm not rushing off. I'll help do what I can tonight."

Mark re-emerged from the bathroom. "Are we good to go?"

"Boss has given me the go ahead so yes. Night guys," he gave Becca a hug, "well done you."

"Night Frankie. Night Mark." She watched them leave knowing she was going to be in the exact situation she had tried so hard to avoid.

Chapter Thirty-two

THE DAY BEFORE YESTERDAY

Dan followed them to the door and locked it behind them. He turned to Becca, "So, are we going to have that nightcap to formally close proceedings?"
Becca nodded her head tightly and played with her necklace, the little voice of reason inside her head telling her this was a very bad idea. She felt like a rabbit caught in the headlights, rooted to the spot unable to avoid the inevitable. Dan picked up two champagne flutes and filled them to the top and handed one to Becca. "We really should make a toast. To Café Swan. To Lehmann's Wine Store. To us."
Becca smiled although it felt more like a grimace and took a gulp of the champagne followed quickly by a second gulp, that little voice warning again that more wine was a stupid idea. By the look of the bottle, the champagne should have been delicious. However it tasted acrid and bitter on account that she had already drunk too much.
"You ok? You're very quiet."
"I'm tired. It's been a long day."
"Are you sure that's all it is?"
Becca made a show of looking at her watch. "I need to clear up in here. Tony will be here soon." She hoped the mention of his name would gently remind Dan that she wasn't available. She moved away from the counter, stumbling slightly and began to remove the floral decorations from the tables.

"Let me help. Where do you want them?" Dan followed her lead and collected some decorations.
"Just take them and the tablecloths to the back room. Most of the dishes and glasses have already been loaded into the dishwasher or stacked in the kitchen. I just need to clear the café floor for tomorrow. Frankie can finish up in the morning."

Once they had finished, Becca was in the TwinkleStarKydz room collecting her things, the mixture of fatigue and too much alcohol made her yawn. She didn't hear Dan approach. He was leaning against the door frame watching her.
"Even when you're tired you're beautiful."
She stood stock still. Her heart started to hammer in her chest again. Dan moved towards her and stroked his finger along the outside of her arm just as he had done earlier. Again a jolt of electricity shot through her body in response. She looked up at him "Dan….."
"I want to see you," he interrupted her, his chocolate brown eyes meeting her green gaze, "away from the café, away from the wine store."
"I'm with Tony," she tried again.
"But you're here with me now." He was standing so close to her now she could smell his aftershave. He delicately ran his fingers though her hair then tilted her face up towards his. Panic flooded her body and she was paralysed realising what was about to happen. He put his lips on hers and kissed her, the unwelcome feeling of excitement in her stomach bubbling up once more. She momentarily broke

away. His eyes searched her face then he kissed her again.

This time she responded.

A few moments later the little voice in her head woke up and started screaming at her, demanding to know what she was doing. She pushed Dan away and took a step back. "No. No. This is a mistake."

"Becca, please," he took a step towards her, "you can't deny it. There's something between us. Could you find an excuse and meet me tomorrow? Either at the wine store or my apartment so we can talk?"

She shook her head, "There's nothing to discuss."

"Don't do that. Don't pretend this hasn't happened." She could see he was starting to get angry.

"You're right. I can't undo it but I can stop it from ever happening again. I need you to go. Now." She suddenly became aware that Tony was on his way to the café and she needed Dan gone before he arrived.

"No. I'm not going anywhere. Not yet." His jaw was set and his nostrils flared.

"Dan you're making me feel uncomfortable. I'm going to ask you to leave once more." She picked up her mobile. "If you don't, I'm going to dial 999." His eyes flicked to her phone.

"This isn't over." He grabbed his coat and stormed out the room. When she heard the front door to the café slam behind him, she exhaled. She hadn't realised it but she had been holding her breath during the altercation. She sat down, her legs suddenly shaking as the adrenaline and relief overtook her. She looked at her watch and nervously fidgeted with her necklace. Tony would be here any minute. She needed to regain her composure and

quickly.
She didn't know it at the time but her relief would be short lived. Dan, fuelled by a combination of disappointment and embarrassment at her rejection, waited outside. He leaned against the wall, waiting. If Becca was determined to deny what had just happened, he wasn't. A few minutes later he saw Tony's Audi turn the corner and pull up outside the café. He took a deep breath and stood up, arranging his features for a friendly welcome.
Tony got out the car, clearly surprised to see Dan outside the café. "Hey mate. Everything ok?"
Dan nodded, "Yeah, yep. Of course. Becca's just grabbing her things and locking up. I was feeling a bit off, told her I'd wait out here. Needed a bit of fresh air."
Tony nodded his head, suspicion beginning to creep into the edge of his subconscious. "Sales ok tonight?"
"Yeah, around the same as the Christmas event."
Tony nodded again and waited, sensing an awkwardness in the exchange. "Good. Good." He gestured to the café, "I'm just going to go and see is if she's ready."
"No worries. I'll just head off then. Night Tony."
"Night mate." Tony wearing a frown of confusion on his face watched Dan walk away. He shook his head and turned towards the café just as Dan stopped and turned back around to face Tony.
"Does she always do that thing with her tongue when she kisses you?"
Tony froze as his mind processed the question. He turned back and took a step towards Dan.
"Say again, *mate*?"

More confident this time Dan took a step towards Tony and drew to his full height, "The way she flicks her tongue. I was just wondering if she always kisses like that." He smiled, "It was a *really* good night.....*mate.* You should ask her about it."
Tony took another step towards Dan so they were inches from one another. "I think you should go. Now."
Dan nodded, "Don't worry, I am, but ask her Tony. Ask her about what happened tonight and what's been going on for months now." Still facing Tony, he then took several steps backwards before eventually turning around and walking off down the street. Tony watched him until he turned the corner and was out of sight. He didn't move for several minutes as his mind raced, conjuring up all sorts of scenarios in his head. His mobile started vibrating in his pocket. It was Becca.
"Hey. Just wondering where you are? I thought you would be here by now."
"I'm outside." Tony hadn't moved. He was still looking down the empty street after Dan.
"Ah ok. I'm just coming then. She hung up and Tony lowered his hand which was clutching his mobile. He was still looking down the empty street. A few seconds later, Becca emerged from the café.
"Hey."
"Get in the car, Becca."
She looked at him then followed his gaze down the empty street. "Everything ok?"
He turned to look at her, "Just get in the car."
She didn't need to be told a third time. She staggered around to the passenger side as a sense of

foreboding grew in the pit of her stomach.

Chapter Thirty-three

NOW

By the time Becca had reached the end of her story they had made their way through a couple of rounds of coffees and a bottle of wine which was left over from Friday night. Mark let out a long slow whistle and sat back. "Wow! That's like something straight out of a Hollywood movie. That was one serious grudge Zoe held against you. Talk about serving revenge cold!"

"What are you going to do?" asked Frankie.

Becca shrugged, "It's not completely up to me, is it? It's really up to Tony. I'm the one who's caused this."

"I think you're being a bit hard on yourself," Frankie shook his head, "you covered *a lot* of ground last night and it wasn't all your doing. It's just as much up to you as it is Tony."

Becca clearly disagreed. "As Tony said last night, it's become too complicated. It's not just about me and him anymore. Especially now I know the extent of Zoe's involvement. I really don't know how he's going to react to *that* bombshell. He's been put through enough already without finding out he's essentially had a stalker for over ten years. If he's not already thinking I'm more hassle than I'm worth then this is surely going to tip him over the edge."

"That's hardly your fault. You can't hold yourself responsible for how *she's* behaved. You have to tell him," pressed Frankie. "Apart from anything else that's the biggest problem you've both had, keeping secrets from one another under the misguided belief you were protecting each other."

"I'm scared, Frankie." Becca's face crumpled.

"Oh sweetie." He enveloped her in a hug, kissed her forehead and looked over at Mark silently asking him to help out and say something. He took his cue.

"If any of us understand how you're feeling right now, it's me," Mark began. "We all know I messed up drastically. Granted it took me a lot longer to accept how I had behaved and the repercussions it caused," he glanced at Frankie, "but once I faced up to the truth it became clear what I needed to do." Becca looked at him expectedly, hoping he was going to impart some secret code. "Take responsibility." She slumped against Frankie, deflated. "Look you're both right. Becca, you can't change what's happened and neither can you force Tony to forgive you and move on. And Frankie, you're right too, both Becca and Tony need to hold their hands up to their part in this mess, and accept they were manipulated by external forces. Then once you've stripped it all back, you've maybe got a shot at rebuilding the relationship."

Becca looked doubtful. Mark tried again.

"You're scared you're going to lose Tony, yes?" She nodded "And you're worried that actually it's already too late and you've already lost him. Correct?" She nodded again. "Then you actually have nothing left to lose. In your head the worst has already happened but by trying your damnedest to fix it, you might actually just get back the thing you're convinced you've destroyed." He smiled,

"Take it from someone who knows what they're talking about."
"I was a bitch to you, wasn't I?" she smiled back.
"Yes. You were. But rightly so. I deserved it."
She shook her head. "I gave you such a hard time after what you did to Frankie and here I am, no better. In fact you could argue what I did was much worse. I've put twelve years of marriage at risk. For nothing."
"Hey, everyone makes mistakes and if anything, I'm living breathing proof that no relationship is ever too damaged to rebuild. You've just got to be prepared to put yourself out there and fight for it."
While they were talking Frankie had stepped into the kitchen and now re-joined them. "Don't get mad but I've just phoned Tony." The colour drained from Becca's face. "We've been here for hours, Becca. He had been calling your mobile but couldn't get hold of you."
"Damn. I forgot about that. After I left Zoe's I was planning on coming here and lying down for a bit. I had turned my mobile off so I could sleep. I hadn't expected anyone to be here. I just forgot to turn it back on again. Is he ok?
"He was worried about you."
"He thought I went to see Dan, didn't he?"
"I'm not going to lie, the thought had crossed his mind."
"See! It's hopeless. He doesn't trust me!"
"Becca it's not even been 48 hours since it happened. Give the guy some time. For what it's worth, he's mostly relieved you're ok. I told him you're nursing a war wound from your visit to Zoe's. I haven't told

him the real reason behind it. He assumes she just gave you a slap for kissing Dan. I'll leave the full story for you to tell him."

"I guess I should head home then."

Frankie shook his head, "No sweetie, you're coming home with us."

"He wants me to leave?" her voice cracked.

"No, nothing like that but you both need a bit of space to do some thinking, that's all. That's why I phoned him, to suggest you stay with us for a couple of days. He's going to pack some clothes and a few other things for you and bring them round to ours later but before he does, you need to tell him about Zoe. Go and phone him now."

Becca hesitated and looked between Frankie and Mark. She picked up her mobile and turned it on then watched as it beeped and vibrated with multiple voice messages and texts from Tony asking if she was ok. She dialled his number and he answered after one ring. The boys could tell he was clearly firing questions of concern at her. "Yes, yes. I'm ok. Uhuh. Yes it does hurt. No, I don't need to go to the hospital. Honestly I'm fine. Well, better for hearing your voice. Did you pick up the kids? Are they ok? Are you ok? Look there's something else you need to know about Zoe. Her reason for lashing out at me wasn't what you think," she looked at Frankie and Mark then stood up and went to the kitchen for some privacy.

They watched her go. Frankie let out a long slow breath, "What a mess."

"Do you think they'll make it back from this?" asked Mark.

"I really don't know. He adores her and would do anything for her. I just don't know if that's going to be enough. The main thing is it's all out there now. No more confessions to make. They can just focus on what happens next, whatever the repercussions and fall out."

PART THREE
CONSEQUENCES

Chapter Thirty-four

ONE WEEK LATER

The girls rallied round. Armed with wine and nibbles, they arranged to come over to Becca's the following weekend. As it was a Saturday, Mick was working so Wendy had organised for the twins to stay with her sister. She brought Austin and Lizzie with her and all three of them were staying the night at Becca's. Wendy had suggested the sleepover under the pretence of keeping Emily and Max occupied but the real reason was her concern for Becca as she wanted to see for herself how she was coping.

Despite being pre-warned by Wendy, when Carol and Susan entered the kitchen they were visibly shocked to see the bruising on Becca's face which for the moment still retained its purple colour although it had started to turn yellow at the edges the healing process under way. Becca organised some glasses, poured the wine and decanted some snacks into bowls. They took their seats around the table. There was an awkwardness and tension in the room as no-one really knew what to say. Sensing this, Becca took the initiative.

"It's ok, you can ask. It's why you're all here, to check in on me," she smiled sadly.

"Good God, Becca," Susan shook her head, "please tell me you called the Police?"

Becca shook her head, "And say what? A twisted, bitter 'friend' created a situation so she could

manipulate me into kissing her boyfriend and break up my marriage because she's been in love with my husband for thirteen years? It sounds a little too 'Single White Female' don't you think?"
"But surely you could do her for assault?" Susan pressed.
This time it was Wendy who answered, "Oh luvvie, we've tried talking sense into her - me, Tony, Frankie.....she won't have any of it."
"Because I've told you all, it's not that simple. It's my word against Zoe's," Becca sighed, clearly exhausted by repeating the same conversation. "Tony had just spent the night in a prison cell because he had stupidly let his anger get the better of him by smashing the wine store window. If I called the Police sporting this," she pointed at her face, "there would forever be a shadow cast over Tony and his reputation. Even when Frankie first saw me he jumped to *that* conclusion and he knows Tony. It wouldn't matter what I said, there would always be a kernel of suspicion that I was trying to blame someone else for something he had done. I couldn't do that to him. I've put him through enough already. I've just got to let it go, accept that Zoe got the better of us. It might not have been the outcome she really wanted but it was a result all the same." Becca took a big gulp of her wine.
"How did Tony react when he found out about Zoe?" queried Carol.
Becca exhaled slowly, "Sheer disbelief. He wanted to go round and have it out with her but thankfully Frankie talked him down. Could you imagine how that would have gone?!"

"And where is he now?" Carol asked softly.
"He's staying at one of his rental properties for the moment. I stayed with Frankie for a few days but I needed to come home. The kids were getting quite unsettled."
"What did you tell them?" Susan nodded towards Becca indicating she was meaning the bruising on her face.
"Just that there had been an altercation at the wine tasting event. Someone was drunk, I asked them to leave and then I got in the way when they lashed out. We told them I had stayed with Frankie for a couple of days because we didn't want them to see me and get worried. But they're not babies, they know something's up especially now Tony's moved out. Again, we've told them he's just busy with work but I know they're not buying it."
"And what about......" Carol faltered.
"Dan? It's ok, you can say his name. He's not Voldemort!" Becca attempted a joke to lighten the mood. It didn't work. "Yeah. I've heard from him, much to Tony's irritation. He heard through the grapevine about Zoe slapping me and felt responsible for it because he had deviated from their 'plan'." She shook her head. "Even that's a mess. He still owes me money from the wine tasting night and he owes Tony *a lot* of money for the wine store renovation and I've put Tony in the position where he's under contract and obligation to a man he *knows* has kissed his wife."
"Can't he just get his guys to finish the job for him and he can stay clear of Dan?" asked Susan.
Becca shook her head, "Not at this point in the job. It

needs Tony to oversee it and he can't just walk away. He's too conscientious. Not to mention something like that sticks to you, to your reputation. It could do him and his business a lot of longer term damage. It's bad enough that he had to pay for a new window out of his own pocket. He's just got to suck it up and get through the next few weeks. No wonder he can't stand to be anywhere near me right now." Her face crumpled and the girls all looked at each other. Wendy went to Becca's side and cradled her the way she would when soothing one of her children.

After a few moments she gathered herself together again, "It's not all bad news. Frankie, Mark and Wendy have been amazing stepping in to run the café and you girls coming here tonight means the world to me. I know I'm not alone and you have no idea the difference that can make. I've been in a situation before when I felt completely on my own and it sent me down a very dark road. Knowing I have you all behind me, well......" she trailed off and took a sip of her wine. Then in an effort to change the subject, she cleared her throat and said, "We can't talk about my problems all night. Please can we talk about something else? *Anything!?*"

"Oh, tell her about your dress, Carol!" Susan suggested. Both Wendy and Carol shot her a look of dismay as if telling her telepathically that now was not the time. Becca detecting the conflict smiled and said encouragingly, "You bought a dress? Of course I'd love to hear about it."

"Oh don't worry, I can tell you about that another time. It doesn't feel quite right talking about my wedding tonight."

"Don't be daft. Getting your dress is a big deal! Please Carol."
"Ok, it was Susan who put me onto the idea - those pre-loved wedding dress websites? Well, there were a few I liked the look of so I contacted the sellers but unfortunately I had missed out on a couple of them as they had already sold but third time lucky and the dress was still available! So it's on its way to me as we speak. I can't tell you how relieved I am to finally get something. I was really beginning to panic."
"So what's it like?" Becca asked, feeling more relaxed now the spotlight had moved on from her.
"Well I've gone for a tea length dress after all. I did get a bit carried away and looked at some other styles but as beautiful as they were, they didn't feel right for the sort of day we're having, you know? They were just too formal. The dress I've got is pretty classic, vintage feel, Mikado fabric, clean lines, nipped in waist, buttons down the back with a Bardot neckline. The only thing is the belt which originally came with it is broken. The seller knocked a bit more off the price of the dress which means it was a brilliant deal but I do need to find a new belt. And shoes. And something to go in my hair. I was thinking about maybe going for a coloured pair of shoes and get a belt in a similar colour?"
"What colour did you have in mind?" asked Susan.
"Maybe some kind of purple? Lilac maybe? I've been thinking that would be a nice colour which would complement the duck egg blue in the café. We could have some simple lavender table decorations wrapped in hessian ribbon and I could have a rustic, wild flower style bouquet."

"Sounds perfect, luvvie," smiled Wendy, "and do you think the dress will need any alterations?"
"Hopefully not, it's my size but won't know until I try it on."
"Well give me a shout once it arrives and we can have a look. I could run up a sash for you too, once you've decided on a colour."
Becca abruptly stood up and left the kitchen. The girls all looked at each other, concern on their faces.
"I knew I shouldn't have started talking about my wedding. It was so insensitive of me when her marriage is hanging by a thread."
"It's not your fault, Carol. It was my fault for changing the subject to your dress," insisted Susan. "Should one of us go and check on her?"
"Give her a few minutes," suggested Wendy, "I'll top up our drinks and if she's not back in five, I'll go and find her."
They didn't need to wait that long as Becca soon reappeared holding a shoe box. "What shoe size are you Carol?
"I'm a size seven."
Becca smiled, "Same size as me. Well, if you're thinking purple, you would be welcome to wear these." She opened the box to reveal a pair of Manolo Blahniks in a lilac shade. "Please don't feel you have to wear them but if you would like to then they could be your 'something borrowed'."
"Oh my God!" screamed Carol. "They are beautiful! Are you serious? I can wear them?" She gently lifted one from the shoebox and turned it over in her hand like she was holding Cinderella's glass slipper.
"Of course. Tony bought them for me one

Christmas," she smiled but it didn't reach her eyes. They had misted over at the memory of opening the shoe box on Christmas morning. In her mind's eye, she could see Tony's delight at her reaction to his gift. The image made her heart constrict, aching at the thought that there might be no more Christmas mornings together. She recovered and continued, "I've only worn them a handful of times so they're still like new. They've sadly been confined to the wardrobe for too long now and shoes like that demand to be worn on a special occasion! I would be delighted if you chose to walk down the aisle in them."

"I would be honoured," Carol stood up and gave Becca a hug.

"If you're settled on purple, I could get a length of satin in the same colour as the shoes and easily make a sash for your waist? That could be your 'something new'," Wendy added.

"And with my dress being pre-loved I already have my something old!" Carol laughed. "I just need my something blue."

"Well if you're borrowing Becca's shoes and Wendy's making you a sash, I'll buy you a garter and I'll make sure there's blue in it. How does that sound?" asked Susan.

"A bit weird," giggled Carol, "but thank you that would be lovely."

"How's Jason feeling about it all?" Becca asked as she took her seat.

"He's so laid back about the whole thing. He doesn't even want a stag night, just a couple of pints in the local with his mates. As far as he's concerned the wedding is a big family party with the two of us a bit more dressed up than normal which is helping to keep my nerves in check. It's without a doubt the best decision we made to keep it small and straight-forward. Whenever I start getting wound up about any detail he just shrugs his shoulders and says, 'Babe, at the end of the day, it's about you and me and we're on the same wave-length. Ignore everyone else.'"

"Wise words," Becca uttered wistfully, "everything else is just smoke and mirrors. Things like the picture-perfect table decorations or guest list, they become a fleeting memory so quickly and even more permanent things like a dream house and exuberant gifts," she indicated to the shoe box on the table, "in the scheme of things, they're not all that important. As Jason says, being on the same wave length, being there for each other - for better for worse - saying those words and then living by them, that's what really matters. You've got a good one there, Carol. Hang onto him." Becca reached over and gave Carol's hand a small squeeze. "Right, enough of the soppiness! Time for a top up."

Becca stood up and made her way to the fridge to retrieve the wine. Wendy joined her with the empty glasses. "You ok love?"

"Yeah I'm fine. I've just had plenty of time this week to think while Tony's been staying at the rental place. Plus organising Carol and Jason's wedding has really opened my eyes. I thought me and Tony were like that, absolutely solid but I realise now a lot of it was superficial and when we scratched underneath it, we've discovered shaky foundations. Look at them," she nodded her head towards Carol, "they've been together since school and still all they care about is each other. Doesn't matter what else is going on around them, it's just about them." She looked down at the ground. "Tony said to me last weekend it's become too complicated and it's not just about us anymore. And he's right."

"Hey, it's early days yet. You're both still hurting and raw. I don't agree with Tony anyway. Zoe's gone and so is Dan so it *is* just about you and Tony now."

"I've been going over all the conversations I had with Dan, replaying them, trying to figure out how it got to the point it did and do you know what I realised? When he started hinting, insinuating he wanted more than a business relationship, I didn't say 'no'. I didn't flat out tell him I wasn't interested. Why didn't I do that? I've been going over and over, trying to work out if I did in some way let him think it was a possibility….."

"Stop it, Becca. Stop right there. You're not figuring anything out. You're just torturing yourself. What does it really matter? It's not going to change where you and Tony are now. You need to forget about Dan and Zoe and the conversations you did or didn't have. You deeply regret what's happened and you've told Tony as much, that's all that matters now." Becca didn't look convinced so Wendy tried again, "I once saw a quote somewhere it said 'Don't look back, you're not going that way'. That's what you need to do now, move forward. Think about what you want and if that's Tony, then that's the direction you need to focus on."

"But how will I know? How did you know it was the right thing to walk away from your first husband?"
"Oh sweetheart, me and Dave were very different to you and Tony. Nothing was right between us and we knew it well before Austin came along. You and Tony have been put in a very specific set of circumstances. I guarantee you if there was no Zoe and no Dan you wouldn't be in this situation. For me and Dave it was intrinsic, fundamental to the very core of us not being suited to each other. The fact that you even need to *ask* how you know when it's time to call it a day tells me that's not what you want."
"Thanks, Wendy."
"We're here for you, me, the girls and Frankie. We'll help you figure this out. Come here." She gave Becca a hug. "Now, let's fill up these glasses and start planning this hen night of Carol's."
Wendy joined the girls at the table leaving Becca to return the wine to the fridge. She took a few moments to compose herself and as she closed the door to the fridge, the magnetic blackboard where she would usually scribble down items for her food shopping caught her eye. She picked up the chalk and wrote the new mantra Wendy had just given her: "Don't look back, you're not going that way." She repeated the words to herself before returning to the table to enjoy the rest of the evening.

Chapter Thirty-five

ONE MONTH LATER

It was almost three weeks after the fateful wine tasting night before the bruising had subsided sufficiently and Becca felt comfortable enough to return to the café. She had been back for almost a week now and after getting over her initial nerves she quickly got into the groove feeling relieved to be back to her normal routine. It was a Friday afternoon, Wendy's classes had finished for the week and Becca and Frankie were seated at a table having a coffee during a lull in customers.

"What a quick week! Maybe I'm just out of the way of things but that felt like a busy one," Becca observed.

"No, you're right, we've been run off our feet," Frankie agreed, "in fact this is the first time we've had the chance to properly chat since you started back. How's things going?"

"I honestly don't know. Tony's still sleeping at the rental property although he's had a few people viewing it so not sure how much longer it'll be available and what he plans to do once it's let. It's all so awkward and polite between us. It's like we don't know how to act around each other. I hate it."

"What about the kids?"

"They're starting to struggle. It's been what, a month now? Max has been really quiet. He just keeps coming over to me and giving me a hug for no reason. Emily is such a Daddy's girl and she's really missing Tony. She started acting up with me last weekend. I let Tony know and he had a word with her. He has this way of getting through to her whereas I just seem to rub her up the wrong way when she's behaving like that. That's when she got upset and told him she was missing him and wanted him to come home. Like I've not had enough guilt heaped on me as it is."

"They're only kids, Becca. She's lashing out because she doesn't understand. What have you told them?"

"We're sticking to the story that Tony has a lot of work on which means working longer hours so for the moment, it makes sense for him to sleep on site but they're picking up on the weird vibe between us. After Emily's outburst last week, Tony's started coming over every night after dinner. He stays for a couple of hours until the kids have gone to bed then he goes back to the rental. He's making it clear that he's doing it for the kids. As soon as they're settled in bed, he leaves. He's not giving me the opportunity to talk to him."

"Ouch. It's still early days. It doesn't mean anything, he's obviously just not ready to talk about it yet. He'll come round." Frankie affectionately squeezed Becca's hand.

"But when, Frankie? It's been a month! How much longer can I excuse his unwillingness to talk as 'early days'?" Becca let out an exasperated sigh.

"Erm, how about now?" Frankie nodded towards the café window. Becca turned around to see Tony cross the street heading in her direction. Her heart skipped a beat.

"He didn't mention anything to me about coming to

the café today." She looked at Frankie, a mix of fear and excitement rippled through her. "What do I do?"
"Christ alive Becca, just talk to him! Don't let him leave until you've had a conversation about this mess. But first things first, take that look off you face. It looks like you're constipated and it's not attractive."
She couldn't help herself and collapsed into a fit of giggles, her nerves getting the better of her.
"Hey." Tony said as he entered the café then looked from Frankie to Becca, confused as to what was going on. "Did I miss something?" he asked.
"Oh it's just Frankie being Frankie," Becca replied wiping a tear from her eye. She was secretly grateful for his well-timed comment breaking the ice just as Tony walked in.
"I'm so glad you find me amusing," Frankie rolled his eyes, "can I get you anything Tony?"
"Nah, I'm good thanks," he replied. Becca's heart sank. His refusal of a coffee indicated this wasn't going to be a long visit. "I just want a quick word with Becca." He held up a pile of papers. He was clearly here on business.
Frankie read Becca's mind and they exchanged a look of disappointment. He quickly said, "Well, I'm just about to finish up, but I'm happy to hang on for a bit longer just in case there's any last minute customers. Save you from being disturbed. I'll give you a shout once I've cashed up and I'm heading off."
Tony went to open his mouth and protest but Becca got in there first, "If you don't mind Frankie that

would be great. I do really need to talk to Tony. Why don't we go through to the back room?" She stood up and walked towards the TwinkleStarKydz room giving Tony no option but to follow. He felt like he had been cornered which irritated him as he wasn't ready to have the discussion which Becca clearly had in mind.

Once they were safely inside the TwinkleStarKydz Room Becca closed the door, took a deep breath and turned around to face Tony.

"There really isn't any need for a secret squirrel meeting," he began, "I just needed to give you these, for the accounts." He handed her the pile of papers he was holding. She could tell he wasn't happy with the ambush but since she had come this far she decided to press further.

"I know you're not ready to talk yet Tony, but it's been a month now and I can't go on like this indefinitely. It's not good for the kids, we're practically lying to them. And it's no good for me." She saw a flicker of something cross his face. "I've seen you every night this week but we haven't spoken other than to exchange pleasantries and pass on any information about Max and Emily. It's like history repeating itself and in case you've forgotten, that didn't work out too well for me before." It was a cheap shot and she knew it but she needed to say something to snap him out of his sulk.

He rubbed his chin which Becca recognised as his 'tell', usually when he was conflicted or annoyed with something. "All right. There are a few things that need to be said." He walked over to the table in the corner which Wendy uses as her desk and pulled out the two chairs. He took one and indicated to Becca to sit down in the other. She crossed the room and did as she was invited.

"Do you know where I've just come from?" he asked.

She shook her head.

"The wine store. We finished the refurb today." At the mention of the place Becca's stomach flipped over. No wonder he wasn't in the mood to talk to her.

"Oh. I didn't know you were expecting to finish this week. I thought you had a bit longer left on the job. Are you pleased with it?" She knew it was a mistake as soon as she asked.

"I'm delighted to be shot of the place and if I never see Dan Lehmann again then it'll be too soon. Does that answer your question?"

"Sorry."

"I left one of the guys taking photos for the website to show we've now got experience in commercial projects then I've just got the final invoice to send *him* and that's me done. That reminds me, can we get some photos of the café too?"

"Sure, of course. You don't need to ask."

"Yes I do. It's your café Becca, I can't just waltz in like I own the place."

"So you're going to pursue more commercial jobs then? I'm proud of you." She knew that would be strike two.

"Come off it. I don't need a patronising pat on the back."

She sighed, frustrated. "I just don't know how to act

around you at the moment. I'm constantly walking on egg shells, desperate for an 'in' to talk to you and you're just putting up barriers. We're not going to get anywhere unless you give me a chance."

This time it was Tony who apologised, "Sorry, but you've got to understand that last few weeks have been nothing short of a living hell. I've had to get up in the morning, go into work and face the man who kissed my wife not to mention all the very personal details he knows about me, my wife and my marriage. It's pushed me to the brink Becca, having to swallow my pride like that and keep my cool under his smarmy grin. It's not that I *don't* want to talk to you and try to sort out this mess, I really do but my God, these last few weeks have taken every ounce of energy I have. When I get to the end of the day I'm just drained. I've not had the strength to talk to you and work out what *we* do. There's nothing I want more than to find a way to put all of this behind us but because of the wine store job I couldn't just cut my ties with him after *that* night, even though I would have loved to just turn my back on him. It's made it so much more difficult for me to forgive you."

"I understand that. But you're done now, it's over with him and we can just concentrate on us now. Neither of us have to see him or talk to him again. Well, once he's paid us what he owes anyway."

"What do you mean, paid 'us' what he owes?"

"He still owes me my share of the money from the final wine tasting night."

"That was a month ago! He's never taken this long to pay up before. He better not even think of playing

that game with the amount of money he owes me. What's he up to?"
"Well at a guess, he knows that once he pays me what he owes then that'll be it. No reason for any sort of contact between us again. He's clinging on to it as his final link with me."
"Do you want me to have a word?"
"I've got it, Tony, I don't need you to fight my battles for me." Her answer came across much sharper than intended and she could see it stung him. She softened her tone, "Are you going to come over tonight as normal? The kids have got something they want to ask you."
He followed her lead and relaxed. "Yeah, I'll be there. Are you going to give me a hint as to what to expect from them?"
"I suppose I should so you're not put on the spot. You know it's my birthday coming up in a couple of weeks?"
"Yeah, I hadn't forgotten." She noticed he had tensed up again at the mention of her birthday.
"Well, I had suggested a day out somewhere and they mentioned the Safari Park, not quite what I had in mind, I was thinking more a museum and lunch but they've had a rough time too, especially Emily, so I've agreed to it but they want you to come too."
"What and play happy families on a day trip? I don't know, Becca. It doesn't sit right. Pretending everything is ok."
"Forget that it's for my birthday. Just……just look at it as doing something for them. Please? It would mean so much to them."
He rubbed his chin again and looked at her, "Ok, but

just because it's the kids who are asking."
She met his eye and nodded, "I know." He noticed the hurt in her eyes from his answer. He cleared his throat and tried to find a way to finally ask the question he had been trying to ask for weeks, "Are you ok Becs?"
"Yeah I'm fine. I know you're only agreeing to it because Max and Emily are asking...."
He shook his head, "I don't mean are you ok about the Safari Park. I mean *you*. Are *you* ok?"
Becca was thrown by the question. She hadn't expected it.
Tony continued, "I've been worried about you. You know, after everything we talked about. When you told me about how you were after you lost your job and I took on this place for you. I know you probably don't believe me given my silence with you but just because I've been angry with you, it doesn't mean I've not been worried about you or I've stopped caring. I've been checking in with Wendy. I know she's been keeping an eye on you and she's been assuring me you're ok. I've been so grateful to her for doing that. It's given me the space I've needed to get through the last few weeks and try to get my head straight a bit. I've wanted to speak to you so many times. I would get up in the morning and say to myself 'tonight, when I see you I'll speak to you' but then I would spend the day at the wine store, and well, by the time I would see you, I would be angry and tired. I know Wendy, Frankie and the girls have been around for you so I knew.....or hoped....you would be ok. But are you? Are you ok Becs?"

It all came out in such a rush it caught Becca completely off guard and it took her a few seconds to respond. "I would be lying if I didn't say I've struggled, of course I have. I was so embarrassed by Zoe giving me a black eye and having to take time away from here. Then you moved out and I didn't know where we stood. And I still don't know what's going on between us so of course I've lain awake some nights worrying that I've put us through too much and we won't recover but having Wendy and Frankie and Carol and Susan, it's really helped this time." She reached for Tony's hand. He didn't pull away. "I know it's not ideal as the person I've desperately wanted to speak to is the one person I've hurt the most, but you're here now, asking if I'm ok. So yeah. I think I'm going to be fine." She smiled and squeezed his hand.

He nodded relieved, "I've missed the kids so much. And I've missed you." Becca felt a tingle of excitement grow in the pit of her stomach. "Now that the distraction of Dan and the wine store refurb is out of the way, you're right, maybe we can focus on us now and what *we* do. I still can't make any promises to you and you need to understand that. A lot has happened and I'm still pretty raw at the situation I've just had to pull myself through."

"I get that but even this today is a step in the right direction."

"It needs to be baby steps, Becca. Don't rush me."

They were disturbed by a hesitant knock at the door. It was Frankie, "I'm really sorry to disturb you guys, I held off as long as I could but I really need to make a move. I've done the last of the tidying up, I've

wiped down and cashed up so we're organised for the morning."
"Thanks Frankie," replied Becca.
Tony looked at his watch, "Yeah I need to head off too, I need to stop by the office before finishing up for the day." He turned to Becca, "I'll come over later. It looks like the rental is going to be let soon so we've got a bit more to talk about."
"Ok, remember to act like you don't know anything when the kids ask about the Safari Park."
"Will do. See you later," and with one last look towards Becca, he got up to leave.
Once he was out of earshot Frankie turned his attention to Becca, "So sorry. I couldn't hang off any longer. I really didn't want to interrupt you."
"It's ok, honestly. I think we had gone as far as we could for now."
"I really do need to go, but am I right in thinking it went well?"
"We've got a long way to go yet, but we might just be able to start considering our future rather than worrying about the past. As a wise friend recently told me 'Don't look back, you're not going that way'."
"Wise words indeed. Hopefully you've broken the stalemate now." He walked over and gave Becca a hug. "Send me a text and let me know how it goes later with Tony but if you need me, phone, don't text. Promise?"
"Promise. Night Frankie."
She followed him to the door of the café and locked it behind him. As she moved back to the kitchen to file the papers from Tony and collect her bag, she

allowed her mind to wander and let herself think, ever so tentatively, that they might just manage to find a way through the maze of chaos she had created.

Chapter Thirty-six

TWO MONTHS LATER

It was Becca's birthday and she had taken the day off from the café. It was well into June and the weather was utterly miserable and not at all like the early summer which the calendar indicated. She got the kids up and out to school as normal then took herself off to the city centre for a hairdresser's appointment and a spot of shopping.

There had been no offer from Tony for them to spend time together, instead he had suggested he stay with the kids so she could go out for dinner and drinks with Frankie and Wendy. He even suggested she stayed at Frankie's under the premise of giving her a break and a night off. So as a birthday treat, Becca had decided to buy something new to wear. She was glad of the distraction and was desperately in need of cheering up as she hadn't heard anything from Tony yet. She had convinced herself he would be in touch today even with just a 'happy birthday' text and as a result, the disappointment increased with every passing hour that her phone remained silent. By the time it was time she was making her way to the café to meet Frankie, Becca's mood matched the gloomy weather.

"And here comes the Birthday Princess now!" announced Frankie as Becca walked into the café. He gave her a birthday hug. "Have you enjoyed your day of pampering and retail therapy? Your hair is gorgeous!"

"Thank you. Yeah, it's been nice. The kids had cards and a box of chocolates for me this morning."
"That was sweet of them. Well, here's another something for you to open." He handed her a present and card. Becca smiled as she opened the gift. It was a personalised birthday pampering pack filled with all sorts of indulgent goodies - her favourite luxury chocolates, prosecco, face mask, bath soak, scented candle and a gift voucher for a full body massage.
"Thank you Frankie, it's really thoughtful."
"Well I thought you could do with a bit of TLC. Any word from Tony today?"
"Nothing. Not even a text."
"Really? I'm quite surprised at that. Thought things were starting to edge in the right direction? How did it go on Saturday at the Safari Park?"
"It mostly went well." Becca took a seat in the sofa in the bay window and Frankie followed. "Not exactly the birthday day out I would normally choose but the kids were really excited about it which was the most important thing to me. Tony picked us up as planned and we did the safari bit first, you know where you stay in the car and drive through the enclosure with the tigers and lions? By the time we did that and parked the car it was time to get something to eat. It was just after that we hit a blip. The gift shop is in the same building as the café and after we had lunch Emily wanted to go there first before heading out to the rest of the park. I told her we would do the shop at the end of the day on the way back to the car as we normally would and she totally kicked off. At first it was just the usual

stroppy nonsense about wanting to go to the shop *now* and then all of a sudden she really let rip at me. Screaming at me that she hated me and it was all my fault that Tony wasn't living at home with us. It was so embarrassing. Everyone at the tables around us just started staring."

"You're joking? What a little madam!"

"Truth hurts though Frankie, doesn't it? I mean she was kind of right but I've never seen Tony properly angry with her before. She's always been able to wrap him around her little finger, usually when she's got herself into trouble she would give him the big sorry puppy dog eyes, shed a tear and that would be it. It's not the first time *he's* ended up apologising to *her* but he was furious with her. He marched her out the door and gave her a right talking too. I have no idea what he said to her but she was *very* apologetic when she came back to the table and was my best friend for the rest of the day."

"Oh Becca."

"After that we had a lovely day. It prompted me and Tony to talk some more while the kids were running around in the play area so it maybe actually wasn't a bad thing."

"What did you talk about?"

"Well, I told him I had done a lot of thinking and I realised that I had been speaking to Dan about aspects of our marriage that I felt we needed to work on when I really should have been having those conversations with him. I made a massive mistake. I opened up our marriage to a stranger when it should have just been between us. I apologised, truly apologised and he accepted it. He even gave me an apology of his own. He said that he needed to take some responsibility for the situation. He acknowledged that he introduced me to Dan and ultimately persuaded me into the wine tasting venture with Dan when he knew I wasn't sure about it."

"Sounds like a breakthrough. And what about the rental property?"

"Yeah it was. The rental's been let and the new tenants move in in a couple of weeks' time so he asked me how I felt about him coming home again."

"Becca, that's great news!"

"So I thought but there are stipulations."

"Like what?"

"Well, he wants to get a sofa bed for the spare room which we currently use as an office."

"Ah, I see, so he's coming back home, but not necessarily back to you."

"Exactly."

"Well look at it as a positive, if he's going to be back home then you'll have more opportunity to talk and work on things."

"I suppose so but I can't help but think that the only reason he's coming back is because the rental's been let, otherwise he wouldn't be."

Frankie shook his head, "Don't question the motive. You've finally begun to open up to one another about what's happened. This is a good thing."

"Then why haven't I heard from him today?"

"I don't know, Sweetie. But your birthday isn't over yet so there's still time for him to get in touch and while we wait, we have cocktails with our name on them! Let's lock up here and go get our glad rags on

or we'll be late to meet Wendy."
As they both stood up, the café door opened and in walked Dan. Time seemed to stand still as the three of them looked at each other like they were in some kind of Mexican standoff situation. Frankie made the first move and stood in front of Becca as if shielding her from him, "What do you want?" He spat the words at Dan.
"I'm not here to cause any trouble, I just need a moment with Becca."
"Why?"
"That's between me and Becca."
Becca put her hand on Frankie's arm, "It's ok, Frankie." He looked at Becca. She had suddenly turned very pale.
"Only if you're sure. I'm not leaving you alone with him though - I'll go and sit over there," he nodded his head in the direction of the tables in the far corner of the café. She nodded her approval and he moved off, glowering at Dan as he passed.
"I think I've made an enemy there," Dan commented once Frankie was out of ear-shot.
"I would say you've made more than just one enemy," Becca retorted.
"Touché." Dan gestured to the present which lay open on the table, "Special occasion?"
"My birthday," replied Becca
He smiled, "Happy Birthday, Becca."
"I'm sure you didn't come here to exchange pleasantries, Dan. Get to the point. What do you want?"
Uninvited, he took a seat in a chair opposite the sofa. Becca retook her position on the sofa with her back to

the window. "I'm just here to settle up for the wine tasting night, that's all."
"You didn't need to physically come here to do that. A bank transfer would have been sufficient."
"I also wanted to see you. I know Tony's all but moved out."
"And why is *my* marriage *your* concern?"
"Don't be like that, Becca. I still think about you."
"I don't believe this. You spitefully tell Tony about kissing me, then he has to continue working for you to finish your god-damn wine store and now he's only just freed himself from you and I'm *just* starting to get somewhere with Tony and you turn up again?" She shook her head astounded at his audacity. "What do you think is going to happen, Dan? Do you think I'm going to fall into your arms? Do you think we're going to give it a go? I put Tony through hell over you and I've very possibly lost the man that I really love because of it. There is no way on this earth I would ever consider any kind of relationship with you, not after what you did to us."

Unbeknown to Becca, Tony stood across the street watching the exchange. He could see the back of Becca's head animated as she talked. Sitting opposite was *him*. He felt like he was watching a car crash unfold in front of his eyes, unable to look away but feeling sick to the pit of his stomach at what he was seeing. He was holding a bunch of daffodils, birthday card and a small jewellery box, all intended for Becca. For the moment he was rooted to the spot considering his options. He flipped between rage, wanting to do nothing more than storm into that café and knock his lights out to feeling utterly crushed watching his wife converse with the man she had kissed. He shook his head in despair. After Becca had cornered him into talking when he last stopped by the café and then at the Safari Park, he had started to let himself believe that they might be able to work through this but seeing her with *him* he realised how fragile their relationship really was. He thought he could get over what happened. He hoped he would be able to trust her again but the reality hit him hard. He couldn't.

Back in the café Becca took the opportunity to put Dan in his place and tell him exactly what he had done to her, her marriage and her family. Making it crystal clear there would be no future relationship between them, either business or personal.

"So I can expect the final wine tasting payment to be transferred to the café account tomorrow?"

"If that's what you want."

"It is and once that money hits my account, then that's us. Over. I never want to see or hear from you again. Do you understand?"

Dan hesitated. Becca continued, "And you'll also pay Tony the last of what you owe him. This week. Then you can get out of our lives and leave us alone once and for all."

"It doesn't need to be like this."

"Yes it absolutely does. We let a fox into the hen house and I'm clearing up the mess. Pay us what you owe and let us get on with our lives. I've avoided the Police this far but don't push me Dan, I'll do whatever it takes to protect my family and get my marriage back on track even if it means court orders."

"You'll both get what you're owed tomorrow."

At that, Frankie made his way back over to where they were seated, "I think you're done here."

Dan didn't move, his eyes travelling all over Becca as if taking in every inch of her, "If you change your mind……"

"I won't. Bye, Dan."

Frankie tried again, "Time to go." His voice sounded sterner this time and Dan responded accordingly. He stood up and moved towards the door, turning back to look at her one last time, "Bye, Becca." Frankie opened the door for him, not out of politeness but to emphasise the point that he was to leave. He followed Dan outside. "You better do as she asked. Next time you won't get anywhere near her. You'll have me to answer to instead and I won't be as polite as Becca."

Dan cast his eyes over Frankie, "Don't worry *mate.* You've made your point and *she's* not worth the hassle." With that, he deliberately shouldered his way past Frankie knocking him slightly off balance. Frankie recovered and turned around to see Dan swagger off down the street. "What an arsehole," he thought to himself and then moved back in the direction of the café door when something on the ground caught his eye. It was a bunch of daffodils and an envelope with Becca's name on it propped up against the wall next to the door of the café. He picked them up and went back inside.

"You ok?" he asked as he sat on the sofa next to Becca. He could see she was shaking.
"It's just the adrenaline," she said, "I'm glad I had the chance to tell him what I thought and I'm so relieved you were here. I don't think I could have done that without you being both my moral support and security. I hope that's it done now. Dan Lehmann will be out of my life for good now and I can focus on Tony."
"I don't think you'll be having any trouble from him again. Oh, I found this sitting outside."
He handed the daffodils and envelope to Becca. She took them from Frankie and looked at the envelope. Her heart stopped as she recognised the writing immediately, "It's from Tony! I know his handwriting." She ripped open the envelope and pulled out the card. On the front it read "To my wife on your birthday." It had an illustrated drawing of a couple walking down a city street which didn't look too dissimilar to Venice. On the inside he had written, "Saw this card and it made me remember the good times with you. I want us to get back there. Love Tony." She started to cry and handed the card to Frankie to read.
"What's with the daffodils?" he asked.
"When we had the big showdown after *that* night, during one of the lighter moments, Tony made a passing comment about buying me daffodils and I pointed out that he had *never* bought me a simple bunch of daffodils. I joked with him that even his choice of flower was always a bit flashy."
"You see? He's starting to create in-jokes with you from this. It's a good sign. I wonder why he left

them outside and didn't come in?" As soon as he finished his question he knew the answer.
"Oh God, Frankie. He saw Dan here with me. He left the card and flowers to let me know he had seen us together." Becca felt sick.
"What does it matter? I was here with you. You weren't 'together' sneaking around behind his back," he said in a vain attempt to reassure her.
"But it does matter, doesn't it? If he saw us it'll just cast it all back up again, remind him what happened, how I hurt him and broke the trust between us. What do I do?"
"Try phoning him. Now. Go on. He can't be that far away. Ask him to come back. Tell him that I was with you all along and you sent Dan packing for good."
Becca was still shaking from her exchange with Dan as she fumbled around in her bag. She found her mobile and called Tony. It rang a couple of times then went to voicemail. She hung up without leaving a message. "Voicemail," she said to Frankie.
"Did it go straight to voicemail? Or did it ring first?"
"What difference does that make?" Becca asked exasperated.
"Because if it went straight to voicemail it means his phone is either out of signal or switched off so he didn't know you were phoning. If it rang first….."
"Then he's ignoring me." She finished his train of thought, understanding what it meant. "It rang two, three times maybe then went to voicemail. He saw it was me phoning."
"Try again."
She redialled with the same result then tried once

more despite knowing what the outcome would be.
She shook her head, "This is turning out to be the worst birthday ever. Forty-four and about to find myself divorced and trying online dating."
"I'll not have you talk like that Rebecca Swanson. Tony came here to see you today on your birthday. He gave you a card where he's telling you he wants to work it out with you. He still loves you. You are not giving up. Phone him again and if he doesn't answer leave a message or text him and tell him that he did not see what he thought he did."
Hands still shaking only this time from nerves, she did as she was instructed. Her heart hammered hard in her chest. The phone rang....once....twice....and then silence "Hello? Tony?" her voice quavered, "I know you were here. I got your card and the daffodils. I.....I......"
"I saw you, Becca. Through the café window. I saw you with Dan."
"You really didn't see what you thought you did. Believe me."
"That right there is the problem. I don't think I can. I want to, I really *really* want to but I don't think I can."
"You've got it all wrong. Frankie's here with me. I didn't know Dan was coming. He just turned up out of the blue to finally settle the money from the final wine tasting night. He's also promised to transfer the last of the money for the refurb to you tomorrow. He's out of our lives for good."
Silence.
"Tony? Are you still there?"
"Yeah, I'm here."

"I told him I put you through hell because you had to finish his job despite knowing what happened. I told him I made such a mess of us. I told him I'm trying to fix it. I told him.....I told him.....I love you Tony. Only you. I don't want to be with anybody else. You've got to believe me. He's not coming anywhere near me again. Frankie's made sure of that. It's done. Over."
More silence.
"Where are you? Come back to the café. Please."
"I don't think that's a good idea."
"Why not?"
"Just go and have your night out with Frankie and Wendy. I'll speak to you tomorrow."
"About coming home?"
"Becca, leave it, we'll talk tomorrow."
"Tony, you're making me nervous."
"Just stop pushing or I'll say something I regret. It's still your birthday."
"Your card, you wrote that it made you remember the good times with me and you want to get us back there. Did you mean it?"
"I did. But that was before……"
"Before what?"
"Before I saw you with him! Alright? Before I saw you with Dan."
"But….but I explained what was going on."
"Even if I believe you, my first thought when I saw you together was that you were with him behind my back."
"So what are you saying?"
"Don't you get it? I can't trust you! No matter how much I really want to. I can't."

Becca felt a coldness creep across her shoulders. The conversation had taken a turn she didn't like. She swallowed hard, "And if you can't trust me?"
"Then I think we're over."

Chapter Thirty-seven

THREE MONTHS LATER

Tony sat alone in his office, not that he was working anymore. It was well after six and he was just delaying when he would make the short journey to the soulless budget hotel. He looked around his office.

It was functional, not flashy.

One side of the office space, where he currently sat, boasted a desk with an office chair and a window. On the other side of the room was the area Tony used to meet clients. It was furnished with a small two-seater black vinyl sofa and a basic coffee table which separated the sofa from two black vinyl bucket seats. On the other side of the door to his office was a smaller room where his part-time admin assistant sat at a similary functional office desk.

On the walls were a selection of framed photos of some of his favourite cars, most of which were Aston Martins. This reminded him of his unused Christmas present from Becca.

He was thrilled beyond words when he opened the envelope which contained a home-made gift voucher for him to redeem a weekend hire of an Aston Martin. He couldn't believe she had gone to those lengths for his present. He was straight on to the company website that night once the kids had gone to bed and had his eye on a DB11 convertible model. He told Becca he was going to hold off until the summer months so he could make full use of his

forty-eight hours with the car. The calendar had just turned the page to July but he couldn't bring himself to go through with the hire.
Tony sighed, his eyes continuing to roam the room. On his desk stood a framed photo of Emily and Max and beside it stood another family photo of all four of them. It had been taken on holiday a couple of years back when they had gone to Portugal. They looked so relaxed and carefree. They all sported genuine smiles, not the kind that are forced for the camera. Tony had fond memories from that holiday as they had taken each day at a time, no plans and no agenda. If they fancied a long lie, they had a long lie. If the kids wanted a day at the pool? No problem! It was just an easy, laid back fortnight. At the end of the two weeks Becca and Tony had vowed to do it again but for lots of reasons, they couldn't get the time last year and this year, well, the less said about this year the better.
He let out a further heavy sigh and looked at his watch again. That little wander down memory lane passed another five minutes.
He really couldn't sit around here much longer, but the thought of leaving his functional office to go to a functional hotel room wasn't filling him with much enthusiasm. After Becca's disastrous birthday he had continued to stay at the rental property but once the new tenants moved in he had no option but to move out. He couldn't face moving back home with Becca as he had originally planned to do so that left him with the only option of a hotel. He had momentarily considered buying a sofa bed to replace the vinyl couch in his office so he could sleep here

but somehow that seemed too tragic. The irony of being a homeless forty-five year old property developer was not lost on him.

He had to keep reminding himself that he wasn't actually homeless. He had a home and a family who he stayed with for half of the week. Without actually agreeing to it, he had fallen into an arrangement with Becca where on Mondays and Wednesdays he would collect the kids from school, take them home, stay overnight, then drop them off at school the next morning. Becca would do the Tuesdays and Thursdays and they did alternate Friday afternoons to Monday, giving them every other weekend with the kids. When Tony was with the kids at home, Becca would stay with Frankie. This arrangement meant that the last time Becca and Tony had actually seen each other was at the Safari Park.

Today was a Thursday which meant it was Becca's turn to have the kids and to make matters worse, she also had them for the weekend. Hence the reason for hanging around the office much longer than was necessary. He had called a couple of his friends to see if they fancied a catch up over a beer but they had plans and commitments with their families.

He checked his watch again. Another five minutes had slowly ticked past.

He abruptly stood up annoyed and fed up with the thought of an entire weekend stretching out ahead of him alone and with no plans. He felt like a caged wild animal pacing back and forward full of pent up frustration but with no outlet for it. He had just decided to go and get something to eat and wash it down with a beer or two when the buzzer to the office sounded. He looked in the direction of the door perplexed. Who would be coming here at this time?

He made his way to the intercom to answer the buzzer, "Hello?"

"Tony, it's Wendy. Going to let me in?"

He closed his eyes. As much as he wasn't thrilled at the prospect of a long weekend alone, a set-too with Wendy was not appealing. "Em, I was just on my way to……"

"To where, Tony? The nasty budget hotel or the pub for a liquid dinner? Don't be an arse and let me in."

He rolled his eyes and relented, pressing the buzzer to admit her.

A few minutes later she bustled through the door in her larger than life way. He decided to take the first of the conversation, "Look Wendy, I'm really in no mood for a lecture," he started.

"Well that's handy because I'm not here for an argument. I'm not about to start playing go-between passing messages between you and Becca. We're not teenagers and she doesn't even know I'm here. Believe it or not I'm just as worried about you as I am about Becca."

Tony nodded and gestured to the sofa, inviting Wendy to take a seat. "Can I get you a cuppa?" he asked.

"Yeah, if you're making one for yourself."

He made his way over to the Nespresso coffee machine and filled up two cups then took his seat in one of the bucket chairs opposite Wendy. They both sipped at their drink, each waiting for the other to begin.

Eventually it was Wendy who broke the silence.
"So how you doing?"
"All things considered I'm alright."
She nodded slowly, holding his gaze, "Uh-huh."
"Seriously Wendy, I am. I'm fine. I don't need an intervention."
She sat her cup down on the coffee table. "So you're ok?"
He shrugged, "Yeah."
"And does that mean you're happy with your current circumstances?"
He didn't respond immediately as that was a loaded question. If he answered yes, he would admit to being happy living out of a suitcase with nowhere to really call home. If he answered no, he would be opening himself to a barrage of questions about why he couldn't just sort things out. He opted for a politician's answer which side-stepped the yes or no question and finally said, "It's not a permanent situation. I'll figure something out."
"Uh-huh."
"I don't know what you want me to say, Wendy. We are where we are and in case you've forgotten, it wasn't my doing."
"I know and Becca's destroyed over it."
The words winded him like a punch to the gut.
"It's hardly a walk in the park for me either."
"Oh really? You just told me you were fine," she said flatly.
"Of course I'm not ok. There's not one part of this situation that's ok. It's a complete mess and there's no way out of it. Is that better for you?"
"Finally. Some honesty."

He sat his coffee down and leaned forward so his elbows were resting on his knees. He looked down at the floor, clasped his hands together and asked,
"How is she?"
"Not good, Tony. Really not good."
He nodded, "I've been worried about this. You know, after what happened before."
"I'm not going to sugar coat if for you, love, it's not my style. She's struggling. Me and Frankie and the girls are doing what we can but we're worried about her. Now I'm not telling you this to guilt trip you into making any decision, but you need to know."
He nodded, "Thanks, Wendy. I knew you would be looking out for her. I just needed some space to try and work out what to do. Just because I'm angry with her doesn't mean I've stopped caring. In fact, knowing you were all there for her made it easier for me to step away for a time."
"I thought you were getting somewhere and had started to move past this Dan fiasco?"
"So did I but then when I saw them together it was just too much - the hurt, the betrayal. I know what you're thinking, it was just a kiss. But it wasn't. She told him things, private things, about us and then I had to go on working for him to finish the contract. It was humiliating."
"Tony, when he turned up unannounced at the café, Frankie was with her the entire time and from what he tells me she put Dan firmly in his place and sent him away with a real flea in his ear."
He laughed bitterly, "Yeah, I believe that. The accountant is still in there somewhere. She can be brutal when she needs to be."

"So what have you decided? Because this flitting between home and a hotel can't carry on. It's not good for you, Becca or the kids. Luvvie, take it from me, I've been in your shoes. If you're calling time on your marriage then there's decisions that need to be made. What happens to the house? Sell and split? Will Becca buy you out? Will you buy her out? And whoever doesn't get the house needs somewhere else to live. Then there's the café. It's under the property development business so that needs sorted out and you need a proper arrangement for the kids so they know where they stand. The school holidays are just a couple of days away now….."
"Woah! Slow down there, Wendy!"
"Like it or not, love, these are the decisions that need to be made. Unless you don't actually want to call it a day with her?" She stopped for a moment to give Tony time to think and finished her coffee before speaking again. "Look, I get that it's daunting and what makes it even more difficult is your complete inability to be able to talk to one another about any of this stuff even the arrangements for the kids! From what I gather from Becca, you didn't even discuss it and just fell into this arrangement. I could honestly bash your heads together." She noticed Tony flinch at the comment. "What is it, Tony?"
"Just a bit of a raw nerve there, that's all."
"Go on," she encouraged. He initially hesitated then continued.
"That's the real problem. I could possibly have gotten over the whole Dan thing, with a bit of time anyway but it's just brought back so many memories of what happened before, when I bought the café

without Becca knowing anything about it and the strain it put on us back then. I didn't know how to deal with that or how to fix it and it's the same again now. I want to be able to sort something out with Becca but I don't know where to start. I find it too difficult so I just back off. When things are going well between us it's great but whenever things get difficult and we hit a rough patch I don't know what to do. When you're married it's supposed to be 'for better or worse' but I'm crap at the 'or worse' part and she deserves so much more than that. She deserves someone who can step up and be there for her when life throws shit at you not someone who silently implodes because they're so scared they're going to do something wrong and make the situation worse that they do nothing and just hope it all goes away." He slumped back in his chair, suddenly aware at how exhausted and worn out by everything he was. "It might not seem like it but I'm doing this for her. She's better off without me. She deserves someone who can give her what she really needs."

"And have you actually asked her what she needs? Sounds to me like you're making a lot of presumptions in there."

"Possibly but there's a healthy dose of truth in there too."

"That may be but do you know what I hear most from what you've said? You still love her and you're scared. You're scared that if you stay with her she's going to hurt you again or hurt you even worse than she already has. Or you might hurt her. You think it's inevitable. So if you pull the plug on everything, then you're going to get that hurt out of the way now even if it means making you both miserable. You're so convinced that's going to be the only outcome that you're not even willing to think there is another possibility."

"Which is?"

"That you can work through this and come out the other side stronger for it."

Tony didn't reply. Wendy looked at her watch, conscious she had been here much longer than she intended to be, "Sweetheart, I've got to go. Mick's due to start his shift soon and I've got to get back for the kids."

"Yeah, no worries. Thanks for checking in on me."

"Of course. You and Becca mean a lot to me." She stood up to leave and Tony followed. She gave him a hug, "What're your plans for the weekend? I know it's Becca's turn to have the kids."

He lied, "Oh I don't know. Work's been busy so I hadn't really thought that far ahead. To be honest I'll be happy just to have a quiet one, catch up on some sleep or I might catch up with some mates."

"Well, I was thinking if you want to talk some things over with Becca I could take the kids on Saturday? Afternoon or evening, whatever works better for your busy social schedule." Tony detected a hint of sarcasm and got the impression she saw straight through his poor attempt at a lie.

"Let me think about it. I'm not making any promises"

"Just let me know, love," she gave him another hug and left him alone in his office once more.

He actually didn't need any time to think about it. He walked straight over to his desk where his mobile phone lay. He picked it up and sent a text to Becca: Can I come see you Sat nite? Wendys offered 2 take the kids

He was still holding his phone when the response immediately came back: Yes. What time? Just so I know when to take kids to Wendys

They sent a few messages back and forward to finalise the arrangements. He even got a cheeky text from Wendy poking fun at how quickly he took her up on the offer of a babysitter, despite being adamant that he needed time to think things over. He sent an equally good humoured cheeky text back to her, which he followed up with a message of genuine thanks. Finally, he typed a text to Becca that simply read: I miss you x He faltered, his finger hovering momentarily over the screen before hitting the send button.

He could see she had read the message, the two blue ticks gave it away. He stared at his mobile willing a response. After only a few minutes which felt like hours, he could see she was typing a response. She appeared to stop then start again. Then again and again. Finally a response popped up on his screen which simply said: I miss you too xx talk Sat xx

He picked up his coat and keys and slipped his phone in his pocket as walked towards the door. Suddenly he didn't feel quite as depressed at the thought of the basic hotel room. Maybe Wendy was right and all wasn't lost. He would know for sure in just two days' time. The thought suddenly jolted him as he realised Saturday's tete-a-tete with Becca took on a whole new meaning. It wasn't just going to be a friendly catch-up to tease out where they were. It was going to be make or break.

Chapter Thirty-eight

FOUR MONTHS LATER

Becca was seated at her kitchen table. Alongside her was Frankie and sitting opposite were Carol and Jason. They were having a planning meeting for the wedding which was now only eight short weeks away. They had met a few times to make arrangements and after her initial meeting with Jason, Becca completely understood Carol's excitement at holding the reception at the café. He was a very quiet, unassuming man. He had that colour of hair which wasn't brown or blonde but somewhere in between. He had kind eyes that wrinkled at the corner when he smiled and Becca could tell that the physical nature of his job as a plumber kept him in shape. He was also clearly devoted to Carol.

"Could we begin with confirming timings for the day?" suggested Becca. "The ceremony takes place at two-thirty? Is that right?"

"Yes, we're adding a couple of extra bits to the ceremony so it'll last around 20 minutes."

"And then we'll need a few snaps of you both signing the register and outside the building," added Frankie, "so I reckon we'll leave the registry office three-fifteen/three-thirty at the latest."

"Ok, so the guests will probably start arriving at the café between three-thirty and four. That's fine. Myself, Mark and Wendy are going to be there to serve drinks on arrival. Did you decide what you would like? You were going between either a glass of fizzy or cocktails."

"Fizzy," confirmed Carol. "I would like cocktails too but I would like everyone to get a glass of fizzy on arrival."

"Or a bottle of lager," added Jason, "I don't get the whole wine thing. It just tastes like vinegar to me."

"No problem, we can have some buckets with bottles of lager set up on the counter for guests to help themselves. We'll fill the buckets with ice to keep them cool. How does that sound?"

"Yeah, that's good. Thanks."

"So everyone gets what, one, two glasses of fizzy?"

"Can we do one fizzy and a top up? Then a cocktail?"

"It's your wedding! You can have whatever you like! Did you have a particular cocktail in mind?"

Carol shifted uncomfortably in her seat, "I did but I'll understand if you're not okay with it."

"Go on," Becca encouraged.

"It's the Toffee Apple cocktail which you served at the Autumn Festival wine tasting. I just thought with us getting married in October it would be perfect."

Becca smiled, "That's ok, we can manage that. I remember the ingredients and Mark has experience in making cocktails, so I'm sure with a bit of practice he'll master it in time for the wedding."

Carol visibly relaxed, "Thanks Becca!"

"I'm assuming you're not heading straight to the café after the ceremony and going somewhere else for photos first?"

"Apparently but I don't see why we need to," Jason crossed his arms and sat back in his chair. Becca got the feeling this was a well-worn discussion.
"Because it's our *wedding,* Jase! I know you hate getting your photo taken but it's important to me to have some proper mementos of the day."
Frankie intervened, "I'll make it as painless as possible for you, Jason. Promise. Carol's going to be the star of the show on the day anyway, I just need a few of you both together and some with little Dylan and then I'll leave you alone. Carol told me how much you dislike getting photographed so I'm planning to do the majority of shots in a reportage style….."
"Reportage? What does that mean?" asked Jason.
"Not posed, natural. I'll just wander around on the day snapping away at you and the guests so hopefully you won't even know I'm taking any photos of you."
"I like the sound of that."
"I do need a few of the more formal shots too but I promise we'll keep that to a minimum. Deal?"
"Ok, deal."
"How long do you think the formal photos will take?" asked Becca.
"We're just going to the Botanic Gardens. Maybe half an hour? We'll probably be in the café just after four."
"Perfect. So if we have the meal ready to serve around five? Are you planning on doing the speeches before or after the meal?"
"Neither, if I could get away with it," sighed Jason as Carol playfully nudged hm. "Before, to get it over

with so I can enjoy my dinner."
Becca continued, "Ok, well let's aim for five-thirty for the meal. That'll give plenty of time to serve drinks and have the speeches. Did you decide on what you would like for the meal from the options we gave you?"
"We want to go with the Italian themed meal please."
"Of course. Two pasta dishes, beef Braciole, Italian baked chicken, pizza slices, Caprese salad and green salad, then for the dessert table we'll have mini tiramisu cheesecakes, profiteroles and cannoli. We'll set up the buffet in the back room and take guests through a table at a time where they can serve themselves. By the time everyone's been through and we clear away the buffet from the back room, I expect we can probably be ready for cutting the cake and first dance by seven-thirty at the latest. How does that all sound?"
"Oh don't get too hung up on timings Becca, I want you to be able to enjoy it too. We know the running order: reception drinks, speeches, food, cake cutting and dance. Doesn't matter if it runs exactly to time!"
Becca smiled. "I'm so glad you're not a Bridezilla. You're going to drop the table decorations into the café the day before?"
"Yes, Mum's making them. She did a sample to show me and they're really pretty, quite simple. I decided to go for a mix of betony, lavender and giant bellflowers. All lilac coloured wild flowers. She's going to wrap them in hessian. Oh and I've been buying up scented candles too and have a guest book and some other bits and bobs for the Guests'

Welcome Table."
"Sounds lovely. Just bring it all round the day before and we'll set it up for you."
"I was thinking Frankie, I know you had drawn a couple of ideas for the cake but I was wondering if we could maybe just have some of the fresh flowers on the cake too?"
"Absolutely! If that's what you would like. We could do the three tiers, just keep the icing simple and clean and have some flowers sat on top and trailing down the front of the cake. It would look really pretty."
"That sounds perfect!"
"Are we still going with the chocolate sponge on the bottom tier, Victoria in the middle and lemon cake on the top?"
"Yes please."
Just then Becca heard the front door open, it was Tony. "Hey! We're in the kitchen," she called through to him. He came into the kitchen and nodded a greeting to everyone before addressing Becca.
"Sorry I thought you would be finished by now."
"It's ok, I think we're pretty much done anyway."
Tony spoke to Carol and Jason, "So you're all organised then? It won't be long now."
"Yeah, just agreed the final timings and details with Becca and Frankie. Oh, that reminds me, now we know how long the photos will take I need to speak to Wendy. Mick has the date in his diary but he needs to know times. I'll be able to let him know now."
"You're not getting a taxi, are you? On your

wedding day!" Tony was astounded.
"You and cars," sighed Becca.
This time it was Jason who answered, "We looked at proper wedding cars but they were a fortune. As much as I really wanted one, I couldn't justify spending that amount on a posh taxi."
"I could maybe help you out there."
"You mean your Audi?" questioned Frankie.
Tony shook his head, "I can do better than that. How would an Aston Martin grab you?" Becca's head snapped up and her mouth fell open in shock but it was Carol who answered first.
"That was your Christmas present from Becca! We couldn't possibly use it!"
Tony shrugged and he felt his cheeks begin to colour at the reaction from around the table. "Between one thing and another I've not been able to use the voucher yet and if I don't use it by the end of the year I'll lose it. This would be the perfect excuse to finally make the booking. I'm sure they had a four seater model. Let me check." He pulled out his mobile phone to check the website as Jason and Carol started chatting excitedly with Frankie about how good it would look in the wedding photos. Becca took the opportunity to speak to Tony. She stood up and walked over to him.
"That's a really kind offer. It's the most animated I've seen Jason all evening. Are you sure about it though? I bought that voucher for you and I know how much you idolise those cars."
He shrugged, "Why not? It's a great reason to finally get around to doing it and I'll still get to drive the car which is the main point of it. To tell you the truth

Becca, I've not been able to bring myself to book it. It just didn't feel right." He cast his eyes to the ground. Becca knew what he was referring to and squeezed his arm. He looked up at her.
"In that case, it's a wonderful idea. I think you've made their day!" She nodded in the direction of Jason and Carol. Tony smiled at her, then returned his attention to his mobile.
"Here you go. An Aston Martin Rapide, it's a four door but every inch the luxury car." He handed his mobile to Jason to let him look at the photos of the car.
"Are you serious? You would do this for us?" He couldn't hide his astonishment.
Tony laughed, "I'd be delighted to be your chauffeur for the day. Call it a wedding gift from us but I draw the line at wearing a chauffeur's hat!"
"Cheers mate!" Jason said with a smile reluctantly handing the phone back to Tony. He couldn't take his eyes off his wedding car.
Carol added, "Thank you, Tony. Jase was gutted when we couldn't stretch the budget to a proper wedding car. It was the only thing he really wanted."
"Honestly, you're welcome. You've really been there for Becca over the last few months. It's the least I can do." Carol stood up and gave Tony a hug.
"Right I'll go and drop them an email now to get it booked in. Are the kids in the lounge?" he asked Becca.
"Yeah, they're playing with Dylan."
"Ok, I'll go and see them. I'll let Becca know once the car's booked and she can tell me where and when

I need to pick you up on the day."
"Wait and I'll come with you." Jason said, then turned to Carol, "I'll go and get Dylan organised." Moments later Becca heard the squeals of delight from the kids as their respective Dads walked into the room.
"I'm going to head off too. I'll see you in the morning." Frankie gave Becca a hug, organised his belongings and, with a wave of his hand, headed off in the direction of the front door.
Once they were alone, Carol turned to Becca, "Things look like they've really turned a corner with Tony."
"Yeah, I think they have. Wendy spoke to Tony a few weeks back. I didn't know she was doing that and I have no idea what was said but I don't really care. First I knew anything was a text from Tony asking if he could come over to talk and saying he had arranged for Wendy to take the kids."
"It must have gone well," she gave Becca a sly smile.
"Yes and no. There were more tears, more apologies and it was exhausting going over it all again but at least this time around there wasn't the raw anger that had been there before. I think we both knew this would be it. We would get to the end of the discussion and decide if we could move past what happened or agree to formalise the separation."
Carol sucked in the air between her teeth and made a whistling sound. "When did he move back in?"
"He went back to the hotel after we talked everything through, again just to give us both a bit of a cooling off period to be sure it's what we.....what he......wanted. Then he moved back home on the Monday but it was with the original stipulations he

set out. So he's home, we're under the same roof again and the kids are much happier but physically nothing is happening between us yet. He's on a sofa bed in the office and I'm in our room."

"And how are you doing?"

"I'm getting there. It just all still feels so fragile though. I'm scared one slip and it'll be gone again.

I'm still not sleeping great and there's a constant anxiety knot in my stomach."

"Give it time, Becca. Think back to your birthday. If you could have told yourself *then* that you would be in this situation *now* with Tony back home, you would have jumped at it. Your marriage has been through the ringer. It's no bad thing taking it slowly. Does Tony know how you feel?"

"Yes, we're starting as we mean to go on, full disclosure. He knows I'm not quite myself yet and he's been so good at talking it through which is a huge step forward for him. He would usually run a mile at stuff like this."

"Then my guess is he's here to stay."

Jason returned to the kitchen carrying Dylan in his arms, "I think Max and Emily have tired him out."

"Aww, did you have fun sweetheart?" Becca asked Dylan who gave her a sleepy nod in response.

"I think we better get him home to bed," Carol stood up, "thanks for tonight. I'm just so excited for The Big Day now. I know we're going to be in good hands."

"Well now all the decisions are made, we can just get cracking on everything. The most important thing is that you both enjoy your day." Becca walked to the front door with them and Tony joined them. "Any questions or if you change your mind about anything, you've still got a bit of time. I'll probably order the food and drinks next month."

"We won't be changing anything. Promise!" She gave Becca a hug, "Oh, I did have one question though."

"What's that?"

"The hen night! Can't you give me any clue about what you've all planned?"

"Absolutely not! I'm on strict instructions from Wendy, Frankie and Susan."and on that note, they said their goodbyes and left. Becca closed the front door and found herself alone with Tony.

"Kids ok?" she asked.

"Yep, but they're asking for something to eat."

"They had dinner early tonight because Carol and Jason were coming over. I'll go and stick some toast on for them." She started to move off then stopped. "Thanks again for suggesting the car to them. I think it's just the cherry on the cake for their day." She looked up at him. He held her gaze and she felt a connection that she hadn't felt since the first wine tasting night when he gave her the necklace. She raised her hand to stroke his face but he tenderly took her hand and gave it a squeeze, interrupting the moment. "I'll go and fix something for the kids if you want?"

She nodded, stung by his gentle rebuff then watched him as he walked along the hallway towards the kitchen. Carol's words rang in her head, "Give it time," and rather than feeling frustrated or worried, she acknowledged it was where they were and, for the moment, it was enough.

Chapter Thirty-nine

FIVE MONTHS LATER

It was Carol's hen night. All the guests had arrived at the café and they were sipping on prosecco awaiting the arrival of the bride to be. Becca had tastefully decorated the café with rose gold and white balloons embossed with the phrase 'Team Bride'. The love heart banners which hung on the walls reflected the same colour scheme as the balloons and rose gold diamond ring confetti was scattered over each table. Each place was set with a 'Hen Night Goodie Bag' which contained party poppers, personalised cocktail stirrers and photo booth props. Frankie had set up the photo booth in the far corner of the café (which was usually used as the play area) and provided lots of extra props including hats, glasses, scarves and an array of inflatables.

The night would be compared by Madam Ruth Less, a friend of Mark's who has her own mid-week drag act in a club where Mark used to work behind the bar. As a favour to Mark, she had agreed to perform tonight at mates rates. As all the action was taking place in the main café area, she had set up her PA system and disco lights in one of the bay windows. She would kick off the evening with some of her cabaret act to loosen up the crowd then host a couple of party games. First up was 'Hen Night Bingo' where each guest had a wedding themed bingo card filled with various words associated with weddings. Madam Ruth Less would randomly pull the words out of a hat and the first person to mark off all the words on their card was the winner. The second game was 'Wedding Truth or Lie'. All guests on arrival were asked to write down an embarrassing story about either their own wedding or a wedding they had attended. They would write one true story and one lie then Carol would have to decide which was which. The evening would finish off with karaoke.

Carol was completely in the dark about the evening's entertainment. The only input she had was a plea that the night was to be 'tasteful not tacky' so no strippers or willy-shaped food or decorations as her Mum and mother-in-law would be at the party and although they were no prudes she didn't want anyone to feel uncomfortable. Mark had come up with the suggestion of Madam Ruth Less and she had been briefed by Becca and Wendy on how far she could take the jokes. Carol also wanted Becca and Wendy to attend the party so Frankie and Mark were drafted in to serve the food and drinks. Again, Carol wanted to keep things simple so the food platters consisted of well-loved buffet favourites (pizza slices and sausage rolls) with one or two Frankie twists (halloumi cheese sticks with chilli jam and savoury cheese and bacon scones). For the sweet toothed, Frankie had whipped up some butterfly cakes, mini millionaire shortcake, gin ice cream and vodka jelly. There were copious amounts of prosecco available and Mark had put together a cocktail menu

for the evening containing a few classics – Mojito, Strawberry Daiquiri and Cosmopolitan. Finally, he had created a cocktail specifically for the night called 'The Blushing Bride' which was essentially a pear martini made with pear-flavoured vodka and elderflower liqueur.
The atmosphere in the café was electric as the guests waited for Carol to arrive. There were around fifteen of Carol's family, Jason's family, and friends in attendance. Carol was due any minute, escorted to the café by her Mum and sister. Becca was seated at a table with Wendy and Susan who were both eager for an update on how things were going with Tony.
"Ok, I'll quickly tell you now before Carol arrives and the night really kicks off. Tonight's about her and I don't want to highjack it with the next instalment of the Becca and Tony show. So, thanks to Wendy here, Tony's back home. I have no idea what you said to him but it really helped."
"Something and nothing, luvvie," she smiled
"We're definitely heading in the right direction now although it's going to be a long process. What happened with Dan exposed some cracks in the foundations of our marriage which we had papered over for years. On the surface we seemed solid but it turned out to be superficial. As long as nothing rocked the boat we were good but the second something remotely threatening reared its head, we just couldn't deal with it so to use Tony's property developer analogy, we're taking our marriage back to brick and starting over."
"What exactly does that mean?" Susan asked.
"A lot of talking," sighed Becca, "and with that come

a lot of home truths which can be painful to revisit and discuss but it's the only way we can move forward. We've both got to acknowledge and accept how we've let each other down over the years. Weirdly, it's not about blame or making the other person feel bad. It's cathartic being able to say 'I know I did this and I know how it hurt you'."

"Sounds pretty full on and intense."

"It is. It's utterly exhausting."

"But just think how close you'll be at the end of it, once you've said everything you need to," Susan added optimistically.

Becca exhaled, "I really hope you're right. We might be making headway in the emotional stakes but physically there's still nothing doing."

"Nothing?" asked Wendy.

"Nothing," replied Becca, "he's been home for well over a month now and we've not even kissed, not even a peck on the cheek. Whenever I try to instigate something he finds some reason to step away from the situation. The last time we were physically 'together', if you know what I mean, was the weekend of the Spring into Summer wine tasting night when everything fell apart. That's five months now."

Wendy and Susan exchanged a glance. Becca read their minds, "There were a lot of confused emotions flying around that night and we got carried away at one point. Heat of the moment." She coloured at the memory.

"Have you asked him about it?" pressed Susan.

"Yep, full disclosure. Remember?"

"And what has he said?" probed Wendy.

Becca shrugged, "That he's not ready."
Wendy responded, "Then I'm not sure there's much you can do, love. You just need to give him space."
Susan nodded her head in agreement, "Listen, it sounds like you're going through quite an intimate process just now. You can't share that sort of experience and not feel closer for it. You've just got to trust that the physical side of things will follow when the time's right."
Just then, 'Going to the Chapel' by the Dixie Cups blasted out from the PA system and Carol walked through the door, wearing a hen night veil and 'L plate' around her neck. The crowd cheered and applauded her arrival. Everyone clapped in time to the music and sang along as Carol made her way around the tables to greet everybody. By the time she reached Becca's table her face was bright red with embarrassment. She gave Becca a huge hug and gushed, "This is just amazing! Thank you so much!"
"Oh, it was a team effort Carol, I can't take all the credit."
"By the way, who is *that*?" Carol nodded her head in the direction of Madam Ruth Less.
Susan laughed, "You'll find out soon enough!"
No sooner had the words left Susan's mouth, than Madam Ruth Less's distinctive acidic drawl boomed over the PA system, "I know it's your night Carol Love, but I'm parked on a meter so we need to get started," and with that the hen night got well and truly under way.

A couple of hours later and the crowd were clearly

enjoying themselves. Madam Ruth Less's cabaret act had struck the perfect balance of being risqué but not inappropriate. The group had successfully completed 'Hen Night Bingo' (which was won by Jason's Mum who received a box of posh chocolates and bottle of prosecco) and Carol had correctly guessed fourteen of the twenty 'Wedding Truth or Lie' stories, many of which made toes curl with embarrassment. The party-goers were happily tucking into the food platters while Frankie set up the karaoke machine. Madam Ruth Less was now officially off the clock as she had finished her set but at Carol's invite had opted to stay as she was enjoying the craic with the group.

"All right ladies! Karaoke time!" Frankie announced through the microphone, "and first up to get us started is of course the lady of the moment - Carol!"

The crowd cheered and Carol looked like she wanted the ground to swallow her up but fortified by the alcohol and atmosphere, she stepped forward and took the microphone and a few seconds later, 'Dancing Queen' blared from the sound system.

"Oh wow! That is a brave choice of song!" laughed Susan. "What are you two going to sing? I'm thinking of doing Neil Diamond 'Sweet Caroline'. Even if I'm rubbish hopefully everyone will join in and help me out."

Becca was flicking through the song book, "I might go for Tiffany 'Think We're Alone Now' or Bonnie Tyler 'Total Eclipse of the Heart'."

"Me and Frankie are going to do 'Islands in the Stream,'" said Wendy.

It was around that point Carol realised how high the

high notes in Dancing Queen actually went. The group around the table collapsed in fits of laughter as Carol tried, and failed miserably, to hit them. They were still in hysterics when Carol joined them a few moments later.

"I am never doing karaoke again! That was so embarrassing!" Carol stated as she flopped down on the empty chair next to Wendy.

"The trick is to pick a song that the crowd can sing along with you," Susan offered as she wiped the tears from her face. "Karaoke aside, are you enjoying your night?"

Carol beamed, "It's been more than I ever imagined. It's been amazing! I'll definitely remember it for the rest of my life. Right, I think I really need another drink to get over my singing embarrassment! What would you all like?" The group decided on a round of 'The Blushing Bride' and Carol put in the order with Mark.

Frankie's voice boomed over the sound system, "Ok Wendy, let's get this over with," and Wendy left the group to go and sing her duet with Frankie.

"Oh my God! Wendy's got an incredible voice!" Carol exclaimed as Wendy and Frankie smashed their rendition of 'Islands in the Stream'. She turned to Becca, "You look like you're having fun."

"I'm not going to lie, I've had a blast tonight. It's been the most I've laughed in months. It's been exactly what I needed."

"Good, I'm really pleased to hear you say that. If you don't mind me saying, you look much better. I was a bit worried about you. You just looked so sad and lost."

"That's because I was utterly lost and completely miserable. I'm really grateful to you and the other girls helping me through it. It's been pretty much a full year since I first met Dan Lehmann and in that time my life has fallen apart and I've had to rebuild it. I'm still not through it yet but I'm definitely feeling more positive about things."
"Then I think that calls for a toast," suggested Susan as she held up her 'Blushing Bride,' "To the future!"
"To the future!" repeated Becca and Carol.

Not long after, the evening was drawing to a close. Many of the party goers had already left including Wendy. Mick had collected her to take her home and just as they did for the wine tastings, Tony had spent the evening at Wendy's watching the kids. He was now on his way to the café to collect Becca and Susan. Carol was making her way home with her family so there was only Carol and her immediate family, Becca, Susan, Frankie and Mark left in the café.
Frankie and Mark had tidied up as much as they could and were seated alongside Carol's family watching Becca, Susan and Carol with their arms around one another's shoulders, swaying to the music, belting out Wet Wet Wet's 'Love is all Around'. They were so engrossed in the song and making such a din they never heard the café door open and Tony come in. He pulled up a chair alongside Mark and Frankie. "Please tell me it wasn't this bad all night?" he asked.
"Oh no, it was much worse. They've actually

improved the drunker they've got," answered Frankie. "Becca's already murdered 'Total Eclipse of the Heart' and 'China in your hand'. They also did a group rendition of 'I think we're alone now'."
"And don't forget Dirty Dancing and the Grease medley," added Mark.
Tony winced. "She's always had a terrible taste in music with the voice to match." The song reached its crescendo and Tony couldn't stop watching Becca.
She looked genuinely happy for the first time in months. She had a real smile on her face, not a forced smile which she put on for the kids' sake to try and convince them everything is ok, or a professional smile for the customers, but a truly joyful smile. He couldn't help but notice how different she looked. For the first time in as long as he could remember she didn't look weighed down by the troubles which had shrouded them this year. At the sight of Becca relaxed and enjoying herself, he felt something stir inside of him that he hadn't felt for months.
The song finished and the spectators gave them a round of applause. The girls turned around to take a dramatic bow and Becca caught Tony's face in the crowd. She was momentarily taken aback as she hadn't expected to see him but recovered in time to take her bow with the other girls. They made their way back over to the table as Mark quickly turned on the overhead lights and disconnected the karaoke machine before the girls decided they wanted to do an encore.
Carol's Mum and sister collected their belongings together and were helping Carol put on her coat. She

was definitely swaying and a little worse for wear. She staggered over to Susan and Becca and gave them a big hug. "Thank you so so much," she slurred, "I've just had *the* best night. Thank you. I love you two."
"Awww we love you toot" the girls responded, giving Carol another hug. Frankie and Tony exchanged a knowing glance. There was going to be some tender heads in the morning.
"Bye girls....hiccup.....night night.....hiccup.......love you.......hiccup," and with that, Carol's Mum led her away and out into the September night. The group remaining inside the café could make out Carol shape, still wearing her veil, waving and blowing kisses to them through the steamed up windows as she tottered along the road.
"Ok ladies, your chariot awaits too," Tony said to Becca and Susan.
"I just need to nip to the loo first," said Susan, "I don't think I could hold it until I get home," and she headed off in the direction of the ladies, stumbling slightly as she went.
Mark and Frankie were preparing to lock up which left Tony and Becca alone. Tony could see Becca was swaying slightly. "It looked like it was a fun night?" he asked.
A goofy smile spread across her face which made her green eyes sparkle, "It was. I had so much fun," she gushed.
"I could tell," he nodded, "you looked happy."
She grinned back at him.
"And you look very pretty tonight," he added, "I meant to tell you that before you left."

Her smile froze in surprise. She hadn't expected a compliment like that from him. It was the first time he had made any comment about her in that way in months. The last time he had made a remark like that was the night of the wine store opening. So much had happened since then if felt like it happened in a different life.

"Thank you," she breathed. He looked deeply into her eyes and nodded. She had the feeling there was more he wanted to say but he was holding back.

Susan re-joined them, "Are we ready then?"

"Yep, yep we are," said Tony as he reluctantly pulled his gaze away from Becca. "Frankie, we're heading off now." Frankie and Mark acknowledged him and shouted their goodnights to Becca and Susan.

Tony held the café door open for the girls and then moved ahead of them to open the car doors. Susan climbed in the back and Becca into the front next to him. She watched him out of the corner of her eye as he drove Susan home. Once they arrived at Susan's house, Tony had to help her open the front door as she was having a problem getting the key in the lock. When she was safely inside and Tony was satisfied she had securely locked the door behind her, he returned to the car.

Becca was desperate to ask him if she was right and if there was something else he had wanted to say in the café but it didn't feel the right time so they drove home in companionable silence instead, Becca feeling her eyes grow heavy as the alcohol worked through her system. She let out a small contented sigh.

"You all right over there?" asked Tony.

"Yeah, I'm just sleepy."

"Do you think you're going to be ok? I don't want to leave you on your own if you think you might be unwell in the middle of the night."
"I think I'll be fine. I'll drink some water first before going up to bed."
He nodded, "If you're sure."
Becca plucked up the courage and asked, "Is that the only reason you don't want to leave me on my own?"
Tony's eyes flickered from the road to Becca and back again.
"Because if you wanted to come in beside me, you could."
"Not tonight, Becca."
She couldn't hide her disappointment, "It's just after what you said in the café."
"And I meant it but it doesn't sit right, tonight being the first night......you know.....after everything. You've been drinking. I don't want it to be like that."
She nodded her head and looked out the side window. They had stopped at a set of traffic lights. She didn't want Tony to see that she was upset. Next thing she knew, she felt his hand on hers. "I do want to," he said, "but when it feels right."
Her heart leapt and she turned to look at him, her eyes searching his face. A car beeped behind them alerting them to the fact the lights had turned green. Tony swore under his breath, put the car in gear and drove off. Becca settled back into her seat and once more acknowledged to herself that it was another step forward and for now, it was more than enough.

Chapter Forty

SIX MONTHS LATER

Becca was busying herself in the café putting the final touches to the tables and organising the welcome drinks for Carol and Jason's guests. The handmade rustic wildflower table decorations which Carol had delivered to the café the day before were very pretty and toned in beautifully with the café's duck egg blue colour scheme. Carol had really liked the hen night balloon decorations and asked if she could get a lilac and silver scheme for the wedding. The extra balloon decorations really lifted the café and made it feel properly dressed for a celebration. The Guests' Welcome Table was all set up with the guest book, favours and table seating plan.

So far, their wedding day had gone without a hitch. Even the October weather which had been ominous with heavy rain and high winds all week had settled to give them one of those gloriously sunny autumnal days where the leaves on the trees seemed to burn red against the piercing blue cloudless sky.

Carol looked phenomenal. Her tea length Bardot-style Mikado fabric dress was perfectly set off by Becca's striking lilac Manolo Blahnik shoes and the handmade sash from Wendy. She had opted to wear her jet black hair in a French-roll up-do with a birdcage veil to complete the look. There was a definite Jackie Kennedy influence about the style she had chosen for her wedding day. Jason looked handsome and extremely relaxed as he waited for Carol's arrival. He wore a classic casual navy

coloured suit with matching waistcoat, crisp white shirt and lilac coloured tie. Becca had a feeling the colour of his tie was Carol's decision but it co-ordinated with her shoes and belt perfectly. As a finishing touch, he had a lavender buttonhole which matched the lavender in Carol's bouquet.
Becca, Wendy, Susan and Mark had waited outside Park Circus Registry Office for Carol to arrive in the Aston Martin driven by Tony. Once Frankie had got the shots he wanted and the bride was safely inside with the ceremony under way, Tony had whisked them back to the café. Becca couldn't help but notice how handsome and incredibly sexy Tony looked. He had bought a new suit and put some extra effort into his appearance today.

Tony had picked up the Aston Martin the day before and it was the most excited Becca had seen him since he opened the gift at Christmas. He had taken the car out for its first spin then and, as it was school half-term holidays, he had arranged for Max and Emily to stay with his parents for a few days. It had made sense for the kids to be away for the weekend and they had been just as excited about the chance to go for a drive in the car as Tony was. Between setting up the café the day before, the wedding day itself and clearing up the day after, Carol's wedding was going to keep them both busy the entire weekend. Tony had alluded to his parents that he and Becca needed a bit of time together. Without going into full details, he mentioned they had had been through a difficult time recently. His parents

were only too happy to step in and have the opportunity to spend some dedicated time with their grandchildren.
Becca checked her watch, it had just gone three-thirty. Mark was setting up the buckets of ice to keep the beers cool when he heard his mobile beep, "Oh. I think it might be showtime." He took his phone out of his pocket and checked his message. "Yep, it's Frankie. They're at the Botanics for photos. That means the guests should be here anytime."
"Ok." Becca felt her stomach flip. It was one thing organising a wine tasting night, but to be responsible for a wedding was a whole new level. "We should probably get the prosecco out of the fridge."
"I'm already on it, luvvie," said Wendy as she bustled through from the kitchen along with Susan, both of them holding a bottle in each hand.
Becca nodded and smoothed down her scarlet red wiggle dress which clung to her curves and kicked out with a peplum hem. She had treated herself to an early morning hairdresser's appointment as she felt her usual high pony tail wasn't enough for a wedding. Her hair was styled in a chignon to keep her curls tidy and off her neck (she expected to get quite warm running around serving drink and food) and a few soft curls fell around her face. "Well let's get this show on the road," and she moved towards the counter to help Wendy pour the drinks in preparation for the guests' arrival.
"The food's all under control and on track," Wendy reassured her, "so I think we're all organised."
A few moments later several taxis came to a halt outside the café window and the well-dressed

wedding guests climbed out. Becca recognised some of the faces from the hen night. Mark made his way to the door to welcome the guests, explaining the choice of welcome drinks as they filed in.

The next part of the afternoon disappeared in a complete blur as the guests relaxed into the celebrations and the café came alive with the buzz of conversation as everyone shared jokes and enjoyed the opportunity to catch up with each other, exchanging memories from previous family get-togethers. Becca, Wendy, Susan and Mark were kept busy topping up glasses and serving the 'Toffee Apple' cocktail as requested by Carol. It was clear the guests were planning to have a good night. It was a free bar as the café didn't have an alcohol licence. Becca initially thought the budget Carol and Jason had allocated for drinks was a bit on the high side but seeing how the guests were enjoying the welcome drinks, she understood why they had been so generous with this side of their planning!

The café phone rang which meant only one thing. It would be Tony giving them advance warning that the Bridge and Groom were on the way. It was Mark who got to the phone first and took the call. He gave Becca the nod as he hung up and Becca delicately tapped the side of a glass with a knife to hush the crowd and announce, "Ladies and gentleman, the bride and groom will be with us in just a few minutes' time." The crowd's excited chatter started up once more as Susan and Becca made their way outside to wait for Jason and Carol.

"It's going well," Susan remarked to Becca.
"Yeah, it really is. They're quite a relaxed bunch. I get the impression that as long as their glasses are topped up they'll enjoy themselves! Oh, I can see their car coming now," and halfway along the street was the unmistakable form of the silver Aston Martin.
"I'll go and get their welcome drinks," said Susan, heading back inside.
Tony pulled up in front of the café and both he and Frankie climbed out first to open the doors for Carol and Jason. "Congratulations!" said Becca as she gave Carol a hug. "You look stunning!"
"Thank you," Carol was beaming with happiness, "I'm having just the best day! Tony had a bottle of champagne for me and some beers for Jason. I think it really helped Jason relax for the photos," she giggled.
"Have you drunk a full bottle of champagne?" Becca laughed.
"No!" she squealed, "Frankie helped me! We left the beers for Jase."
"She was a real star," Frankie winked at Carol, "the camera loved her. Just you wait until you see the shots I got."
"I felt like a real film star! It was so much fun, thank you Frankie. Even Jase enjoyed himself and you know how much he was dreading it."
Susan re-emerged from the café with a silver tray which boasted a selection of drinks. "Congratulations Mr and Mrs Evans! We weren't sure what you would like so Mark made up a couple of Toffee Apple cocktails, or there's prosecco or

beer."
"Oh I've had enough fizzy wine for the moment. Think I'll have a cocktail," said Carol.
Becca picked up a martini glass from the tray and passed it to Carol. "What would you like Jason?" she asked.
"Just a lager, thanks Becca."
She passed a bottle over to him and said, "Ok, well if you're ready I'll let everyone know you're here."
She made her way back inside. This time it was Mark who hushed the crowd. Becca announced, "Ladies and gentleman! Please welcome Mr and Mrs Jason Evans!" A huge cheer erupted as a glowing Carol and a rather shy looking Jason walked inside to be greeted by their guests.
Susan and Frankie filed in next with Tony behind them. He stopped to speak to Becca, "Hey," he said and was just about to continue when Wendy appeared looking flustered. "Now the love birds have arrived can you give me a hand in the kitchen? We need to start getting the food ready to serve and I can do with another pair of hands. Mark's been run off his feet keeping their glasses topped up. They like a drink this bunch, don't they?"
"Yeah, I think we're in for a lively night. I can help Mark with the drinks?" offered Tony.
Becca nodded, "Ok. Frankie's still on photographer duties until the cake's cut. Ask Susan to come and help in the kitchen too and I'll be there in a minute."
Plan in place, Wendy went off to find Susan and also let Mark know Tony would step in to help with the drinks. Becca, sensing Tony had something he still wanted to say, turned back to him, "Can we catch up

later?"
"Yeah sure. I really do need to talk to you," he said.
"Oh. Ok." She felt a familiar uneasiness spread out from her stomach, "Let's get this lot fed first then I'll come and find you."
"I'll hold you to that," he said. He looked annoyed, his jaw was set and his piercing blue eyes firmly held her gaze.
"I better go and help Wendy. I've never seen her flap like that before." She smiled weakly and made her way to the kitchen feeling slightly faint as she walked. A sense of dread was nagging at the edges of her thoughts. Things had hit a plateau with Tony. They were still sleeping in separate rooms and there had been no further progress since their discussion in the car on the way home from Carol's hen night. Maybe he had finally come to the conclusion that there could never be anything physical between them again. It suddenly made sense. She couldn't understand why he was so adamant the kids went to stay with his parents for several days when they lived over an hour's drive away instead of just going to her parents who were around the corner. Despite everything he was going to call it a day. She gave herself a shake. She couldn't think about that now, she had a café full of wedding guests who needed food in their stomachs to take the edge off the alcohol they had consumed.

Becca felt like she was in a time warp. Once she was in the kitchen alongside Wendy and Susan, the hands on the clock seemed to spin in double-quick time and before they knew it the speeches were done and they were leading each table through to help themselves to the wedding buffet dinner. Now the guests were all eating, it gave them the chance to catch their breaths and also have something to eat. Becca, Susan, Wendy, Mark, Frankie and Tony were huddled together around one of the booths in the café, all the wedding guests seated at tables in the middle of the floor.

"It seems to be going to plan," commented Wendy, "although I'm shattered and the party hasn't even started yet!"

"It's been really full on," replied Becca and she indicated to the guests, "but they seemed to have calmed down now they're eating." For the moment the raucous chatter had been replaced with a quieter hum of conversation as everyone enjoyed their meal.

"The speeches were lovely," remarked Susan. "Jason looked so smitten when he was talking about Carol. It made me feel all warm and fuzzy inside"

"That's the prosecco, love," joked Frankie. She responded by gently elbowing him in his side.

"So you're just about there with the photos?" asked Becca. She was deliberately avoiding Tony's gaze. He had tried to speak to her again but she had made her excuses. She knew she couldn't put him off all night but she was delaying the inevitable for as long as she could.

"Yep, just the cake cutting and first dance to go and we're done."

"And how are the drink stocks holding up?" she directed this question to Mark.

"Surprisingly well. After the initial flurry during the

welcome drinks they've settled down. We've got more than enough to see us through."
"Good," Becca nodded her relief as she had worried they would run out. Out of the corner of her eye, she saw Jason and Carol stand up to mingle with their guests. "Looks like we're on the final stretch now. Mark, Tony, can you go and check how everyone's doing for drinks? Frankie, can you go and set up the disco and check the cake? Wendy and Susan, can you clear the dishes? I'll help you. One final push and then once the disco starts we can all relax."
Becca, however, felt like she would never be able to relax again. She knew the second the disco started she would be out of reasons to avoid Tony.

Soon enough, the formal wedding day traditions were complete. The cake was cut, the lights were dimmed, candles lit and the first dance was underway. Jason and Carol had chosen Brian Adams' 'Everything I do (I do for you)'. They had been together for so long that Robin Hood Prince of Thieves had been the film they had gone to the cinema to see on their first date and it had been their song ever since.
For the first time all day, Becca found herself alone as she stood in the kitchen. She had slipped out unnoticed halfway through the first dance. She had suddenly felt overwhelmed watching two people who had been together for so long, still clearly and utterly in love with one another. The comparison between Carol and Jason couldn't be starker to the situation she and Tony had recently been through

and just now, it felt too much to be in the same room as them.
She leaned against the sink with her back to the door as she drank a glass of water. She was completely unaware Tony had seen her leave and followed her.
"You ok?" he asked. Becca jumped at his words and turned to face him. "Sorry," he continued, "I didn't mean to give you a fright. I saw you slip out and just wanted to check on you."
"Just thirsty and a bit of a headache. It's been a long day."
"It's been an amazing day, Becca. You did them proud. They've really had a wedding to remember and it's down to you." She smiled although she was dreading what was coming next. "I'm glad I managed to get a moment with you. I've been wanting to talk to you all day." He moved towards her and her heart began to thump against her rib cage. This was it. No avoiding it now. "There's something I need to say," and he produced a small jewellery box from his trouser pocket and handed it to her.
"What's this?" she asked.
"Open it."
She did as she was instructed and inside was a gold necklace with a Daffodil pendant, small diamonds placed to indicate the stigma and anthers of the flower.
"Do you recognise it?" he asked. She looked at him, confused.
"It is......was......your wine bottle necklace. After it got broken I took it to a jeweller to ask if they could fix it but it was broken beyond repair so I asked if

they could make it into something else and I got them to do this." He nodded towards the box she was holding. "At first I was annoyed they couldn't mend it but then I realised this was actually better. It's a bit like us. Even when you think something's broken beyond repair, with a little time and effort the parts that are worth saving can be used to create something even better. I was going to give it to you for your birthday but it didn't quite work out….." his voice trailed off as he realised she was trembling. He took a step towards her and took her in his arms, "Hey, hey, shhh. Everything's going to be ok."

"I thought you were going to tell me tonight we were done. That's why I've been avoiding you all afternoon."

He took a step back, "Why on earth did you think that?"

"The way you looked at me when you arrived with Carol and Jason. You looked so annoyed. I thought it made sense. You were so determined the kids should go to your parents for a few days. I thought you needed them out of the way so you could tell me you were leaving me and have the time to move out before they came back."

"Christ, Becca, no! I was annoyed with Wendy. I was just about to give you the necklace but she pushed in and got in my way. I was already kicking myself for missing you this morning. I had planned to give you the necklace first thing so you could wear it today. I hadn't realised you would be up and out to the hairdressers so early. Then when I saw you standing outside the Registry Office waiting for Carol, you looked stunning. And sexy. Very, very

sexy."
Becca started laughing. A combination of relief and hysteria overwhelmed her. "We're not quite there with the communication yet, are we?"
"Hah! Obviously not but why change the habit of a lifetime?" and he took her in his arms once more.
"So why were you so desperate to send the kids off to your parents? They could have just gone to my folks. It would have been easier," she asked.
"Ah. That was my other surprise. I've booked a trip and we'll be away for a few days. Just the two of us. We go tomorrow."
"But what about the café? I need to clear up and get everything back to normal again for my regulars."
"It's all sorted. Wendy, Susan, Frankie and Mark are going to see to that."
"The Aston Martin! It goes back tomorrow."
"All arranged. The company is going to collect it from us at the airport."
"Airport! Why? Where are we going?"
"Venice, where it all started for us, before the kids, and the café, and everything else came along. It's also where I fell in love with you and where I realised I wanted to spend my life with you. I thought where better for us to properly start over, to remember why we're together and put this year behind us once and for all."
He momentarily pulled back so he could look her deep in the eye. "I love you, Rebecca Swanson," and with those words he kissed her. As Becca relaxed into the kiss which she had longed for, all the tension released and the weight finally lifted. They had found their way back to each other.

THE END

Epilogue

Two days later, Becca rolled over in bed, the late morning sun cascading through the window gently waking her. She opened her eyes and took a few moments to recall the last forty-eight hours. After the excitement of the wedding, her feet had barely touched the ground. She had arrived in Venice yesterday afternoon with Tony and they spent the most incredible evening together. She smiled to herself as the details returned to her, how they had talked and laughed recounting memories from their previous trip to the city and then, after much anticipation, finally gone to bed together. She smiled again in the knowledge that they had a further two days to selfishly enjoy one another.

Realising she was alone, she sat up in bed. The room was silent but the hum of Venice outside the hotel window provided enough of a background noise that she had to strain to listen for Tony in the ensuite, but nothing. She got out of bed and wandered in the direction of the bathroom. As she drew near, she could smell his aftershave in the air and there were visible signs he was already up and showered. She located her mobile and was about to climb back into bed to phone him when something on the coffee table caught her eye. It looked like a plate of brioche and pastine with a coffee pot standing alongside it. She sat down on the sofa and saw there was also a note scribbled on the pad of headed paper. It was from Tony:

'You were sound asleep and I didn't want to wake you. You obviously needed the sleep after last night! Just gone out to check arrangements for the next couple of days, got a few surprises lined up. Be ready for 12.30, I have lunch booked for us – you'll need your posh shoes and a dress to match. I had room service bring up a light breakfast to keep you going until then. I'll be back soon x'

Becca checked her watch. It was already after eleven. The last time she had slept that long was before the kids had arrived. She clearly needed it! She quickly ate the breakfast and drank a lukewarm cup of coffee before getting ready for the day. Her stomach was in a flurry of anticipation as she wondered what Tony had planned for them.
As she selected what she was going to wear, her mind wandered. She wasn't naïve. She recognised that right now, she and Tony were in a bubble. The kids and the café were physically over a thousand miles away and psychologically even further. It would all still be there for them when they stepped off the plane at Glasgow airport in a couple of days' time so for the moment it all could just remain as a distant hazy thought. They may have been able to finally put events behind them but the scars were still there and always would be, even if only to serve as a reminder of just how close they came to losing everything. In the meantime and for the next forty-eight hours, it was just going to be her and Tony. And right now, that was all she needed.

Cocktails from the Café Swan Menu

From the "Late Summer Sun" Event:

Classic Mojito

Juice of 1 lime
1 tsp granulated sugar
Small handful mint leaves, plus extra sprigs to serve
60 ml white rum
Soda water to taste
Step 1: Mix the lime juice, sugar and mint leaves in a small jug, crushing the mint as you do this. Pour into a tall glass over ice.
Step 2: Pour in the rum, stir and top with soda water to taste. Garnish with mint and serve

Dan's Sex On The Beach

50 ml vodka
25 ml peach gin liqueur
50 ml orange juice
50 ml cranberry juice
Step 1: Pour all ingredients into a cocktail shaker and shake to mix.
Step 2: Pour into a tall glass over ice to serve.

From the "Autumn Festival" Event:

Witches Brew

50 ml vodka
25 ml blue curacao
100 ml pineapple juice
Step 1: Pour all ingredients into a cocktail shaker to mix.
Step 2: Pour into a tall glass over ice to serve.

Toffee Apple

25 ml salted caramel gin liqueur
25 ml apple flavoured vodka
Splash of grenadine
Lemonade
Step 1: Pour gin liqueur and vodka into a cocktail shaker to mix. Pour into a chilled martini glass.
Step 2: Add a splash of grenadine and top up with lemonade.

From the "Winter Wonderland" Event:

Classic Mulled Wine

1 small orange - sliced
1 bottle red wine
50 ml brandy
1 whole cinnamon sticks
1 star anise
4 whole cloves
Step 1: Pour the red wine into a large saucepan. Add the sliced orange, cinnamon stick, star anise and cloves. Heat very gently until simmering then turn off the heat.
Step 2: Remove the cinnamon stick, star anise and cloves. Stir in the brandy. Ladle equal measures into mugs or heatproof glasses to serve.

Clementine Bucksfizz (Makes 6)

Juice from 1kg clemantines
175 ml pomegranate juice
6 tsp Campari
½ bottle of prosecco
Step 1: Mix the fruit juices in a jug and chill until needed.
Step 2: Pour 1 teaspoon of Campari into each glass. Half fill each glass with the juice mixture and top up with chilled prosecco.

Santa's Little Helper

25 ml blueberry vodka
15 ml Chambord
15 ml triple sec
50 ml cranberry juice

Step 1: Pour the blueberry vodka, Chambord, triple sec and cranberry juice into a cocktail shaker to mix.

Step 2: Pour into a chilled martini glass to serve.

From the "Spring into Summer" Event:

British Sunset

25 ml Pimms

25 ml vodka

25 ml fresh lemon juice

25 ml orange juice

25 ml apple juice

Step 1: Combine the Pimms and vodka in a high ball glass over ice.

Step 2: Add juices to the glass and gently stir to combine.

Elderflower Fizz (Makes 2)

50 ml elderflower gin liqueur

15 ml lime juice

20 ml sugar syrup

Prosecco

Step 1: Pour the elderflower gin liqueur, lime juice and sugar syrup into a cocktail shaker to mx.

Step 2: Pour mixture equally into two chilled champagne flutes. Top up with prosecco.

From Carol's Hen Night:

Blushing Bride

25 ml pear flavoured vodka
15 m elderflower liqueur
25 ml lemon juice
15 ml sugar syrup
Step 1: Pour all ingredients into a cocktail shaker to mix.
Step 2: Pour into a chilled martini glass to serve.

About the Author

Mary-Grace Burinski is originally from Ayrshire in the south-west of Scotland but now lives with her husband, two sons and cat in Fife which is on the east coast of Scotland.

When not writing, Mary-Grace has a regular day job and also runs a grass roots charity with her husband and friend (who also doubles as her red-penned editor!). To relax, she enjoys reading as much as writing, drinking wine and eating chocolate while talking rubbish with friends. She can also be found binge watching Say Yes to the Dress and Curvy Brides Boutique, usually on a Saturday morning with her feet up while drinking coffee.

Follow me on Instagram and Twitter @mgburinski
www.mgburinski.com

Thank You

I never thought I would actually get to the stage of writing the 'thank you' part of the book. I have been incredibly lucky to have so many people around me who encouraged and supported me to do this. Not one of you laughed at me when I told you this secret of writing a book and for that I am grateful. It gave me the confidence to keep going and really follow a dream I've held for years.

First of all to my husband Craig. When I told you I was doing this, you never dismissed it as a crazy notion or thought I was bonkers, you just encouraged and supported me. Thanks for giving me free advice on the legalities of buying and selling commercial properties……albeit imaginary properties (although I did notice you rolling your eyes on one or two occasions). Love you.

Now onto my peer review groups. Hopefully all of you will appreciate the reference to the red sparkling Shiraz!

First of all the ASHS girls: Emma, Tracey and Joanne. You were the ladies I first disclosed my secret too and the first to tell me to go for it. That belief and encouragement in those shaky early days of letting 'actual people' read my book was invaluable as you built up my confidence and really helped me believe I could do this. Emma I need to say a special thank you to you. Your commitment to read through and dissect the story and characters meant so much.

My BFFs Clare and Lynn. You've both always been there for me in the best and worst times. Love you both. PS - if I make enough royalties from this book, the next weekend in Nice will be on me.
To Sharon and Rachael my wine tasting partners in crime! No guesses for where *that* inspiration came from!
Judy, thank you so much for getting the red pen out and helping me get my debut novel over the line. It meant a lot to me and there was no-one better I could have asked.
To my big bruv Jippy, maybe I'm no such a daftie after all, I've written a book! And finally, Mum and Dad. Love you.

Printed in Great Britain
by Amazon

62459688R00173